TALES
from the
EMERALD CITY
by Ray Gerring

All names in this book are fictional.
Similarities to actual names are purely
coincidental.

Publisher: Ray Gee Books
rjgerring@yahoo.com
ISBN 978-1-4928-3447-2

Cover design by the author.

Dedicated to June Elizabeth Gerring,
my sweetheart.

INTRODUCTION

Seattle, the "Emerald City" has been my home town for over four decades. Some of the following short stories are taken from my own experience. Some are true, some are from my imagination. I sincerely hope that readers may find them amusing, entertaining, and in some way meaningful.

Ray Gerring, 2013

CONTENTS

THE GEEZER MAFIA

CHAPTER 1

Harry Larson gazed wistfully at the blue waters of Puget Sound across a four-mile wide channel to the Kitsap Peninsula and the clear silhouette of the snow-capped Olympic Mountains beyond. Unusually blue water, he thought, almost a cobalt hue because of the bright sunshine on this gorgeous spring day. There I go, he thought, thinking in artist's colors again. Harry was pondering the scenery through the bayside windows of Oscar's Boathouse restaurant, a favorite seafood eatery in Ballard, Seattle's Scandinavian district, three miles north of the city center.

Harry was seated at Oscar's in a glassed-off dining space, separated from the main restaurant. He and his five friends met bi-monthly for lunch, usually at Oscar's, where the wait staff fondly referred to them as the "Geezers." Now in his eighty-first year, Harry had enjoyed a close friendship with four of the other Geezers for over fifty years. As he sipped his martini, a husky tank of a man appeared at the doorway. "Hey man," grinned Harry, admiring the still youthful athletic movements, the crew cut, the bull neck and alert eyes of Max Hanson, Harry's lifetime friend and favorite Swede. "Hello, Svenska poika," said Max, looking directly with intense ice-blue eyes into Harry's face. Max's usually stern look, the result of his contrived expression as a former police captain, was entirely different when he was around Harry Larson, his old pal. Max's expression reflected friendship, respect, and was a kind of special affection old geezers would understand. "I see you have lost more hair," chided Harry, interrupted by the arrival of Andy Lindstrom, 82, who shouted, "Which one of you old farts is man enough to buy me a drink?"

Tagging along with fat Andy was Victor Lundberg, his face expressionless, cautiously selecting his chair at the table, facing away from the view windows. Always a serious and sensitive man, Victor Lundberg, 81, had enjoyed a career as a professional graphic artist and was admired by his peers. He was productive and confident in his creative years, but recently a victim of progressive dementia. Despite Victor's debilitating handicap, his lack of understanding, forgetfulness, halting speech and expression of a profound sadness of spirit, his old friends encouraged his presence at each meeting. Usually it was Andy who drove Victor to and from these bi-monthly luncheons. Big hearted Andy enjoyed every opportunity to be helpful. A World War II army veteran, Andy loved to reminisce about his experiences in the Big War. In his working years Andy was employed in the often-dangerous occupation of commercial fishing, mostly in Alaskan waters.

The remaining two old friends noisily joined the others as they staked out their locations at the table. Gus Stenval, age 84, and Sammy Aaron were the last to arrive. Tall, slightly hunched over with wild looking hair, unkempt mustache, a bit buck toothed, pop eyed and potbellied, Gus took his seat.

The geezers sometimes teased Sammy for looking too "Jewish" as if he represented some kind of an anti-Semitic caricature. When they started bombarding him with "friendly" ethnic insults he gave as good as he got. "If I am a greedy money grubbing Christ killing little Kike, I can certainly call you guys a bunch of dumb headed herring chokers, or snoose chewing anti-Semitic square heads," Sammy retorted. Sammy was only 68 and the newest member of the group. Harry Larson invited him after meeting at a "Fifty Five Alive" driving class. The two-session driving class is offered to seniors usually by AARP at some senior centers as a means of reminding seniors about driver's legal responsibilities, ethics and roadside manners. Class participation resulted in a significant discount on driver's car insurance.

Not much was known about Sammy Aaron's past, the others accepted him by virtue of Harry's sponsorship. They all knew about the past lives of each of the other five. Harry Larson was born of Swedish immigrants in Ballard in 1926. Tall white haired with even features, Harry appeared more like 70. He was perceived by his peers as a grand combination of loyal friend, intellectual authority and all around good guy, a former professor of art history at the University of Washington. Harry took pride in his past career. Situated in Seattle's north end on a lovely campus, the U of W shares a shoreline with the stunningly beautiful Lake Washington. Twenty miles long running north and south, Lake Washington borders the east shore of downtown Seattle.

As the acknowledged leader of the Geezers, Harry took pleasure in exerting a kind of gentle informal control of the content of each meeting. The preliminary drinks were mostly water and diet soda, although Harry usually had one martini and Sammy ordered a shot of straight bourbon. The lunch choices were varied. Victor needed toasted cheese, fat Andy demanded pork chops, Harry ate seafood salad, Max, Sammy and Gus were happy with poached salmon.

As they began the meal, the usual "How ya doing?" small talk prevailed until Harry Larson asked, "Why don't we have a joke? Who's got one?" "OK," shouted Sammy, "here's a limerick: There once was a pirate named Bates, who cut a fine figure on skates, but he fell on his cutlass, which rendered him nut-less, and virtually worthless on dates!" Chortling and mild giggling escaped from the mouths of the five octogenarians, much as if they were dirty-minded fourteen-year-olds.

"Anybody else," asked Harry? "OK, then let's have the health report. Why don't you go first Gus, and we'll proceed around the table." "I've got the same arthritis pain in my knuckles, had constipation last week and the damned asthma has returned," said Gus. Suggestions followed including home remedies, drug recommendations and suggestions to quit his present HMO.

4

Victor was next, his glassy eyes, vacant look and halting voice eliciting silent empathy. "I will be having sur-surgery next week," he stuttered, "left knee replacement." This was no surprise, as poor Victor described the same ailment at each get together. Andy was next, describing how he has learned to administer his insulin shots each day, adding that an attack of dermatitis has come and gone during the past weeks. Harry described a nagging back pain, and the exercise program which supposedly affects a cure. Max gave his usual lecture on keeping fit through exercise and a healthful diet. They all knew Max was right, well, mostly right.

They were all aware of the fact that most of their friends, family and acquaintances had died before the age of eighty. They all felt somewhat fortunate, but humbled because they knew their time would be up in the near future. Try not to think about it, be thankful to have lived this long. Remember the happy times and keep going the best you can. Hope that when your time comes it will be quick.

Sammy reported that he had been informed that he would need a hip replacement. Otherwise, for now, he seems to be OK except for a strain or a sprain of the right wrist. "I hope it isn't broken," said Sammy. He was vague about explaining how his wrist had been injured. As a matter of fact, the injury had happened the previous day in a rather bizarre occurrence. Thoughts of the incident ran through Sammy's mind. His image of himself as a ladies man was quite the real thing.

Unmarried, rather short with a trim build, Sammy, at age 68, was in very good shape. Balding with a neat fringe of dyed black hair and a black mustache, he was smart, well-spoken and witty. The trace of a New Jersey accent was apparent from time to time. Sammy was a fastidious dresser always decked out in tasteful jackets, ties and two-tone spectator-style wingtip shoes. Sporting his stylish aviator eyeglasses, he was very attractive to the single ladies at the senior center dances he frequently attended. Sammy had lost count of the lovely ladies that had fallen victim to his charms, mostly as brief affairs. Sammy liked his affairs to be brief, two or three weeks of intense intimacy was about right.

The very day before the Geezer meeting Sammy had escorted his present lady friend to a small boat moorage on a little bay on Lake Washington, adjacent to a well-known slough. The slough featured boat channels intertwining among cattail swamps and reeds with overhanging weeping willow branches and secluded little grassy islands. The calm waters and quiet intimate little inlets, ponds, and water passages were ideal for canoeing and romantic getaway rendezvous. Since there was a spell of sunny warm weather Sammy had taken Edith, his current lady friend, on a canoe ride through the slough. After a picnic lunch on a grassy bank, Sammy paddled his rented canoe slowly through the lovely little waterways enjoying the sunshine, the smell of the water, the water plants and the spring air. Later in the summer the slough would be crowded with canoes, rowboats, rafts and other watercraft; however, at this time of year very few people were present. Sammy slowly maneuvered his canoe into a secluded area and allowed it to sit quietly, securely wedged into a grassy area covered with reeds and cattails. Seduction was a specialty with Sammy, so in no time he had his lady's clothes completely off. The couple immediately engaged themselves in vigorous coitus, ingeniously performed inside on the deck (floor) of their canoe. As they finished and began to put on their clothes, they were shocked to hear a loud voice shout "You sure have a nice big pussy!" After a pause, it was repeated twice more. Sammy looked at Edith and said, "I can't see anybody out there, but I might have to deal with him when we paddle out of here." Seeing the frightening look in his dark eyes, Edith quietly said, "Embarrassing as it is, please do not create a scene or a confrontation. Look Sammy, I'm sure that you are a brave and upright man, so you do not need to do anything to prove it, just let it go. Let's just get out of here." Sammy had formulated a plan as to what he would do if a confrontation occurred. Edith, humiliated, felt sick as she sat in the front of the canoe. Sammy slowly paddled out from their secluded spot into a wider channel, which ultimately would wind around back to the canoe rental boathouse. The air was still, no boaters or people in sight, when suddenly another canoe appeared headed for the stern of Sammy's canoe. Sammy turned his head slightly as the canoe approached. A tall blond boy in his late teens was slowly paddling toward Sammy. The kid wore a T-shirt, cutoff jeans, a ponytail and a wide smirk. He was obviously enjoying the quiet confrontation as he spoke in a loud voice: "Hey old man, I saw you making it back there in your canoe! How was it?" Loud laughter ensued. Just as the boy's canoe got close, Sammy turned suddenly, grabbed the bow, and with surprising quickness and strength flipped the canoe on its side dumping the tall kid into the water. At the same time in a lightning move, Sammy raised his paddle and swung it straight down in a chopping motion, splitting the young man's head with a deep gash revealing his shiny gray brain tissue. The blood spurted into the water in globs and droplets, like a small fountain. Grabbing a small length of rope lying in his canoe Sammy looped it tightly around the dead boy's neck, secured the rope and towed the body to a small inlet close by. Fortunately there was still no one in the vicinity a far as Sammy could tell. Edith, crouching in the bow covered her head as her body stiffened in a state of shock. Sammy covered the corpse with cattails and branches before paddling rapidly back to the boathouse.

As he drove Edith to her home, Sammy contemplated doing away with the old broad, but decided to let her go for now since she was a quivering basket case. He would decide what to do with her later. Sammy wore that dark satanic look, almost like the stereotype hit men portrayed in the Godfather movies. For the rest of the day, he favored a painful right wrist. Sammy felt no tug of conscience. It was almost like he had done such things before. In Sammy's mind, the "canoe encounter" was simply a matter of self-defense, protecting one's honor, so to speak.

Sammy half-listened to the guys at the table as

they proudly discussed their volunteer activities in the neighborhood community, in the two weeks previous Gus and Andy had spent several hours collecting litter in and around the streets of south Ballard. Their job consisted of filling large plastic garbage bags with beer cans, plastic cups, paper and plastic wrappings along with the occasional used syringe. After disposing of the litter into the appropriate recycle dumpsters, they usually headed for a Scandinavian lunch at the local WASA lodge hall.

Harry and Andy spent Wednesday of each week delivering boxes of food to people on a list compiled by the charity committee of the Ballard First Lutheran Church. Generous donations of cash provided a large quantity of storable food in a small building next to the church. The church was located on a quiet neighborhood street in the heart of the Ballard community. Members of the Lutheran Men's Club took care of the donations, bookkeeping, storage, references and delivery of the large food boxes to those on their reference list. Harry fulfilled the role of deliveryman once or twice a week. He carried a booklet of vouchers that were as good as cash for needs such as rent, second hand furniture and dental bills. The men's club ultimately redeemed the vouchers.

At times, Harry sent out some letters of complaint to the Seattle mayor's office, reminding the city officials that certain Ballard streets had holes and ruts needing repair. He often chuckled to himself as he composed these letters to the city big shots. Harry, happily married to his wife Judy, of almost sixty years, spent one morning each week lecturing on art history in a classroom at the local senior center. The lectures were concerned with the arts of ancient Rome, and were part of a free educational program at the center offered to retired seniors.

Max Hanson spent much of his free time chauffeuring handicapped men from the local senior center to and from their medical appointments. He arranged his schedule around his three weekly workouts at the Ballard fitness gym. Of the two men, Max had the most free time. A single widower, he lived in a small condo with a view of the Ballard marina. Max enjoyed viewing the scene of over a thousand colorful boats of every description moored neatly in perfect rows. The shimmering shapes reflected in the water were a source of endless fascination for the old cop. He also loved keeping in touch with his old buddies from the Seattle Police Department, all retired by now. His one son, Butch, a Seattle police officer, kept in close contact with his old dad. In spite of the inevitable aches and pains of old age, the Geezers derived satisfaction in their volunteer activities.

After the meal only Andy ordered desert, apple cobbler ala mode, his usual choice. Harry complemented the guys on their generous volunteer efforts, after which he asked for opinions about the effectiveness of what they had been doing in the community. "Doing good!" blurted Victor. All seemed quite pleased with their do-gooder accomplishments. "There's more we can do," said Harry, "but we are busy enough for now." "Any suggestions for a topic to discuss next time?" "Yeah," exclaimed Gus, "how about if each of us brings a list of their favorite movies?"

"Great idea," said Harry, "until next time." Raising his coffee cup as if giving a toast, "Din-skoal, min-skoal." (A toast to you and a toast to me) "La chaim," (to life) shouted Sammy as he took his last sip of cold coffee.

After leaving Oscars, Sammy attempted to call Edith Nyberg. No answer. "Leave a message," said a voice. Sammy decided to drive to Edith's house. Opening the front door, Edith, 65, appeared disheveled and distraught. "We have to call the police. I am so upset I think I'm going crazy after what you did." "Calm down, Edith, don't worry about it. The blame is all on me, so you are not guilty of anything." "I was there, I am an accessory." "No, no, Edith, anyway it was self-defense. We'll just keep quiet and it will all blow over. You'll see. Just keep cool, it will all blow over, and we can forget about it."

Edith, an attractive widow, had never witnessed a violent act in her entire sheltered life. She always enjoyed her role as a church going homemaker with a comfortable life in a quiet suburban neighborhood. "We have to tell the police. Please, Sammy, we have to do the right thing." She began to sob, to cry bitterly and to wail. "You're too upset right now Edith, but you must understand that you have to keep your mouth shut." "If I don't tell the police, when I die I will go to everlasting hell," screamed Edith. Sammy lowered his voice to a sinister tone, "I'm going to leave now Edith, and I'll be calling you on the phone tomorrow morning. I want to hear you say, 'It's OK, Sammy, and I swear I will never say a word to anybody.' If you do not say those words you will be in real serious trouble, real serious trouble."

On the following Thursday Harry arrived at Oscar's before the others, as usual. Despite an overcast sky and the gray water out on the Sound, Harry was trying hard to put on a happy face. Two close friends had recently died. We just keep toppling over, he thought. Harry did not look forward to their memorials. "Hey-hey Harry, min bra lille Svenska poika!" shouted Max as he entered the private dining area. (Hello, Harry, my good little Swedish boy.) "Hewr mor du, Herr Hanson?" replied Harry. (How are you, Mr. Hanson?) "Mycka bra, tak." (Very well, thanks.)

After all were greeted, after the usual teasing and small talk, Harry asked, "Anybody got a joke?" "Here's a punch line," said Gus. "If you don't tell anybody about the baby, I won't tell anybody about the sheep." Some genuine appreciative chuckles pleased Gus. "Another punch line," said Andy, "OK, bartender, help me get this Norwegian off my ass." The guys seemed amused but puzzled. "OK," shouted Andy, "the frog on the guy's head was talking to the bartender!" Some guffaws partly salvaged the effort. "That was a good one," screamed Victor, head thrown back with both hands gripping the edge of the table.

"How about a health report?" said Harry, "Why don't you start, Andy?" "My diabetes is a bit worse. Dr. Quack says my feet are really bad; so bad he might not be able to save them." "How long?" asked Max. "Maybe a year or less," said Andy. "Old age ain't for sissies," offered Harry. "My bones and spine keep getting weaker," said Gus. "I may have to take some back-stretching treatments. What happened to the golden age?" Victor repeated his knee-operation story. "I'm doing OK for now," said Sammy. "I've had some kind of acid reflux, but it comes and goes." "There have been times in the past," said Max, "when I've had temporary diarrhea. No fun. Nothing recently." Commenting on his own health, Harry was vague but mentioned some suspected hearing loss.

The do-gooder report was about the same as last time. Max, however, reported that some of the community leaders were very disturbed about the opening of a strip-club on fifteenth avenue Northwest, only four blocks from the high school. "What's it like?" asked Andy. "Some say it's kind of a table-dance joint serving overpriced drinks. It features young half-nude girls go-go dancing or whatever they call it now." "Where do the girls come from?" asked Gus. "From what I hear, it's easy to recruit them. They have lots of girls working in clubs in Lake City and Kirkland that can earn five hundred bucks or more on a good night." "What do the girls do in those joints?" asked Sammy, as if he didn't know. "Sexy dancing, provocative behavior, all kinds of flirting, playing up to the men and teasing, all that sort of stuff. Not to mention the fact that the girls are often seduced into prostitution," answered Max. "What's the name of this joint, and who runs it?" asked Gus. "They call it *Girlies*. It's rumored that some Russians are involved in the operation," answered Max. "Maybe the do-gooders should look into it," suggested Harry. "Let's all see what we can find out about it."

"OK," said Harry, "let's move on. Who has his list of favorite movies?" Andy volunteered: "Here's three of my favorites, Casablanca, The Searchers, and High Noon." "How about the Godfather, Inherit the Wind, and On the Waterfront?" spoke Harry. "I liked Alien, The Exorcist, and the original Frankenstein," said Gus, with a twinkle in his eye. "Linda Blair is cute," said Victor. "A real horror aficionado," Sammy blurted out. "I used to like war movies," said Max, "like All Quiet on the Western Front (which I remember from the early thirties), Apocalypse Now, and Platoon." "Those were all anti-war movies, Max," said Harry in a soft voice. "I liked them anyway," retorted Max. "Spoken like an ex-Marine, Max," said Gus. "A man's man," chuckled Andy.

Everyone knew that Max was a decorated ex-marine, having served in the South Pacific combat areas in World War II. "Once a Marine, always a Marine," Gus offered. Gus served in the war as well during the Allied invasion of Europe. He had been wounded and captured during the battle of the Bulge in 1944. Trained as an army explosives technician, he found himself in an army infantry squad after deployment to the battle line in Belgium. His capture only lasted for a few weeks as the combat lines shifted. Taking advantage of chaotic circumstances, Gus managed to escape. His wounds were minor and he was soon back into the fighting until the European war ended in May, 1945.

After the usual closing toast, Harry adjourned the meeting. Max drove Victor to his home a short distance away. Victor's wife Karen guided him to his couch for his afternoon nap. Max thought Karen looked a bit distraught. "To tell you the truth, Max, I'm really worried about our granddaughter, Kira." "Why?" asked Max. "She's in with a really bad group of kids. She's seventeen, a senior in high school. I suspect all kinds of terrible things are about to happen to her." "Like what?" "I'm sure they drink and probably do drugs and that's bad enough." "What else?" asked Max. "I've heard that a couple of the girls are dancing at that *Girlies*, the new strip joint on fifteenth," replied Karen. Max felt his big body stiffening. "You think Kira would do that?" With a look both anxious and fearful, Karen answered, "She's been kind of swept into the influence of those wild kids. She's underage, impressionable, very pretty, vivacious and prone to the cultural pressures we have nowadays." Max stood, straightened his back and said, "Do you mind if I look into this, Karen?" Despite his advanced years, Max sometimes thought of himself as a kind of warrior of righteousness.

The next night Harry was watching Godfather II on the movie channel, when the phone rang. "It's me," said Max, "Can you get away tonight?" "Max, it's past my bed time." "I'm with my son Butch. We are going to check out *Girlies*," said Max. "The strip club on fifteenth? You're too old for that sort of thing, Max." "Victor's granddaughter is in some kind of situation. We think the guys who run that club may be trying to recruit her," said Max, in a taut tone of voice Harry remembered all too well from their younger days. Teenagers often hung out in groups somewhat equivalent to today's gangs. When confrontations occurred with other gangs, they usually sent out their toughest boy who then fought the other gang's champion. Max was always the anointed one back in the 1940's. It was a kind of teenage rite of passage, a machismo thing. "Are you with me, Harry?" Max asked his old friend.

Max, Butch and Harry took their seats, barely visible through the cigarette smoke. Harry was tempted to cover his ears. The noise (this is music? thought Max) was pure cacophony and almost unbearable to Harry and Max. Butch, age 46, was conditioned to the music, and almost liked it. The three, like any strangers, were carefully observed by three or four tough looking guys, all in their thirties. Obviously bouncers, they all wore the unmistakable surly look as they hovered around the fringes of the crowd. On the tiny stage danced three lovely young girls. Their sexy gyrations in very skimpy costumes, lots of tits and ass, provocative movements, and flirtatious expressions were all designed to arouse the libido of the glassy-eyed men in the audience. Along with the performance on stage, a half dozen other girls were performing table dances three feet away from their seated customers. "How much do they charge for table dancing?" asked Harry. "Twenty bucks or more," said Butch.

A scantily clad waitress appeared at their table. They ordered three beers which she quickly delivered and announced, "OK, gentlemen, that will be fortyfive bucks, plus a nice tip, please." "If I were still on the job I'd make sure to close this place down tomorrow," said Max as he dug to come up with fifty bucks. "It was your idea," grinned Harry as Butch kept scanning the premises, looking to see if he recognized anyone. "Hey pop," said Butch quietly, "Do you see the two bozos standing in that corner?" Max and Harry strained to see. "Bouncers," said Max. "Yeah, I think I remember busting that one guy a few years ago for something." "Was he convicted?" asked Harry. "I think so but I can't remember." After turning down some aggressive offers for table dancing, the three left *Girlies*. "Come again boys," said the doorman, a nasty looking, buffed-up kid in his early twenties. "Did that kid speak with an accent?" asked Max. "Yeah," said Harry, "Russky."

CHAPTER 2

Edith Nygard boarded the plane for Puerto Vallarta and Sammy felt greatly relieved. Getting the money together was not difficult, but it ticked him off when he wrote the three thousand dollar check for the vacation package. He was still leery that Edith might open her mouth to her companion about that bad day at the slough. Her companion, Ingrid Petersen, was thrilled to accept Edith's offer of a free vacation for two weeks to sunny Mexico. Maybe I've scared her enough so she won't talk about it, thought Sammy to himself. She had damned well better not.

Andy's favorite pastime was visiting old buddies at the marinas nearby. He loved to inspect boats, cruisers, sailboats, trollers, purse seiners, hydroplanes, canoes and rowboats. He loved 'em all. As a former halibut fisherman he had spent most summers of his working life in Alaskan waters. During the past generation all fisheries had suffered a devastating decline.

Improved technology, more efficient methods and over-fishing a finite resource had resulted in a pale shadow of a prosperous fishing community in Ballard. Even so there remained hundreds of ex-fishermen, mostly retired, still living in the area. Andy knew many of them and hung out with them often. A definite bonding existed among the rugged weathered and often taciturn old codgers. Most were Norwegian, immigrants or American born, but their numbers also included Finns, Swedes and Croatians. When bumming around the docks and marinas Andy often took Gus along. Growing up in a Norwegian family Gus understood Scandinavian lingo, body language, attitudes and typical characteristics. Although easily assimilated, Scandinavian immigrants often hung onto familiar traditions. Gus still loved lutefisk. At Christmas, partying at the Sons of Norway Lodge, he could still dance the polka, hambo and Swedish waltz. Not as well as when he and his wife were young. Those were the days.

At times, Andy and Gus enjoyed visiting with Arne Arneson, who worked as a part-time guard and caretaker at Shilshole Bay Marina, on the shore of Puget Sound. The three old codgers enjoyed walking along the mooring docks commenting on the sea worthiness of each boat. After a morning of visiting the boats, Gus and Andy usually had lunch and headed home for their afternoon naps.

Heartbroken over Victor's mental condition, Karen Lundberg felt she needed to intervene in her granddaughter's life. Kira had lived with her grandparents, Victor and Karen, ever since both her parents had died in a car accident when she was nine years old.

Although Kira had always been a naturally sweet and respectful girl, lately she had changed, "just the opposite," thought Karen. "Please listen to reason," went the discussion. "You must change your ways." "Don't tell me what to do, I'm of age, I can do what I want," Kira retorted. Kira usually ended these arguments by slamming the door as she left the house. Karen found moral support from her close friends but the problem and the anxiety remained.

As a longtime friend of the family, Harry Larson was also seriously concerned about Kira. He took it upon himself to contact the principal of Ballard High School, who referred him to a student counselor named Cora Angelos. At their initial meeting, Harry tried to describe the anxiety felt by the Lundberg family over Kira's recent behavior.

Miss Angelos seemed to grasp the seriousness. After a conference with Kira, Miss Angelos called Harry to report the results of their meeting. "I tried to convince her that she was headed down a dangerous path. She seemed to understand my attempt to advise her, however, I wasn't convinced that she would change her attitude. She is very intelligent, beautiful and a real charmer, but headstrong like so many other kids her age. I even went so far as to describe how attractive young girls are sometimes enticed into illegal activities resulting in prostitution, prison and broken unredeemable lives. As Kira left my office, she looked back at me smiling and asked if one of her Grandpa's nosey old friends put me up to this...

"Anyone have a joke?" asked Harry at the next luncheon meeting of the Geezers. "A horse walks into a bar," said Andy. "The bartender looks at him standing at the bar and says, "Hey Fella, why the long face?" A good laugh from the guys rewarded Andy, along with a shout from Victor, "A goddamn horse!" More jokes came forth, including another bar joke, an old traveling salesman joke and an old doctor joke.

The health reports got worse. Everyone had at least three ailments from a stiff neck to a serious heart problem. Old age continued to wear the guys down, even 68-year-old Sammy, who suspected he might be coming down with shingles or some other itchy disorder.

The assigned topic was discussed, dissected and argued over without a consensus of opinion, but the fun was in the verbal exchange. Enlivened by the good natured debate, the old guys were very much aware of the value of the kind of mental exercise they were enjoying. Old men need mental stimulation to keep their minds from rotting away, thought Andy. Look at poor old Victor.

Since first starting their little luncheon klatch, they had discussed almost every topic imaginable: politics, religion, history, sociology, science, education and war. Fortunately, the various individuals had diverse opinions, which always afforded stimulating discussions.

Except for Sammy, there existed an invisible unspoken subtle bond between the Scandinavians who shared a common cultural conditioning. Is there a genetic factor that determined behavioral characteristics? Sicilians have always thought so. What about Jews, American Indians and Japanese? Who knows?

The subject turned to Victor's granddaughter, Kira. Andy suggested approaching the guy who manages *Girlies*. "You gonna try to muscle those Russian mafia guys, Andy?" asked Sammy. This got the undivided attention of all. "You got it all wrong, Sammy," said Andy. "Just suppose that we are the mafia and those Russian punks need to be brought into line."

Grinning at the thought of six, no five, very old crippled-up square heads physically intimidating anyone, was rather far-fetched. "Andy, you old goat," yelled Max. "If we were all fifty years younger we might make a pretty good gang," said Gus. "We've got the perfect Vito Corleone," said Sammy, looking at Harry. "Going along with the gag," said Harry, "and who have we here?" looking at Max, "Luca Brazi?" "Damned if we don't have Clemenza," pointing at Andy, "and Tessio," gesturing with an imaginary pistol at Gus. "Here's Michael Corleone," said Max, pointing at Sammy. "Or he could be Tom Hagen." "What about Victor?" "Let's make him Fredo." As all were familiar with the Godfather book and movies, they all enjoyed the silly fantasy.

"What did you have in mind about the manager at

Girlies," asked Harry? Andy looked thoughtful. "I would be willing to pay them a visit along with Father Ryan, my priest at church." Andy enjoyed the distinction of being the only Roman Catholic in the group. He was converted to Catholicism over fifty years ago in order to marry his Catholic sweetheart. Andy was a true believer, but in a quirky way, often attempting to impress his friends with his knowledge of the rituals of the church. The guys did not particularly enjoy religious rituals but never gave him any guff over it. Their religious convictions, with the exception of Max the Lutheran, drifted between secular humanism, rationalism, agnosticism and the Golden Rule.

"I think it's worth a shot," said Max, "That nice little granddaughter could be seduced into becoming a whore in no time." The meeting concluded after a loud discussion about the wisdom of allowing eighteen-year-olds to vote.

Betty, Andy Lindstrom's wife looked up *Girlies* phone number. Andy had found Father Ryan willing to participate in a meeting. All Andy had to do now was make an appointment.

The surly Russian manager of *Girlies* strip club was suspicious of Andy's motives but agreed to meet the following afternoon. After all, arrogance must take a back seat to maintaining a good relationship with community leaders. "That's a joke," thought Yuri Zharkov, "but let's see what these jerks want."

Although Father Ryan made a convincing argument in favor of protecting the innocence of young Kira

Lindstrom, Yuri was adamant. Andy felt as if he was over his head in the conversation and realized he was totally ineffective. After the meeting, Father Ryan and Andy were left with the feeling of frustration and disappointment.

"This guy is impossible!" exclaimed Andy over the phone to Harry. "He's like an underworld mobster or something. He's immoveable. He even admitted he's about to hire Kira. Damn it, we couldn't reason with him." Andy sounded distraught. Harry was silent. Then he almost growled, "Then maybe the Geezer Mafia has to deal with him."

"What possible action could be taken against these thugs?" Andy's question had been on the minds of each of the men in the Geezer group. "We need to make them an offer they can't refuse," chuckled Andy.

The five functioning members of the group were gathered at a lunchroom table at the Ballard WASA Lodge, otherwise known as the "Swedish Club." The lodge offered a workout gym, a swimming pool, lunchroom, meeting rooms, dance hall and fraternal rituals, much the same as the Sons of Norway Lodge six blocks away. The old neighborhood lodges suffered from lack of attendance, as members grew older and died off. Other lodges such as the Elks, Eagles and Odd Fellows, have either disappeared or were struggling to survive.

The Geezers, including Sammy, enjoyed the WASA lodge for social interaction, entertainment and a comfortable refuge. "Maybe I could get my son Butch to send some cops in there to find some legal violations or something," said Max. "With all due respect, Max," remarked Sammy, "these Russians are probably taking care of the cops, if you know what I mean." Sammy's comment drew a fierce glare from Max Hanson, but he did not respond. "Maybe we could picket the place," said Andy. "You know, some gentle picketing might just get those creeps to back off on Kira," said Harry. "You old herring-chokers are really naïve," growled Sammy. The five old men were silent as they thought over Harry's suggestion, wondering if he was serious. Their silence allowed the sound of the pool players in the next room and some old fool practicing the accordion in the dance hall. They recognized the Schottische. Hearing the music, Andy was reminded of the happy times in the past. "The forties and into the eighties, those were the days," said Gus. "Remember the old Bert Lindgren dance hall in Lake City? Our old ethnic music is still fun to listen to."

"Did I tell you guys about my cousin in Sweden?" asked Harry. "The same kid that stayed with you about twenty or twenty-five years ago?" asked Max. "Yeah, he's into politics. After serving as Mayor of Stockholm, he now serves on the Federal Cabinet." "As what?" blurted Victor. "Minister of Democracy is his title, in charge of all kinds of things; immigration, gender equality and some environmental policies." "You were pretty close, as I recall," said Max. "Yes, he stayed with us for a year and attended the university where I taught. We took him on trips all over the state for his American experience." "How many times have you gone to Sweden?" asked Andy. "A half dozen times over the years, we love the family over there and enjoy the different culture," answered Harry. "Is that why you have become a sort of half-assed socialist?" Max grinned. "Quit trying to bait me, you neo-fascist," charged Harry. "I also have another Swedish cousin who has moved to St. Thomas in the US Virgin Islands." "No virgins there, anymore," giggled Victor. "I suppose he moved there to avoid taxes and to enjoy the warm weather," Harry suggested.

The next morning Harry had occasion to discuss the *Girlies* problem with a cousin, Leo Nordland. Although twenty years younger, Leo and Harry had in the past enjoyed a fairly close relationship. When Leo was twelve he joined the Boy Scout troop sponsored by the Ballard First Lutheran Church, where Harry taught Sunday school and served as the scoutmaster. Leo worked his way up the ranks and identified with Harry, his mother's nephew. The weekend hikes in the nearby Cascade and Olympic mountains was the favored activity in which Harry and Leo participated with great enthusiasm for three or four happy years of scouting. Hearing of Harry's concern for Kira, Leo thought his son Bruce, an eighteen-year-old explorer scout, might be interested. "I don't know, Leo, these Russian guys running the strip club are rough customers." "Let me talk to Bruce," said Leo.

One week later a group of five clean-cut teenage boys walked back and forth on the sidewalk in front of the *Girlies* strip club. The boys were all explorer scouts, friends of Bruce Nordland. They each carried a sign stapled to a stick. The signs carried different messages, carefully hand lettered with colored markers. "Leave Kira alone," "Indecent," "Close this place down," "Russians, get out of Ballard," all displayed by the wholesome looking young men who were careful to not physically block the entrance. One two-hour shift of pickets in early evening was replaced by another group of five, from seven to nine p.m.

At first Yuri Zharkov was amused. After three days of continuous picketing, he and his staff inside the strip club became angry. Word quickly spread around the community about the picketers. When Harry learned of it, he called Leo. "That's enough Leo, please tell Bruce to stop picketing. Maybe they have gotten the message." Bruce responded to his dad's phone call by promising to call off the picketing after one more day.

Two days later, after a frantic all night search, Leo and some friends found Bruce unconscious lying in a heap next to a dumpster behind the Safeway store badly beaten, his right arm fractured. Emotionally shaken, Harry couldn't stop apologizing to Leo and Bruce, as they were gathered around Bruce's bed in the Ballard Hospital.

Sammy was seeing Edith almost every day since her return from Mexico. Still very concerned about her ability to bury the slough experience in her consciousness, Sammy was keeping a close eye on her. He was attentive , constantly taking her to dances, dinners and the occasional movie. All the attention seemed to provide the diversion she needed for now, thought Sammy. You can never fully trust secrets to anyone, especially those with some kind of phony conscience.

He had half expected a visit from a detective after reading about the slough murder in the papers. Maybe it's just sloppy police work. He had carefully wiped down the canoe and paddles, he recalled, at the time he returned the canoe. The attendant at the boathouse may have remembered him or Edith, but then again, maybe not. Could there have been any witnesses? No chance. For now, he would just keep in close touch with Edith and keep her happy.

After the usual jokes, the bi-monthly luncheon get-together got under way. The "sunshine report" revealed the ongoing problems as well as disturbing newer ailments. Both Andy and Gus had recently been diagnosed with cancer, prostate and colon respectively. Both were hopeful they would receive effective treatment. "Every day past seventy-five is borrowed," stated Andy.

Except for Victor, all the guys in the group were in a state of serious concern about the fate of Kira. What could become of her in the hand of those Russians? What could be done about that awful strip club right there in the heart of their peaceful old neighborhood? Were these Russian guys part of some version of the new Russian Mafia they had all read about? "What can we do?" "Make a list," said Harry, "use the old brainstorm method." "OK," said Max, "try to get more action from the police vice squad. They should be able to dig up something." "The community council should pressure these organizations," said Harry. "How about vigilante action?" shouted Max. "Strange talk coming from a cop," said Gus. "You guys are supposed to hate vigilantes."

"OK, then," said Max, "How about some Viking raids, you all have Viking blood. You have all inherited Viking courage, haven't you?" "Not me," protested Sammy, getting a chuckle all around. "Here's a suggestion. We organize our own Mafia. You know, a Cosa Nostra organized criminal Mafia family," exclaimed Andy. "We have five families right here." "What do we call this family?" asked Gus. "How about the "Geezer Mafia"?" blurted Andy. "It looks like Andy, Gus and Victor are the button men," laughed Harry. "When do we go to the mattresses?" snickered Andy. "How many of you have seen the Godfather movie – OK, movies – more than twice?" asked Harry. All raised their hands except Victor. Max took Victor's hand and raised it above his head. All the men chortled and looked at each other. "Geezer Mafia it is," shouted Andy. "You don't need to kiss my ring," stated Harry, the new Don in a playful tone. Speaking in Norwegian, Gus addressed the group, "We're going to do something about those goddamned Russians." "We're going to find a way," said Harry, speaking in English, "to make them an offer they can't refuse."

CHAPTER 3

Two days later Harry, Max and Andy met for lunch at Sven's, a hole in the wall eatery in downtown Ballard. They all ordered the lunch special, a small pickled herring appetizer, followed by köttbullar and potatoes (meatballs, potatoes and gravy), supplemented by hardbread and beer. The real thing, thought Max, remembering his mother's cooking. "I've made some calls to people I know who might still have a voice with some of the city hall politicians," Harry's voice carried no conviction. "Ditto with some of the guys I know from the police department, but no real influence anymore." Max's voice betrayed his lack of confidence that any police pressure could be applied to the *Girlies* operation. "I found some information about those Russian guys," said Andy. "Arnie Arneson says those guys rent a forty-two foot cruiser twice a year to go salmon fishing up in the straits. They take a boat load of their guys with names like Yuri, Alex and cornball names like Boris." "When do they go next?" asked Max, his eyes narrowing. "What are you thinking, Max? You want to sink their fishing boat?" Gus asked. "I would if I wasn't worried about my immortal soul," murmured Max, with his big jaw jutting out and his ice-blue eyes flashing. Surprised, Harry spoke, "I knew you were a good Lutheran and devout Republican, Max, but are you serious?" Max just looked at Harry, then into Andy's eyes. "As a Catholic, I think about that too," said Andy. "You don't have to think about spiritual things, Harry, being a damned atheist." "You guys still don't know the difference between atheist and agnostic," said Harry. "You are also dumb enough to believe every word in the Bible." "What's not to believe, Harry? I never knew you were an authority on the Holy Bible." "C'mon guys," said Harry, "You know as well as I do that the Bible was written before we knew there were germs, not to mention gravity." "Which part of the old or new testaments do you think are lies, Mr. Don Corleone Larson?" "I don't think there are very many lies in the Bible, but I think the great truths in the text were written as allegory." "It is all supposed to be the inspired word of God," grunted Andy. "Look," said Harry, "this discussion is maybe for another time, but I'll give you a couple of examples of Biblical pronouncements that are unacceptable in today's world. For example, the Old Testament references like this one: to those people you may not associate with. The "unclean, you know who they are: Outsiders, prostitutes, lepers, cripples, handicapped people, sick people, blind people and the uncircumcised. Also women, during their menstrual period should be shunned because they are unclean. In Exodus 20:7, it says it is OK to sell your daughter into slavery. There's a whole lot more." "Never mind," blurted Max, "We don't need to hear it." "Speaking of violence, as a mortal sin, there are plenty of examples where violence and murder is condoned. An example of righteous violence is when Jesus drove the money changers, the bad guys, from the temple. Violent action against those Russian bastards running *Girlies* strip club may not only be permissible but expected of righteous people in a position to drive them out of the temple," Harry expounded showing some passion. "Never thought of it that way," murmured Andy, his double chin quivering. "Let's keep doing all we can," said Max. "Then we'll talk it over again," stated Harry.

Three nights later Harry and Judy Larson were hosts to Harry's cousin Leo Nordland and son Bruce, now a nineteen-year-old freshman at the University of Washington, near downtown Seattle. The conversation at dinner turned from small talk to Bruce's academic plans.

"My goal is to have a career involved with protecting the environment," stated Bruce.

Apparently fully recovered from the vicious beating he suffered months ago, Bruce was enjoying his college experience. New to a fraternity, he enjoyed the camaraderie. Courses in math, English and chemistry kept him very busy along with his participation in the martial-arts club. What a big handsome kid, thought Judy Larson. Bruce is like a symbol or prototype for an ideal American kid, thought Harry. Strong, athletic, bursting with youthful energy, how could Bruce not be successful at anything?

After dinner, Harry and Bruce found a chance to talk one on one. Bruce asked if Harry had any new information about the thugs that had beaten him three months ago. "Not a thing, Bruce, but we're all pretty sure it was those Russians who run the strip club." Harry was struck by the expression that came over the handsome young man's face, as it seemed to darken, contrasting with the blond hair and the intense penetrating steely gray blue eyes. Oh my god, thought Harry, can the kid be thinking revenge? I guess I can't blame him.

Two days later, Bruce happened to see Kira Lundberg in a local drug store. Creeping up behind her, Bruce whispered in her ear, "Caught ya, you're it!" Kira laughed as she turned to face Bruce. "What are you doing here I thought you were at the UW?" "For classes only, how are you, Kira?" "I'm fine, but I heard some guys beat on you, I'm so sorry Bruce, are you OK now?" "Yeah, I'm OK," said Bruce, his features hardening. "What about you? I hear you are in some kind of danger, is that right?" "It's a part time job, but the pay is good. I'm saving for college." "Yeah, it's really expensive, but are you sure you want to have anything to do with those mugs at *Girlies*?" "No problems, it's been OK so far," said Kira, looking so unbelievably pretty, that Bruce couldn't help feeling nervous. "You sure have grown up since I knew you as a skinny little Swede in high school." "You too, Brussie," said Kira, using an old nickname. They both laughed. "I think the guys who kicked hell out of me are the same underworld bozos that you work for." "I can't believe that," replied Kira, looking somewhat doubtful. "Anyway, take care of yourself Kira." "So long Bruce." "You're gorgeous, Kira, bye."

Meeting Kira aroused feelings, which confused him a bit, but fueled the flame inside his guts, a primitive need for revenge. Gritting his teeth as he walked home, Bruce heard himself say: "Beating the living shit out of those guys may not be enough for me."

CHAPTER 4

"Well guess what old-timer, the Geezer Mafia got something done," hollered Max over the phone. "What did we do?" Harry answered. "Didn't you sic the Health Department on those guys at *Girlies*? Well they've closed them down for violations for about a week, something about a dirty kitchen or bar or something." "That's good news Max, but our efforts to wear them down is going to take more than this I'm afraid," said Harry. "Yeah, but maybe we can think of something else," sighed Max.

At lunch after their volunteer roadside trash pick-up, Andy said, "Gus, you were an explosives expert during the war, right?" "Yep, World War Two, Battle of the Bulge, Belgium, France and Germany. In case you have forgotten, that was almost sixty five years ago," Gus said proudly. "You remember any of that?" "Actually, I think I remember most everything about it in spite of my old age disabilities. What do you want blown up? I used to be good at bridges." "Maybe we'll have to blow up that *Girlies* place," said Andy with a grin. "I know you are kidding you old fart," teased Gus, "but I'm in favor of the idea. Where do I get the explosives?" Andy chuckled and said, "Just having fun fantasizing, but I found out how to get explosives, contraband, dope, cars, whores, anything you want as long as it's illegal." "I take it you've been talking to Arnie Arneson again down at the Marina," said Gus. "It's amazing," said Andy, "all the smuggling that goes on, there's all kinds of stuff hidden on boats between here and Canada only three hours away." "Get me some Cuban cigars sometime," said Gus. "You quit cigars twenty years ago," sneered Andy. "I can still dream," sighed Gus. "Tell you a secret," confided Andy, "Arnie keeps a little storehouse of illegal stuff he trades back and forth, even has plastic explosives." "Too bad we don't still smoke cigars," said Gus.

The following Saturday night found Harry, Andy and Victor in attendance at the Leif Ericksen Branch of the Sons of Norway Lodge midsummer festival dinner, a fancy smorgasbord, with aquavit and beer. The wives of the three looked forward to these happy occasions at the lodge, a lovely Scandinavian-modern three story building in central Ballard.

The after dinner entertainment featured a Norwegian accordion band direct from Oslo via Chicago, Minneapolis and Fargo. The band repertoire included old-time waltzes, schottisches, polkas, snoas and hambos, seldom-heard folk melodies from the old country. Shortly after the music began, the sound of sirens penetrated into the hall. Sounds like a three-alarm fire, thought Harry. Everyone hated the fire sirens.

Entranced by the lovely old-time music, Harry felt someone touch his shoulder. "Come out to the lobby, Harry," said Hjalmar Dahlbeck, manager of the lodge. In the lobby three men with sober expressions gently put their hands on Harry's arms and shoulders. "We think it's your house, Harry," said Hjalmar.

CHAPTER 5

Harry gazed thoughtfully through the large view window overlooking Puget Sound. The dark gray rain clouds were lowering and advancing southward toward the city. Big storm coming thought Harry. In the living room of son Daren's home the family sat quietly close to each other. Daren, his wife Linda, daughter Alison and husband Chip and son Craig, had responded quickly to the bad news of the night before. Daren was speaking: "I told Mom and Dad that we want them to stay here with us until their house is repaired."

All in their fifties, Harry and Judy's family had always enjoyed a loving relationship. Daren, a Boeing

Company engineer, Alison, a high school English teacher and Craig, an architect employed by the State of Washington. The four grandchildren were employed in out-of-state jobs.

"What did the fire chief say about the fire, Dad?" asked Craig sitting on the sofa, his arm around his mother. "He said our house was about half-destroyed, and suspects arson. It usually takes four months to fix the damage," said Harry softly. Strange, thought Alison, Mom and Dad don't seem to be really devastated. I'm sure I would be but I'm glad that they're still pretty tough. "When we think back," said Craig, "anytime things took a bad turn, Mom and Dad were at their best. They kept us going through thick and thin."

The one-week closure imposed by the Health Department was both infuriating and frustrating to Yuri Zharkov. Gathered in the office in the back section of the *Girlies* building were four other men, legal immigrants from Russia. They kept things running at the club. Zharkov's two partners, Ivan Temkin and Igor Vorsky could be described as career criminals. Boris Pochenko and Josef Chimskey, in their late twenties and slightly younger than the other three, enjoyed their roles as bouncers and bullies. That was easily observable by their grim expressions and the body language of designated tough guys.

"We may have taken care of these efforts to close us down," growled Yuri, "But we can't be sure." "We may have to do more," added Ivan. "These old square-head Scandinavians have been such a pain in the ass. We

35

might have to lean on them again, only harder." "Maybe we just ought to kill one of 'em," muttered Josef.

Boris Pochenko had watchman duty at the *Girlies* parking lot on the night the strip club reopened. The parking lot was crowded with perhaps a hundred cars, including those of the manager and his henchmen whose cars were parked in the far corner of the lot. As Boris strutted in between the cars, he was sure they were secure from vandals or thieves but he almost wished for some action. How he loved to smash people's faces with his powerful arms and huge fists.

Distracted by some movement in a shadowed corner of the parking area, Boris collapsed and fell between a new BMW and an old Ford Impala, victim of a powerful blow behind the left ear. "Hope I didn't kill him," said Bruce Nordland, as he tucked a blackjack into his back pocket. The blackjack was inherited from his great uncle, Axel Nordland, who used it back in the days where violence was common on the docks of downtown Seattle.

Bruce had no doubt that the guy crumpled at his feet was one of those involved in the brutal beating he had received a few months earlier. Just a sharp rap behind the ear was all it took to flatten a big cowardly Russian bully. No doubt the other Russian assholes inside the building deserved a "blackjack massage" as well. I wonder, thought Bruce, why we never hear about blackjacks anymore?

Bruce and his explorer scout friends carefully selected the cars belonging to the Russians. The tires on each of the cars were purposefully slashed with large razor sharp hunting knives carried by each of the boys. Smashing the windshields was strangely enjoyable to them all as they wielded heavy sledge hammers with wild abandon. The parking lot was soon littered with shards of broken glass. "That's enough, let's get out of here," shouted Marty Owens, Eagle Scout. All five boys, all Bruce's age, gathered their knives and hammers and ran quickly into the shadows.

Three days had passed when Max received the phone call. It was his son Butch. "Hi Dad, some stuff has been happening in Ballard I have to tell you about." He sounded seriously concerned. An honest hard-working cop, Butch was much like his father. He worshipped his dad whom he regarded as an exemplary human being.

"What's up, Butch?" asked Max. "There were two incidents last night. The watch Captain has assigned detectives to investigate. Those Russian operators of *Girlies* had their tires slashed and their car windshields busted out. They didn't report it. That's very strange. The really bad news is that Kira Lundberg, Victor's granddaughter, was abducted and raped last night. As many as four guys kept her in a motel over on Aurora Avenue and they went after her all night taking turns. Busted her up pretty bad. She's at Harborview Hospital. They say she's out of her head. Victor and Joyce are down there now, but old Victor probably doesn't know what's going on." "Do we know who the guys were?" "No, not yet Pop. I know this is really upsetting for you. Gotta go now. I'll call you tonight."

"Thanks for showing up on such short notice guys,"

said Harry. "I don't think we're in the mood for our regular jokes." "I have one," said Andy. "What do you call ten thousand dead Russians at the bottom of the sea?" "A good start!" No laughs. "That's a lawyer joke," shouted Max.

The meeting was brief. The only topic discussed was the tire slashing and the attack on Kira. "Who could have done those cars?" asked Harry. "I have my suspicions, but that would be a tragedy as well," said Max sadly. "I think I can find out and I'll get back to all of you." All were there except Victor. "We have to put some intensive effort to find out every damn thing we can about those Russians!" exclaimed Max. Churning through their thoughts were questions about their capability to do anything, to have any impact, any positive effect on the Kira situation.

Compared to most eighty-year-old men, Harry, Gus and Max were in fairly "good shape," but age takes its toll. Between them they suffered the usual octogenarian disabilities: cancer, prostate problems, arthritis, worn-out tendons, muscles and joints, Parkinson symptoms, failing eye sight, deafness and perhaps the worst of all, impotency. As if that were not enough, they were also dealing with memory loss and the tendency to misunderstand, misinterpret and the inability to effectively communicate. Did they possess the necessary strength, stamina, mobility and courage to take any action at all? Maybe we will need to rely on Sammy Aaron who is younger and shrewder, thought Harry. There is something about my friend Sammy that is not only mysterious but dangerous as well.

"Ok, then it's decided," declared Harry, "We will spend all the time we can gathering information about those bad asses at *Girlies*." "Maybe Butch can help find out something," said Gus. "We're working on it, Gus," said Max. "One more thing," interrupted Andy, "remember what we heard about how those guys all go salmon fishing every fall? They rent a boat here at Shilshole wharf and spend a week fishing in the straits off Vancouver Island." "When is their next trip?" asked Max. "Four of 'em are leaving the week after next." "Find out everything you can about their fishing trip, Andy," said Sammy. "I'm curious."

"Hi cousin, I'm returning your call, what's up?" Bruce Nordland liked Harry, his father's cousin. His voice was a strong youthful baritone. "I need to see you," replied Harry. "Do you still jog down at Golden Garden's park on Saturday mornings?" "Yeah, every Saturday about nine a.m. You want to meet me there by the boathouse?" "OK Bruce, I'll jog along with you, if you go slowly, and we can talk." Harry arrived finding Bruce doing his stretches. "Let's walk," said Harry. "What's on your mind, cousin?"

Bruce was such a great kid. Hell, he's the perfect kid, thought Harry. "Are you responsible for harassing those Russkies at *Girlies*?" "How did you know?" Bruce grinned. "I just guessed. You must quit that nonsense. You'll have to get your revenge in a different way. This way is counterproductive. Besides, it's dangerous. Those guys are really nasty and unpredictable." "I didn't think anybody knew it was me and a few of my buddies," said

Bruce. "Oh, god, now you have your friends involved. You've got to back off now, Bruce. I'm not kidding. Promise me." "I know you're thinking of my best interest, Harry. I promise I'll think about it. I really respect you and I will back off for now. Kira is recovering from that brutal rape but she's a mess, mentally. I've gotten to really like her. I still think the same guys who beat hell out of me that night attacked her. I'd bet anything on it."

At eight a.m. Sunday morning, it was foggy with a misty rain in the cool air. Max Hanson was briskly walking along the gravel path near the Government Locks. The locks provided access to boats of all sizes to travel to and from the spectacular Puget Sound connecting the freshwater lakes in the heart of Seattle. Despite his eighty-two years Max was still physically strong. He took pride in his physicality. As he strode briskly along the path, he was suddenly aware of two men walking behind him, big guys in their twenties or thirties wearing caps and dark wind breaker jackets. From behind some bushes about twenty feet ahead stepped two more men, one short and husky and the second one very tall. Max had seen similar body language many times before. These guys are looking for trouble. What do they want with me? Max could feel his heart beat faster and his senses sharpen. Brave Max couldn't help feeling genuinely fearful.

CHAPTER 6

"OK Geezers, it's time to start the meeting," said Harry. "Everybody's here but Max. He's never late. We'll go ahead anyway. Who's got a joke?" After some bad lowbrow jokes and a disturbing health report, the good works reports were brief. As they ate lunch the discussion was mostly about the *Girlies* mob. Were those guys really some kind of Russian Mafia? Who is it that has been slashing tires and smashing windshields in their parking lot? Where the heck was Max? The animated conversation, comments and questions continued as they picked away at their food. Just as everyone was finishing the last vestiges of Oscar's lunch special, the waitress showed up with a package. "A messenger just left this box for you gentlemen," she announced as she entered the door of their partitioned little lunchroom. "There's a note you're supposed to read first," she called as she left the room.

"Read it Harry," said Gus. "Is it a cake? Big cake box. What a surprise. Who sent it?" Harry read the attached card aloud. "Here is delicious dessert for you." "Open it," said Victor. As Harry started to pry open the lid, Sammy shouted, "Hold it, Harry, don't open that box! Don't open it," screamed Sammy. It was too late, partly open, Harry gasped in horror as he looked at the staring eyes and bloody head of his lifelong friend Max Hanson.

The next morning found Sammy striding into the local Wells Fargo Bank carrying an empty black bag on a shoulder strap. After a quick visit to his safety deposit box, he got into his car and drove twenty-five miles south on I-5 to Tacoma. Pulling up to an old decrepit looking warehouse near the old Tacoma dock area, he climbed two flights of stairs to a dingy office with no name on the door. Sammy knocked. "Come in, Sammy," hollered a voice. "I saw you pull in. Long time no see." The voice belonged to a huge dark complexioned middle aged man with thinning gray hair, a black mustache and furtive squinty black eyes. "Do you have the stuff I called about?" asked Sammy. "It's right here. You got the cash?" "Yeah, and I'm kind'a in a hurry, Jimbo," said Sammy. Leaving with a large heavy black satchel, Sammy put it carefully in the trunk of his car. That afternoon, back in Ballard, Sammy called Gus and Andy. "Let's get together right away," he said over the phone.

The neighborhood had never seen so many police uniforms, plain-clothes detectives and city officials. The news of Max Hanson's murder spread throughout the county. Seattle had seldom seen such a media craze. It seemed that everyone expressed shock, outrage and a desire for justice. Where is the line that separates justice and revenge?

The police had quickly organized teams of investigators. Grim-faced Seattle detectives visited each of the five Geezers. Strangely, none of the old guys accused the group of Russians at *Girlies*. Hard-faced couldn't describe the grim expressions when questioned by the police. It could be described as a combination of profound personal loss, intense anger, a deep hatred beyond description and an unstoppable determination for revenge. Outwardly however, to the authorities each man projected sadness over the loss of a friend, and hoped the killers would soon be brought to justice.

"Did Max have any enemies that you know of?" "No."

"Did he hang out with any shady characters?" "Not that we know of." "Do you suspect anybody?" "No." How could the detectives know that these ordinary apparently good hearted eighty-something old fossils had agreed before any interviews on exactly what to say to the cops?

The initial shock of having poor Max's head delivered to them in a bloody box had sent them home in a profound sadness. Devastated, they needed support from each other in the worst way. Consequently, the day after the unforgettable experience at Oscars, they talked on the phone to each other, depending on Harry as a coordinator. Perhaps because they all felt an overwhelming anger override their grief, even though they all cried during their discussions, they knew that revenge (justice?) belonged exclusively to them. They had to, they needed to, they felt compelled because of their love for their wonderful faithful friend, to kill the guys who had murdered and beheaded, beheaded! Max Hanson. Don't tell the cops anything. We are not too old, too decrepit. We may be falling apart, but we can – god damn it – avenge Max. Whatever it takes those Russian bastards are going down.

Max's memorial a few days later was held at the WASA Lodge. The crowd overflowed into the street, where loudspeakers had been set up. A Marine color guard gave full military honors to Max, a WWII Pacific area combat veteran, a decorated hero. The Seattle police department color guard led the funeral procession through the Ballard streets. Police cars, the police drill team and the police pipe band all participated in the

43

funeral of a good and decent man.

"Where do we look for the body?" Police Captain of Detectives Lucas Carter asked of his investigative team. Lieutenant Nat Maxwell answered: "We may never find it captain. It's likely that Max's body is at the bottom of Puget Sound, sleeping with the fishes, so to speak." "What is Butch Hanson saying about this?" queried Captain Carter. "He's strangely quiet. He's so shaken up, I think he's in shock," answered Maxwell.

The day after the funeral Andy and Gus paid a visit to Arnie Arneson at the Shilshole Marina. "Their plans haven't changed. They're leaving Sunday for their fishing trip and will be gone for a week." "Who will be aboard?" asked Gus. "There will be five of them on that forty-two footer. You can see her from here. The Sea Swan, nice boat, only three years old. She'll cruise in good water at twelve knots." "How far are the Straits?" asked Sammy. "About forty miles," replied Arnie. "Who did you say would be on board?" Andy persisted. "Oh, I am required to turn in a list? Here it is in my jacket: Yuri Zharkov, Boris Vochnsky, Ivan Temkin, Josef Molotov and the fifth guy, Rocco Bella." "An Italian," murmured Sammy. "Yeah, they said he's a friend from out of town."

The salmon fishing trip on the Sea Swan was scheduled for departure on Sunday at seven a.m., September fourteenth. On Saturday the thirteenth, it was drizzling a bit at five a.m. when Arnie unlocked the gate, allowing three men to enter. The first man aboard the Sea Swan, carrying a large brown satchel, was Sammy Aaron, wearing a dark hooded raincoat. Andy and Gus both carrying tote bags, followed. After quickly inspecting the handsome forty-two foot cruiser, they held a brief conference, then set to work carefully placing the plastic explosives, programming the detonators and timing devices.

Twenty minutes later they sat in a booth at the Pancake House in the Fremont neighborhood a few blocks east of the Ballard Bridge. All agreed that their project had gone well. "Let's hope the eleven a.m. setting will see the Sea Swan right in the middle of the Straits," said Gus in a grim quiet voice. "Should be perfect," murmured Andy, swallowing a big piece of pancake covered with sweet Pancake House syrup.

"The detonator technology is a lot more sophisticated than it was a few years ago when we used 'em on cars," said Sammy, with an evil grin. "You're kidding, right?" Gus asked, a surprised expression coming over his face. No answer from Sammy, just a knowing smirk. "Yeah," said Gus, "the stuff they use now is a hell of a lot more powerful than the explosives we used to blow up bridges in Belgium and Germany in the Big War." "With what we put in that boat, that blast will be heard for twenty miles. Won't be anything left of the boat or any of those bad guys in it," growled Sammy.

CHAPTER 7

Still in a mental fog, Kira Lundberg was well enough to be released from Harborview Hospital. Bruce Nordland was there to drive her home. Poor lovely Kira, he thought, what an awful humiliating experience for her. Then there's the shame, as if it was her fault. She may never be able to shed the horror of it. Somebody has to pay. Those guys who did this do not deserve to have a life.

Kira sat quietly in the car with eyes lowered, shoulders sagging, as Bruce drove toward Victor and Joyce's Ballard home and Kira's home as well. I wonder how she will adapt after all this trauma.

On Friday September 12th, Harry Larson and Sammy Aaron were enjoying the late summer sunset. As they walked along the path at Shoreline Park, a few blocks from Daren Larson's home, Harry marveled at the dramatic colors in the sky above the blue waters of Puget Sound and the blue-violet snow-capped peaks of the Olympic Mountain range in the distance. "No matter how many thousands of times I must have seen this," said Harry, "I'm always completely awed by it. Every time."

"Do you think the cops are through interrogating us about Max's death?" asked Sammy. "Yeah I think so. I'm cleared to take our vacation to Sweden." "Staying with cousins?" "Yes." "That's good, Harry. Listen," said Sammy, "I've got something to tell you. You have been a terrific friend. I can't tell you how much I have appreciated your friendship." "Don't get too sentimental on me Sammy," laughed Harry. "You know I've always liked you too Sammy, ever since we met at the driver's safety class, even though we didn't have a whole lot in common. Maybe we just have some kind of mysterious rapport." "Then you invited me into your group of friends," chuckled Sammy. "We met for lunch, we had poker sessions and we volunteered for charity work together. You even got me to join the WASA Lodge. Imagine a Jew interacting with a bunch of crazy Swedes." Both chuckled, as Sammy continued, "I really have admired the unselfish work you old duffers do for the community." "Geezers," Harry corrected. "And the way you work with those guys. You're their leader. They really respect you Harry." "They loved Max too, damn it," said Harry choking up.

"Didn't you tell me your relative over in Sweden is a Government official?" "Yes," said Harry, "his name is Erik Limback, a second or third cousin. He's a cabinet member with the title of Minister of Democracy and in charge of immigration, among other things." Sammy spoke softly in a confidential tone; "I think you should stay over there for a longer time, maybe live in Stockholm for awhile." Harry gave him a quizzical look, which hardened into a grim expression. "What's going on, Sammy?" "Okay, listen Harry, it's time I leveled with you. You've never really asked me about my history." "Only that you talk like a New York or New Jersey street punk, at times," grinned Harry. "Well, there's more to it than that. Why do you think I suddenly started to live up here in no-man's land?" "You got smart?" "Part of it, I got sent here. You've heard of the government witness protection program?" "Oh Sammy," said Harry, "not you." "Yes me, I didn't have a choice. Death was my only other option. I have to leave here for good before next Sunday. I can't say where to, but give me your Stockholm address and some day I'll be in touch." "Wait a minute," said

Harry, "you have to tell me about this." Sammy spoke in hushed tones as they walked together. "Organized crime operations are everywhere in New Jersey. Not like out here. I grew up with it. All my friends, everybody I looked up to in my neighborhood were all connected in some way on some level with the mob. I started as a fifteen-year-old messenger boy for the wise guys on the street, advanced to a bag-guy, eventually as a stooge for some of the big players. After that to a button man, an enforcer, a soldier, a god damned hit man."

Harry could hardly believe what he was hearing. They stopped walking and sat on a park bench. "At some point, the Feds got enough evidence to take ten or fifteen big shots in our family to trial. They gave me a choice, testify against them or face prison. Either way it meant I would get whacked. My life would be over. So they offered witness protection, a new name, a new city, a new life. I testified, but not before I was able to get into their safe in the back room. I was able to boost over a million. So I betrayed everybody, my bosses, my fellow executioners and leg breakers, my friends, and my family. What a wonderful guy I turned out to be." "Aren't the crime families mostly Sicilian?" asked Harry. "Those are the ones you hear about," said Sammy, "but Jews have played their parts to. Remember Dutch Schultz, Meyer Lansky, Mickey Cohen, Bugsy Seigal and there were lots of others. New Jersey is full of Italian, Jewish, Black and Hispanic mob-connected criminals." "What do those crime organizations give or offer their constituents?" asked Harry. "Protection from other parasites mostly. They don't really give, they take. You don't fool me, Harry, I'm sure you have read all about the mob sub-culture." "I know they have their own rules outside the main society," said Harry. "Yeah rules, their own code of behavior, their own version of morality, their own form of justice." "How can organized crime exist if it functions as total evil?" "Not totally," said Sammy. "The mob rewards loyalty; actually rights certain wrongs when the legal authorities can't get it done. It thrives on legalized hypocrisy and takes advantage of crooked cops, lawyers, judges, politicians and freelance hoodlums. Imagine all the millions the big families have made from numbers, prostitution, loan sharking, extortion, bribery, illegal payoffs, blackmail, drugs and now gambling casinos, which they have managed to get legalized all over the country."

"Where does the Geezer Mafia fit in?" asked Harry with a twinkle in his eyes. "Harry our group of old Geezers have been heroes in the local community. Lately they have tried to deal with some very tough characters but I think that even that problem may be solved soon enough. I believe," said Sammy thoughtfully, "that these old men in spite of their years, have the guts to take action against guys who deserve to pay a price for Max, for Bruce, for Kira, for Victor and Joyce, and for burning your house down. These guys have it coming. You know as well as I do that these creeps will continue just as they always have. The authorities will never deal with them." "What's going on that I don't know about, Sammy?" "It will all be resolved just after you leave for Stockholm," said Sammy grimly. "You mean you guys are planning something without my knowledge?" "Look Harry I know your kids are taking care of restoring your house while you're in Sweden. Take my advice, plan to stay there for at least a year."

"You guys don't need to go around me. I want to get rid of those Russians just as much as the rest of you do." "We wanted to protect our Don," said Sammy. "We had just enough soldiers to do the job without involving you Harry." There was a long pause. "You should have let me in on it. Remember after they killed Max I knew we had to do it ourselves. That's why I asked our Geezers not to finger the Russians. The cops were never going to nail those guys. The Geezer Mafia carries out its own justice, right Sammy?" "Right, Harry. Stay in Sweden at least a year. Sammy stood up and looked intently – affectionately – at his friend. "Goodbye Harry, " he said as he turned and walked quickly down the walkway.

A few hours later alone in his apartment, Sammy worried about this man Rocco Bella. He seemed to remember the name. From Chicago, he thought. Bad news. He never would have suspected a connection between these Russians and the Chicago mob. Sammy decided to try to get all the Geezers out of town by Monday.

The going away party was at Daren Larson's house. Harry and Judy, despite a few awkward or uncomfortable moments here and there, had been enjoying their stay with their son and daughter-in-law, Linda. Enjoying drinks and a tasty buffet, the group included Harry's and Judy's relatives and closest friends along with Bruce and Kira.

Kira and Bruce had become close friends during her recovery. Bruce had been very attentive and spent a lot of time with her. In fact, Bruce had fallen head over heels for Kira who was still in a kind of post traumatic shock. No more table dancing for her. She was slowly becoming the truly sweet person she had always been except for the brief period of teenaged craziness that led to a psychological disaster. With Joyce and Bruce's help, she longed for the wholesome life she had always known. Sammy was present, quietly enjoying seeing Harry at his happiest since Max's death. More drinks, jokes, stories, dessert, coffee and the party was over at an early hour.

Harry and Judy enjoyed every moment and felt very lucky. "We should be back in three weeks or less," said Harry, avoiding Sammy's look from across the room. "And we'll get together then."

Suddenly a dark thought came into Harry's mind; something tells me I won't be seeing some of these friends again. I want that thought to go away.

Saturday afternoon Harry and Judy Larson boarded the SAS plane at SeaTac airport. When landing at the Stockholm airport they anticipated a hearty welcome just as they had in other previous visits.

CHAPTER 8

The information about the Russians scheduled movements seemed to be accurate, coming partly from

Arnie Arneson and partly from Kira and the girls she had met while working at *Girlies*. The Russians in charge always met early Sunday morning in the back office to count the money from Saturday night's take. The money was kept temporarily in a big security safe. Yuri and Boris usually took the cash deposit to the Ballard Bank of America to be kept as part of their permanent account. After that they shared clean up duty and prepared for next week's business.

Anticipating a Sunday morning arrival of the Russians, Sammy and Bruce sat in the *Girlies* office, Sammy holding a 9mm Glock automatic pistol and Bruce gripping a .38 special revolver. Inherited from his great uncle Axel, Bruce treasured the revolver along with a nasty little blackjack that he had put to use a few weeks before.

Entering the locked building was no problem for Sammy, the professional, who could effect a break-in almost anywhere. Sammy took pride in his lock-picking, safe cracking and assassination abilities as well.

Since four of the regular strip club managers were cruising north on Puget Sound today, Sammy and Bruce weren't sure whom to expect. They guessed there would be only two or three guys and should be easy to handle. Sammy hoped the Chicago goombah was not one of them. "Are you sure you're ready for this, Bruce?" "I'm so damned infuriated over what these guys did to Kira, I'm ready to smoke these bozos right now," growled Bruce. "You have to be very cool when the time comes kid, a bad mistake now would be letting down the Geezer Mafia," warned Sammy.

Josef Molotov and Nick Polovsky, both in their late twenties swaggered up to the front porch and unlocked the door. Josef, about 6' 2", two hundred ten pounds was a very tough looking Russian, with dark hair, thick black eyebrows, unshaven, with a broad black mustache. His companion, who was shorter, with close cropped blond hair and the beginning of a potbelly, echoed Josef's arrogant expression. Both were dressed in dark rumpled clothes, Josef sporting a brown turtleneck sweater.

As the two came through the office door, a loud shout startled them, "Stop right there and put your hands up." Sammy yelled again, with professional authority, "On the floor face down, hands behind your backs, or goddamn it, we'll kill you right now!" "Which one of you opens the safe? If you tell me you can't, we'll shoot both of you in the head in five seconds. Then we will leave. You'll be dead." "Okay, I'll do it," said Josef, in a shaky voice. "Faster," shouted Sammy. "Put all the cash in this bag." "Okay," said Nick, "you have money now you can go, we say nothing." "Shut your mouth. I'll tell you when you can speak." Surprised at his own words, Bruce blurted, "Let's just kill them now!" "Just a minute," said Sammy, "we might let you two pieces of shit live if you tell us something. It had better be absolutely true or you both are dead." Surprised, disoriented and crazed with fear, both Russians began to beg for their lives. "Shut up! Tell us which one of you raped Kira Lundberg, that little blonde dancer?" Josef and Nick began to babble, "No, no, not me! It wasn't us, it was Yuri and Boris." Other names were shouted out. Sammy said quietly, "I told you the absolute truth… we won't kill you if you tell us the truth. We can tell if you lie." "We all did it," said Nick, "But Yuri ordered us to do it. It was not our doing!"

Both Josef and Nick were securely tied to office chairs. Bruce and Sammy stood opposite them leaning over them with their guns pressed against their necks. Sammy was surprised to hear the blast of Bruce's revolver as he shot directly into Josef's genitals, and then a second shot as Josef shrieked. "How about you, are you going to tell us you didn't burn Harry Larson's house down?" yelled Bruce. "Yes we did it," screamed Nick. "You also killed Max Hanson, didn't you?" "No, no, that was Boris and Igor. Yuri told them to do it." "Please don't kill me!" Blood gushed from Josef's crotch, running over the chair onto the floor. "He's still alive," said Sammy, looking at Josef hunched over in his chair moaning his last moans. "You deserve to die," said Sammy, blasting two powerful slugs into Nick's chest and one more into Josef's heart.

"Just a minute," said Sammy, pulling a small .22 caliber Smith and Wesson revolver from a waist holster hidden at the small of his back. The little pistol popped twice, the first shot penetrating Josef's head just above the left ear. The second shot entering Nick's right temple, each shot spraying a burst of blood and brain tissue out the opposite side of the heads. "That'll make it look like a mob hit. It could be a nice distraction for the cops," Sammy hissed. Bruce kept strangely calm but was eager to dash out of the place. "We'll go back through the rear window the way we came in. Grab that bag of cash and let's go," said Sammy the professional.

In Sammy's apartment twenty minutes later, the money was swiftly counted, divided and tucked away, eighteen thousand and change each. "Now we're both murderers and thieves," said Bruce, as he prepared to leave. "First time for you kid. Today you have made your bones. Maybe I told you I never whacked anybody who didn't have it coming. These guys had it coming and don't ever forget it. You can use this money for Kira. She's going to need more therapy. I'll use the money to get myself lost. Again." "Where will you go?" asked Bruce, his voice trembling. "I need to get out of the country for a while. Maybe I'll visit Castro, or maybe I'll find Shangri La. You don't need to know. Get out of here Bruce. Good luck to you."

Bruce drove nearly thirty miles east on I-90 across the floating bridge leaving the highway at Issaquah, onto side roads, taking a turn into the parking lot marking the entry trail to Tiger Mountain. "Where have you been?" yelled Tim Rogge. "You're late man," said Ted Scalzo. "Let's get going," said Porky Katz, "times a wasting." All three were dressed for the six mile hike up Tiger Mountain and back, equipped with hiking boots, shorts and day packs, with their carefully packed lunches and water bottles. Close friends since kindergarten all were former Eagle and Explorer Scouts. At almost twenty-one years old they enjoyed the special bond of friendship and anticipated continuing comradeship as they entered adulthood. "Okay, okay, just give me a couple of minutes," yelled Bruce as he retrieved his hiking gear from the trunk of his car.

Just before starting up the trail, Bruce gathered the group together. "Listen, I need you to back me up." "Why, what's up?" asked Porky. "If anybody ever asks you are to say I have been with you since eight this morning, all of us together." "How come, you need an alibi or something?" asked Tim. "That's right. I'm trusting you," said Bruce with a serious tone, "I want you to swear to it." They all murmured assurances. "Yeah, okay, you got it. Let's get on the trail," said Ted Scalzo.

Sammy had been right. The Sea Swan blast was heard for almost twenty miles from the spot in the Straits of Juan De Fuca, at eleven a.m., exactly as planned. Television and newspaper reports described the explosion of the Sea Swan as "spectacular." Witnesses in fishing boats nearby reported a waterspout rising sixty feet into the air and bits and pieces of the boat (and occupants) spattered as far as fifty yards in all directions. Most of what was left quickly sank into two hundred feet of water.

On the run, Sammy drove rapidly to Sacramento, where he sold his car to a dealer and boarded a plane to Mexico City. Pleased that he had engineered the demise of Yuri Zharkov and his gang of rapists, arsonists and murderers; Sammy felt that his accomplishment was a noble one for the good of a community of civilized kind-hearted people. Nice people, even if they are a bunch of naive herring-chokers. Sammy was still uneasy about the possibility that the Dago Mafia was connected to those mob guys he had just capped up in Seattle. They have ingenious ways of finding people they want to snuff.

All in all, Sammy was quite proud of himself and looked forward to starting a new life. Whatever it turned out to be he could always adapt and take pleasure, especially with a brand-new name.

One year later Harry Larson was on the phone from Stockholm talking to his kids, gathered in Daren's Shoreline home. "We have good news, Mom and Dad," said Daren, "and some bad news." "Your house is completely rebuilt. The neighbors keep a close eye on it," said Craig. "Kira and Bruce are getting married," Alison chipped in. "She's taking classes at the Udub and Bruce is anticipating his degree in only 2 years," said Craig.

"Dad," said Daren, "that *Girlies* place has never reopened. I guess you may have heard about the killings and the fishing boat blowing up." "Yes, we heard about it," said Harry slowly. "What's the bad news?" asked Judy. "They had to put Victor in a nursing home. Andy and Betty have gone to live in a retirement home. There both sick. One of those assisted living places with a built-in clinic." "What about Gus?" asked Harry. "Sorry to tell you Dad but Gus passed away just last week. Pancreatic cancer. It was quite sudden." Harry's eyes filled with tears. "I'm so glad you are all well," said Judy. "How long will you be staying with our fabulous cousins there in Stockholm?" asked Craig. "They are really wonderful," said Judy. "We like it here," said Harry, "we miss you all but we're going to stay here for a while. Maybe for quite some time."

"We love you Mom and Dad..."

The private dining room at Oscar's waterfront

restaurant was noisy with happy laughter and conversation. Present were Bruce Nordland, his three buddies, Tim Rogge, Teddy Scalzo and Porkchop Katz. Butch Hanson, two decades older than the others, sat quietly at the table sipping a bottle of Danish beer. "Okay you guys, let's settle down... Who has a joke?"

THE RATIONALIST

Gayle Westbrook raised the spoon to Billy's lips. "Come on Billy, eat your breakfast. It's hot cereal, nice and sweet, with little fruit bits just the way you like it."

Unwilling to feed himself, Billy grimaced, but opened his mouth allowing her to feed him. "I hate this," growled Billy Ortega. "And I hate you too, you filthy bitch."

Gayle smiled as she continued to feed the uncooperative Billy, carefully wiping his mouth after each bite. "There," she sighed, "All finished for now. Later this morning we will put you into the van and go to the park."

Billy glared at her and replied "Why go to the park if you can't walk?"

"You know you enjoy the park, Billy," she said. "Anyway I enjoy pushing your wheelchair, as we take in the fresh air."

A paraplegic, Billy Ortega had lost the use of his legs two years before. An unfortunate accident had resulted in a severed spinal cord and the loss of his bodily functions from the waist down. Billy was unable to accept his condition. Along with severe depression, he was immersed in self pity alternating with profound sadness. Gayle had taken over as Billy's full time caretaker for the last eighteen months. She had convinced the welfare authorities (those caring for Billy Ortega after his accident) that she was willing and capable of assuming complete care of the sixty-five-year-old paraplegic. No family support was available for Billy's care. The relationship was a bizarre case in which Gayle Westbrook had abruptly left her husband of forty-one years to care for a hopelessly crippled, homeless, poverty stricken man. How could such an unexplainable, illogical, incredible thing come to pass?

Vincente Ortega, Billy's father emigrated from Mexico in the early forties. As the United States furiously geared up for wartime production of almost everything, there was a great demand for workers. Vincente found work on California farms, orchards, and later in construction projects. His income made it possible for him and his wife Rosa to raise a family and enjoy the fruits of middle class American life.

They named their first-born son William, a nice gringo name. Assimilating into American life was all-important to Vincente and Rosa Ortega, even though they still spoke mostly Spanish within the family. In the case of their two daughters however, they could not resist giving them Spanish/Mexican names that seemed appropriate. Esperanza and Margarita were perfect names for their two little girls.

Everyone in the family doted on William (always called Billy) because of his perceived importance as the first son in a Mexican-American family. Billy had an alert mind, and realized from the very first that he was special. He got anything he demanded, and behaved like a perfectly spoiled brat. Billy seemed always to be able to get away with aberrant behavior, resisting discipline and a defiant attitude became "natural" to Billy.

There were a few times in his early life when his father whipped him with his big leather belt after Billy had been caught shop lifting, smoking, lying or tormenting his sisters, but for the most part Billy did as he pleased and got away with almost everything.

Billy Ortega was not only a handsome kid, with flowing black hair and a charming smile, but he was a natural athlete, apparent even at age ten. At about that time his father signed him up on a local Little League baseball team, where he quickly became the star shortstop. Unfortunately, Billy played for only half a season, continually in some sort of squabble with his teammates, coaches, umpires, and anyone involved with his team.

Suspended from his team, Billy turned to other activities, mostly with a neighborhood gang. The group was a ragtag hostile mix of Hispanic and black teenagers, eager to make trouble and steal whatever they could get away with. As a teenager in the late 50's, Billy's family moved between cities in California, wherever Vincente could find work.

In 1960, the Ortega family had settled in Seattle, Washington where Billy and his sisters, Esperanza and Margarita, attended high school. The girls were excellent students and made friends easily. As a high school junior, Margarita Ortega found a lifelong friend. Gayle Talbott was a vivacious, lovely sixteen year-old cheerleader, class officer, and homecoming queen. Her friends could never figure out why she befriended the little Hispanic nobody, but Margarita and Gayle became very close friends.

Brother Billy had turned out for sports, and proved to be an outstanding athlete, even though he was kicked off both the basketball and football teams. "A defiant undisciplined troublemaker" was how his coaches described him. Billy did manage to play a complete season on the high school baseball team where he was the leading batter. His baseball teammates mostly avoided him however, because of their perception of him as cocky and selfish, "a loud mouthed hot shot."

It was well known around school that Billy Ortega was hanging out with groups of boys involved with drugs and other nefarious activities.

The irony was that Billy was very popular with the girls. They couldn't help but be attracted to Billy's dazzling smile and charismatic personality. Billy Ortega was a charmer, and most girls he met fell for him right away. He became rather famous within the high school underground for his many sexual conquests.

In large high schools students can attend for the entire three or four years without getting to know many – if not most – of their classmates. Billy Ortega met Gayle Talbot only once, late in their senior year. Billy's sister Margarita introduced them at a school dance. There was no following social interaction. Billy never remembered

Gayle, but Gayle was quite taken with him at the time of their brief meeting.

After high school Billy attended a community college on a baseball scholarship for one year. As usual he couldn't handle prosperity, and dropped out. Almost by accident however, he was signed into a Real Estate class in which he received a big surprise. He liked it. He took to it. He decided he wanted a career in the real estate business.

Gayle Talbot followed her brother to the University of Washington in Seattle. The opportunities and challenges of a big time prestigious university were perfect for Gayle Talbot, a straight-A student, intelligent, beautiful and charming. Gayle had everything including a wealthy father, doting mother and two very supportive siblings, an older brother Bradley, and younger sister Lacey.

Gayle's father, Carter Talbot, was a prominent Seattle attorney and partner in one of Seattle's largest corporate law firms. Money was no problem for the Talbots. Bradley Talbot eventually finished medical school and became an MD specializing in cardiac research and treatment. Sister Lacey became a college professor of psychology at Reed College in Portland, Oregon. Married to a professor of paleontology, Lacey Smoot was totally engaged in her work and her family of two daughters, Carol and Beth.

From the start Gayle Talbot thrived on her college classes and outside activities. After her freshman year, she became drawn to classes in philosophy and logic. Becoming acquainted with the great philosophers, she was inspired to learn what connections she could discover between the opinions of the great philosophers and the objectivity of the systems of logic. Gayle became obsessed with finding rational and objective truth. The search led to classes of interest in religion, mathematics and anthropology.

Gayle's interests were not strictly confined to her studies. She participated in women's intramural sports; volleyball and swimming were her favorites. She enjoyed an active social life as well, attending sorority and fraternity parties and dances. It was there that she met handsome Franklin Westbrook. From their first meeting they sensed that they were fated to be together. Franklin was the perfect physical specimen, with his blond, blue-eyed Aryan features and muscular 225-pound athletic body. "How is it we haven't met before?" He asked when they first met.

Gayle quietly asked, "Where have you been hiding?" "Out on the practice field," Franklin grinned. In his first year of varsity football Franklin was emerging as the starting tailback on the Washington Husky Rose-bowl bound football team. For his senior year, he was dubbed "Frank the Tank," by virtue of his ability as a powerful running back, one of the best in the Pacific Coast Conference.

One date led to another and soon Gayle and Frank were inseparable. Franklin Westbrook graduated two years ahead of Gayle Talbot and entered law school. They were married soon after. Successful in everything he ever did, Frank became a big time criminal attorney.

Gayle continued her education, earning a master's degree in philosophy. Along with two successful careers, Gayle and Frank Westbrook enjoyed their son and daughter, rarely missing the opportunity to share their growing-up experiences. Both were proud beyond words of their kid's successes, Julie the high school teacher, and Tyler the doctor.

While the Westbrooks were perceived as a "typical" upper class family, enjoying the fruits of wealth and privilege, Gayle sometimes had to disguise her inner feelings about the inequities and hypocrisy she felt she was part of.

Gayle and Frank enjoyed their membership in the prestigious Broadmoor Country Club. The parties, golfing and other activities were pleasurable enough, but to Gayle the prevailing political and social attitudes were sometimes difficult for her to reconcile with her own liberal concerns about social and economic disparities in the American culture.

To compensate, Gayle became an enthusiastic worker for charitable causes. Heart disease, cancer, child abuse, women's rights, homelessness, you name it. Gayle contributed, recruited and organized, always with sincere intentions to help those less fortunate.

Gayle's friends were continually amazed at how she managed a growing family, supported charitable causes, seemed an ideal partner for her husband in his busy career, and continued to educate herself.

In those years, Gayle involved herself in social, political and spiritual interests. She often described herself as a secular humanist, sometimes as an agnostic rationalist.

"A rationalist," she declared, "is someone who values objective evidence over blind faith. Actions must be based on common sense and concern for others. The alternative will ultimately be the end of any kind of rational world. It's clear that greed and excess will take over unless people understand what is happening."

Raising a family and their busy careers kept Gayle and Frank from the friends they had made in their college days. Many of the friends from that time still sent Christmas cards. But with few exceptions, they remained out of touch.

One exception was Gayle's friend from Garfield High School, the vivacious Margarita Ortega. Mostly through the years they had written notes, letters, and the occasional e-mail. On the evening of Gayle's sixtieth birthday she received a call from her old friend Margarita Ortega. "Happy Birthday Gayle, I think of you often and I've missed you so much over the years." Gayle's eyes moistened. "Margarita, it's so sweet of you to call. What a wonderful surprise." "Can we get together for lunch? It's been so long. Can you find the time?" Margarita's voice seemed to imply an earnest need.

Meeting for lunch at a downtown restaurant brought back happy memories for both Margarita and Gayle. Both bubbled over with reminiscences, family stories and accounts of the past thirty-five years. Like Gayle, Margarita was deeply involved with a loving family, but voiced serious concern about her older brother, Billy.

Margarita looked earnestly at Gayle and spoke, "My older brother Billy has had a crazy up and down life, not exactly a model of virtue, but I still love him and he's in a bad situation right now. I thought with your charitable connections you might possibly be able to help him." Big hearted Gayle agreed, along with Margarita, to visit Billy that very afternoon. Gayle vaguely remembered meeting Billy Ortega. It was only one brief introduction, but she recalled being a bit stunned at Billy's devastating good looks. She soon forgot about him, but she was only one of many girls who sensed a compelling sexual aura that Billy projected.

The care center building was five miles from downtown Seattle. The old brick building was in need of repair and the grounds appeared unkempt. Margarita ushered Gayle past the reception desk, down a dark corridor into a small dimly lit room. As they entered, Margarita whispered, "Billy is a paraplegic and in a very depressed state. We won't stay but a few minutes."

Sitting in a wheelchair in the middle of the room under the ceiling light, sat Billy Ortega, sixty-two years old and unable to use his legs. The light reflected off Billy's face in such a way that he appeared to effect a strange radiance. Gayle was shocked, stunned and strangely attracted to the handsome old cripple. To her, he appeared to project an indescribable glowing presence.

"I brought a visitor, Billy. Maybe you remember my old friend from school, Gayle Talbot Westbrook."

Billy's dark eyes flashed as he looked at Gayle, "I remember you," he said softly. "All the boys in school wanted you, and all the girls envied you." Then he showed his perfect white teeth in a welcoming smile.

Sitting next to Billy, Gayle experienced feelings she struggled to identify. Was it a strange sympathy? Was it a longing to help the poor guy? Why was she feeling a weird irrational affection for him? As they quietly talked, Gayle was strangely entranced by the sound of Billy's voice. It was time to go. As they left the room, Gayle said, "I'll be back to visit again soon."

"I love the way you talk," said Billy.

"He used to be such a cocky guy," said Margarita, as they drove away. "But he's pretty humble now."

"He has a compelling presence," said Gayle.

"Can you help me get him into a better place? The care is really lousy. He is bitterly unhappy there." "I'll see what I can do," replied Gayle. She immediately sought a better solution for Billy Ortega through her many influential friends and acquaintances. She found that some charitable and public assistance programs could be made available to Billy through her insider friends.

She also visited Billy the following week, then a few days after that, then regularly every other day. She could not explain the compulsion to be near him. She tried to rationalize the relationship by explaining it to herself. It was simply a matter of trying to help an unfortunate person, crippled, down on his luck, homeless and despondent. Hadn't she always worked for those less fortunate? Hadn't she always come down on the side of the generosity of spirit, kindness, consideration and social justice for those unable to help themselves?

Not only that, but her philosophy of life that humanity must be served beyond the self-interest and greed of the rich and powerful. Wasn't she an example for those who subscribed to take a rationalist approach in solving the problems plaguing mankind? It was there that a bit of doubt clouded her rationalist thinking. Rejecting dogma, blind faith and romantic emotionality, how could she justify her unexplainable affection for Billy? Her feelings seemed to transcend her good sense. She was out of control. She was deeply in love with Billy Ortega and she desperately needed to be with him and care for him.

Many years before, the girls at the community college went for Billy Ortega in a big way, often humiliating themselves just to be with him, to date him, to enjoy his sexual advances.

Billy's abilities in baseball could have led to a professional career, but the necessary discipline was nonexistent. Even so, the league's coaches selected him as the all-star shortstop for 1963. He was awarded a replica of a Louisville slugger baseball bat. The bat was eighteen inches long and meant to be displayed as a trophy. Billy carried the trophy with him on salmon fishing trips with his friends. The nearby bays and rivers were a great source for salmon during fishing season. King salmon sometime weighed in at up to thirty pounds. Billy's trophy baseball bat came in handy when landing a big fish as it was used to club the fish over the head. A sharp blow to the fish's head stopped it from thrashing about by stunning it. Often the blow was fatal.

Billy's friends sometimes felt uneasy when they

stopped into a bar or tavern and Billy carried the weapon with him. Billy often tapped the heavy end of the bat into his open palm. Knowing Billy's unpredictable temper, his friends were never sure if Billy might become a real threat.

After showing interest in real estate and dropping out of community college, Billy caught a break. His mother prevailed on her distant cousin, Armando Diaz, to give Billy a job. Diaz was a principal in a real estate firm in Bellevue, a suburb of Seattle. After interviewing Billy, Armando Diaz hired him as a "gopher," a general helper around the office. It was explained to Billy that in his spare time he could study for a real estate license and work his way into the business. His minimum wage was enough to keep him going while he studied and lived at home.

For the first few months Billy did well in his job at the agency, running errands, cleaning the offices and generally serving the wishes of the agents and their secretaries. Cousin Armando provided him with study materials he needed to pursue his goal to eventually become a full-fledged real estate agent. Billy really did want to amount to something, but could he overcome his lack of discipline and self serving laziness?

Sometimes Armando took Billy along to post real estate yard signs. At times they entered their unoccupied listed homes to inspect and evaluate the marketing possibilities. After these visits, Billy sometimes availed himself of the access opportunities to enter such homes at three a.m.to steal whatever he thought could bring himself some extra cash.

Billy's fellow gang members sometimes joined him. Their underground connections provided access to fences that resold stereos, computers, television sets and furniture.

Billy's capture, one rainy night in possession of stolen goods, led to the loss of his job and a ninety day sentence in the county jail. While there, Billy met some very accomplished professional criminals. These contacts provided Billy with opportunities to continue a life of small time crime after his release from jail. So it was that Billy Ortega subsisted by delivering stolen cars to illegal chop shops, smuggling and transporting illegal drugs, occasionally rolling drunks, and various kinds of industrial burglary.

Five years after his first conviction, Billy was caught in a sting operation, a clever set-up by the county sheriff. Billy and his cohorts were arrested as they pulled up in front of a huge warehouse near the Duwamish riverfront. In the truck were a dozen five gallon cans of gasoline and other fire starting paraphernalia. The timing of the arrest was a bit off, since the police had planned to catch the gang in the act of setting fire to the warehouse building. Instead of arson, the best the prosecutor could get was a conviction for conspiracy to commit arson. Instead of a twenty year sentence, Billy got five years in the Washington State penitentiary at Walla Walla.

Billy had a very rough time while there. Rumor had it that sometime in the past Billy had escaped from an arson fire, abandoning his fellow arsonists whom he could have saved. If only he hadn't been so quick to run away and save himself. Billy always denied the story but the rumor persisted and every criminal in the Puget Sound area knew the story.

The underworld wise guys had their own rules, ethics and standards of acceptable behavior. Betraying or abandoning a fellow criminal was unacceptable and called for some kind of punishment. Since gangland betrayal was common, the hypocrisy of their code of behavior was ludicrous. That didn't stop the prison inmates from setting their sights on Billy Ortega, looking for a chance to teach him a lesson. As a result Billy's life in prison for the first year was a living hell. The tough guys in the joint jeered him, stole his clothes, spit in his face, gang raped him and beat him bloody at every opportunity. Billy was finally given protection through an association with a Latino gang. After two years in the "joint," Billy was paroled. Assistance from State social workers helped him find a job as a laborer for a building contractor working in downtown Seattle. Although humbled by his prison experience, it wasn't enough to change an angry, defiant attitude toward everything and everybody. His sister, Margarita, tried her best to stay in touch, but Billy was a hard case through the years. He was able to keep his head above water financially, but always seemed to be on the verge of retreating into involvement with the bad guys he couldn't seem to resist.

With bouts of drunkenness, abusive relationships with women, two disastrous marriages and the occasional part-time jobs for some other crook, Billy somehow was able to avoid prison and keep himself going until one day, at age sixty, his life changed forever.

At his age Billy Ortega had no business working as a laborer at a construction site. One day while suffering from a fierce hangover, Billy found himself on the roof of a three-storey apartment building. He had just finished delivering supplies for the roofers. As he hesitated on the steeply sloped roof he suddenly felt faint, his brain spinning as if some kind of vertigo was taking over. Slipping to his knees he frantically looked for something to hang on to. His struggle swept him over the edge of the roof to the asphalt parking lot below. Landing on his back Billy miraculously survived but the injury to his spine was irreversible.

Billy was to be forever deprived of the use of his body from the waist down. A paraplegic, his arms and hands, as well, never seemed to function properly after the accident.

Billy's parents had died some years before, leaving his two sisters to help him adjust to his life as a cripple. His sister, Margarita, had helped him through the trauma of recovery. Weeks and months passed in which Margarita helped with the problems of industrial insurance, social security, medical care, rehabilitation therapy, establishing a decent environment, and continuing care. As the time passed Billy had no choice but to accept his new life. Through it all he rarely spoke or showed interest in anything. Billy could be described as a wheelchair zombie, caring for nothing, wishing he could die.

As a self-described "rationalist," Gayle found it exceedingly difficult to explain to herself how she came to her decision to move out of her home, leave her husband and change her life forever. The worst part was how to explain it all to Frank.

When the time came for disclosure, she told herself she would find a way to tell him and hope for understanding. The meeting Gayle had with Frank did not have the desired result. Frank was confused, stunned and saddened. Franklin Westbrook, the irrepressible, highly intellectual, emotionally stable, consistently logical, always in control courtroom attorney found himself completely unprepared and desperately pleading with Gayle for answers.

"You are leaving me? After all we've been through as a family? We love each other. You have fallen in love with another man? Have you gone completely crazy? Gayle, you need medical help, counseling. What has happened to you? I've given you everything. I've given you my life and myself. Your family needs you."

"Surely you are not serious. This is a strange dream, a nightmare! This isn't you. All your life you have been an example to everyone as the ultimate in logical thought, in critical thinking, making thoughtful, sensible decisions, rational judgment and objectivity. Gayle, you are the ultimate rationalist, transcending romanticisms, phony idealism and emotional excesses! Gayle, what can you say to all that?" "I don't know what to say, Frank. All I know is that an unexplainable love has driven me to this decision, I can't help myself." Gayle began sobbing, then crying and wailing, totally uncharacteristic of Gayle Westbrook, the self-proclaimed rationalist.

Frank took a leave of absence from his law firm, unsure of what he could do to dissuade Gayle from her plans to leave. If only he could figure a way to bring her to her senses, to reason with her.

Life as Billy Ortega's caretaker was – as expected – entirely different from her life of the previous sixty years. Gayle had given up virtually all of her social connections, her charitable activities, her friends and family. Most of her time was spent taking care of Billy's physical needs. Cooking, feeding and bathing him were the first priorities, after that came trips to the physical therapist and doctor's appointments. In the time remaining, Gayle managed the everyday laundry and housekeeping chores.

Doctor Tyler Westbrook, Gayle's son, talked with her frequently on the phone. Tyler had no thought of condemning his mother but was at a loss to explain her actions. He wished he could be of help to her, to his father, Frank, and his sister, Julie, as they suffered from Gayle's unexplainable decision to live with Billy Ortega, the lifetime loser, the enigma.

Gayle's daughter Julie had managed to talk her mother into a meeting at a local coffee house. "I tried talking some sense into her but she acts like she hears nothing I say to her. Poor Mom, she acts so strange. She's not herself. Why can't we get some help for her?" Confiding to her Aunt Lacey, Gayle's sister, Julie was beside herself. Lacey spoke softly, "It may be some kind of temporary malfunction, Julie, maybe a kind of madness.

Maybe it has something to do with Karma." "Karma? Oh come on, Aunt Lacey, get real." Lacey answered: "I have read about women who find fulfillment in taking care of others, of someone besides themselves, even when their lives are miserable. Maybe it's payback from a previous life, how can you explain someone like Mother Theresa?" "I think she needs a shrink and we should all be working on it," replied Julie.

For their first few months together, Billy maintained a fairly mellow presence. He was accepting and grateful for Gayle's attentive care and obvious love for him. He was much more content in the pleasant apartment overlooking Green Lake, than in his previous venue, a dingy room in a crumbling old building at the hospital.

Billy made sure his baseball bat trophy was nearby where he could look at it often during the day. As time passed however, he became grumpier and withdrawn, interspersed by moments of shouting displeasure over little things he expected Gayle to do, or not do. "He gets bored," she thought, but her attempts to amuse, entertain, or engage his interest, came to no avail. As time went on, Billy seemed to get nastier, more demanding and personally insulting. Gayle's response was to increase her efforts to please his every whim.

After two years it came to an unhappy conclusion when Billy grabbed Gayle by the neck and began slapping her for some imagined oversight. Despite his being confined to a wheelchair Billy retained surprising strength in his shoulders, arms and hands. Slapping led to punching her in the ribs and face. His hand felt for his trophy baseball bat. In a fit of unexplainable madness, Billy smashed the Louisville slugger bat across Gayle's ribs, neck, and head, beating her senseless and close to death.

Fortunately their downstairs neighbor, hearing the sounds of a serious fight, called the police. Gayle was taken to the local hospital's emergency room where frantic efforts by the staff pulled her through. Billy was sent to the psycho ward at the county jail.

The Westbrook family tried to overcome their feelings of shock and anger at the news. They all rushed to Gayle's bedside at the hospital and began to make arrangements for her return to the Westbrook home. Frank, Tyler, and Julie would make sure she was cared for and protected from that day on.

After release from jail Billy was sent to a police supervised medical care facility where he was to stay, pending charges, awaiting a hearing and ultimate trial. By a strange coincidence, Gayle's son, Doctor Tyler Westbrook was one of the attending physicians at the facility.

Much of Tyler's medical career had been spent researching and treating spinal injury patents. Some suffered limited use of their body and limbs. Others were classified as paraplegic, or quadriplegic. Some were bedridden for life unable to move.

Attempting to find answers to the spinal injury dilemma, a frustrating problem for the millions of unfortunate cases of life-changing accidents, Dr. Tyler

Westbrook was considered an outstanding authority and was assigned cases that provided opportunities for research, for breakthroughs and new insights that ultimately might lead to cures.

In the examining room at the county clinic, Dr. Westbrook stood over Billy Ortega sitting calmly in his wheelchair. As their eyes met, Billy flushed with the realization that Dr. Westbrook was Gayle's son. They had never met, but Billy had heard all about him.

"So what's it gonna be, Doc? You gonna cure me or are you thinking about killing me?" Billy said it with a sneer, like a challenge. "I am supposed to examine you and that's what I'm going to do right now," said the Doctor. After a cursory exam, Dr. Westbrook asked, "It says on your record that you have experienced a serious breathing problem in the recent past. Has it bothered you recently?" "It was pretty bad a few weeks ago, but it seems to be OK now," muttered Billy. The doctor continued, "It appears to be connected to a heart problem due to previous damage. If you have any trouble breathing during the night, be sure to let someone here on the staff know. It could be life threatening if you let it continue." Making notes for the record as he spoke, he glared at a smirking Billy and left the room.

Dr. Tyler Westbrook arrived for his morning rounds at eight a.m., and went to the isolated room where Billy was officially incarcerated. Twenty minutes later he issued an emergency call. Attendant's rushed to Billy's room to quickly transport him to the emergency room for resuscitation. His breathing had completely stopped. His vital signs showed no response. All emergency procedures were followed. Billy was pronounced dead.

"Sometime during the night his breathing stopped, then his heart. It was a recurrence of a previous life-threatening pulmonary condition. Poor physical condition was certainly a factor." That's what the medical report stated. All the physicians on duty at the county medical facility, including Dr. Westbrook, signed the document.

The Westbrook family members were all seated around Gayle's bedside. "Yes, I'm much better," she smiled. "You don't have to talk about the past two years, dear," said Frank, "Let's just pick up where we left off." "We're with you, Mom," they all seemed to be saying. "I still can't explain it all," she murmured. "I will try to make it up to all of you." Strangely enough, Gayle the rationalist said, "You will have to understand that I have no regrets."

The members of the family stared. Gayle had not yet been informed of Billy's death.

In spite of all that had occurred, there was collective hope in each of their hearts that somehow, in time, all would be well in the Westbrook family. Gayle knew that she had a way to go psychologically. What she was to never fully realize was that people in her family loved her so much that they could kill for her.

UNCLE VIC

If Mark Novak were to live to be a hundred he would never forget what took place on a sidewalk one drizzly day in downtown Seattle. Walking briskly along, he was suddenly confronted by a grungy-looking old guy who he thought was looking for a handout. "Don't you recognize me, Markie?" he asked. "How do you know my name? Who are you?" Mark responded. The man drew close enough so Mark could smell whiskey on his breath. "I am your Uncle Vic, kid. Victor Luchinski, your mother's brother and you are my only nephew. Long time no see, eh kid?" "Uncle Vic Luchinski," Mark breathed, "you have been gone for years, where have you been? Last time I saw you I was only about eight or nine." "Never mind that right now, Markie. I have to talk to you about something very important." "Call me Mark, Uncle Vic, I'm twenty six, I'm not a little kid anymore." In his mid-sixties, Vic couldn't help being a bit envious of his tall handsome nephew who looked to Vic like a version of a younger boyish somewhat tousled Rock Hudson. A devoted fan of old movies, Mark saw Uncle Vic as a Strouther Martin look-alike, short, round-faced, balding, with a strange cockeyed stare, an expression at once comical and scary. "OK, Mark it is, kid," said Vic, "I have to talk to you about a matter of life and death. You are the only blood relative I have and I need you. Come over to that coffee shop across the street and I'll tell you about it." "I'd like to hear about it sometime," Mark exclaimed, "but I have another appointment and I'm going to be late." Vic took Mark's arm in a vise-like grip as he hustled his nephew across the busy street and into the coffee shop. As they settled themselves into a tiny booth, Vic spoke in a low hoarse voice, "Get the coffee, Mark, and I'll tell you something that's about to happen that will change your life forever. You can make another appointment later. Now please sit there and listen."

Mark felt annoyed but his curiosity trumped his impression that Uncle Vic's obnoxious behavior revealed him to be a fraud and a weirdo. Mark assumed a submissive posture, sipped his coffee and listened. Vic spoke in a slow growl, "First let me tell you that I didn't mean to stay away from the family as long as I did, but I got tangled up with the wrong people and I couldn't break away. These people were the worst you could imagine. They are thugs, thieves, criminals, and mob guys, killers. If you're just an honest guy in business and you let them help you through a tough spot, they'll call on you later and expect you to do things for them that you don't want to do and the first thing you know you are actually committing unthinkable crimes. If you try to break away they track you down and snuff you. I should have never relied on their offer to help me on that one occasion. They helped me solve a very tricky problem with some nasty crooks that were putting lots of pressure on me at a time when I was trying to make good running a small business in downtown L.A. You know I come from a good decent family – your family – I always loved everyone in our family, especially my sister Marion, your mother, God rest her soul."

"So what do you want from me, Uncle Vic?" Mark asked. Vic fixed his nephew with an intensive stare and softly said, "Some very serious bozos are gunning for me and they're closing in. I expect them to find me in a couple of days or so. They won't stay in Seattle for more than a week or two. I need a place to hide. I will be safe if I could stay under cover for a while at your house." Mark stiffened and exclaimed, "At my house? Are you crazy? You would put me and my family in danger for some stupid thing *you* did?" "I promise you there's no danger to you or your family, I swear." Vic's expression was serious as he continued, "There is no way anyone could possibly connect you and me. Some of my criminal skills include an unofficial PhD in computer hacking. I have already manipulated the county records that connect the two of us. It was fairly easy to scramble our ancestor's names, birth certificate information and that entire sort of stuff." "Why did you do that?" asked Mark, "That has to be illegal, so what's the big idea?" "Ok Mark, I see that I have to come clean and tell you more of the story. You need to see why we have to trust each other. First, I have to tell you that I am going to make you rich beyond your dreams. Just imagine how a million bucks

– free and clear – will benefit you and your family for the rest of your lives and your descendant's lives. I'm serious, one million bucks with no strings attached for very little work on your part. After just a few days I will be gone and you will never hear from me again. Consider it a gift from your long lost Uncle Vic. What do you say, kid, is it a deal?" Mark downed his last drop of coffee and signaled a waitress for more. "Of course not." he said, "You haven't told me the whole story, and it sounds like you are playing me for some kind of sucker. Just what is this all about?" "I have to swear you to secrecy," said Vic. "After I tell you what has happened, you will be committed to secrecy yourself. As I told you before, when those mob guys got their hooks into me, I was very well paid while hanging out with them and doing their dirty work. It turned out that I developed a latent talent for being a very effective criminal. I'm ashamed of all the things they made me do." "Be specific," demanded Mark, getting more suspicious than ever. "Well," sighed Vic, "I was involved in beatings, robberies, burglaries, a couple of kidnappings, mostly of some rich snobby jerks who didn't want to live up to their agreements. I have to admit that I was ordered to cap a few very bad wise guys. I am ashamed of it all, even though every one of those rats had it coming. But here's what happened. The gang I was working with took on the job of knocking off an armored truck in Vegas at a time when the truck was carrying an unusually big load of cash on a certain day when our guys knew it would be profitable. There were five of us doing the job. I was the wheel man and lookout. The job was a success, a really big score, over ten million in cash. We hid the loot temporarily in one of the gang's hiding places, a hidden room in a vacant office building in a suburb of downtown Las Vegas. The next day another guy in the gang and I decided to hijack the cash and disappear. It would have to be forever because when the boss found out our lives wouldn't be worth a nickel and we would be on the run. If we had plenty of money though, we could live in luxury in another country and enjoy ourselves with plenty of women, booze and anything else we could ever want. The guy who helped me hijack all that money is now dead. The cash is buried in a place that only I know about, not exactly near Las Vegas.

Here's where you come in, Mark. If you help me retrieve and transport the cash to a safe place, your share will be one million in hundreds, fifty's, and twenties. There are a few easy conditions. You need to hide me at your house for a week or so, and then you and I will travel to where I have the loot stashed. I will show you how to invest, to hide and spend the money. There are some conditions to this part also, but it's pretty easy if you do as I say. You will have to take a few days off work. Well, nephew, are you game to go for the big reward?"

Mark Novak finished his third cup of coffee before speaking to Vic. "I'm sorry for the trouble you're having Uncle Vic. It's not up to me to judge whatever you've done, but how could I ever trust you?" "Listen Mark, these are the facts and this is the truth. I've gotta trust you because my life depends on it. If you have to hold your nose and trust me, then do it because this is the most important turning point in your life; that is, if you're not too dumb, or too chickenshit, or too cowardly to give your old uncle the benefit of the doubt. Take this," he said, as he pressed a thick envelope into Mark's hand. "There's three thousand bucks in there," murmured Vic. "Take me home with you as soon as it gets dark, in an hour or so. Tell your wife to buy herself a mink coat or something. Just tell her you are helping out an old uncle, down on his luck. I'll stay cooped up in your basement. I'll sleep on that couch you have down there. I'll use your downstairs bathroom. Yeah, Mark, I know all about your house."

Mark's displeasure seemed to fade a bit as he thought about sharing Uncle Vic's fortune. Vic used his salesman's voice: "I'll have my own food. We will stop on the way home and buy a microwave, some of those frozen dinners, a small reefer, and some six packs of sports drinks or whatever. No booze. I'll be very quiet. Now let's get going, we have to do the shopping and make a stop first at a little place in Chinatown to order some passports." "Passports?" exclaimed Mark, "why passports, for whom?" "For you," said Vic, "we may not need them, but just in case. I've picked out some good names for you. How do you like Robert Matson and Neal Bigelow?"

Now in her twenty third year, Kelly Novak, the former Seattle Pacific College homecoming queen, could hardly be more pleased with her life. Married at nineteen to the love of her young life, the handsome

Mark Novak, she doted on him and their vivacious three-year-old daughter, Janna. It seemed that she couldn't stop her continual excitement over their lovely new house in the upscale neighborhood in the Seward Park suburb of Seattle. Growing up as an only child in the Carl and Greta Olson family, Kelly Olson was provided with everything a child in a working class family could wish for, including an ideal loving environment.

"Honey, meet my Uncle Vic. This is my wife Kelly that I have told you so much about." Mark's eyes locked on his wife's questioning look as if to say "please be patient and give me a chance to explain." "I'm very pleased to meet you, Uncle Vic," said Kelly, sweetly. Mark continued, "You may remember my telling you about my favorite uncle from a long time ago. Uncle Vic's military career is over, but he still suffers from wounds he got in combat some years ago. Actually he is a victim of what they call PTSD." Vic smiled as he shook Kelly's hand. "I'm so proud of my favorite nephew's successful career, his beautiful wife and your lovely home here at Seward Park. I'm sure you two have worked very hard to get where you are. Who's this, your little daughter? What a beautiful little girl. What's your name, sweetie?"

As hard as it was for Mark to feel comfortable about Vic's presence in his basement, his concern was mollified to a great degree by Kelly's acceptance of the situation. Uncle Vic behaved just as he had described to Mark, keeping entirely secluded, preparing his own food and watching television for hours at a time. Vic's experience in the underworld had at times, required him to endure stakeouts, hideouts, and uncomfortable physical situations. Kelly occasionally called down to Uncle Vic to see if he needed anything and Mark visited him every evening. During those visits Vic insisted that Mark learn some important techniques used by the cleverest underworld wise-guys, such as using assumed names and aliases, driving lookout and getaway cars, pickpocketing and shoplifting techniques, renting cars, switching license plates, using weapons and explosives, picking locks, handling money and securities, tapping phones and disposing of bodies. Although Mark told himself he was not interested, the criminal issues they discussed fascinated him. "OK Mark," said Vic one night about a week later, "we have to plan our next move. Tomorrow you can buy us each a new cell phone. Use one of those names on your new passports when you register the phone. Next, tell your boss you need to take time off from the fourth to the ninth next week. Remember that little import shop in Chinatown that we stopped at the night you first drove me out here to the house? Stop by there tomorrow afternoon and pick up a package addressed to Abner, just one name, Abner. Pay the guy who gives you the package. It will be about the size of a shoebox. Take this roll and pay the guy two hundred fifty dollars. Bring me the change." "What's in the shoe box, Uncle Vic?" "I'll tell you," answered Vic, "but you are not to open it, just bring it to me unopened. It's a disguise kit," grinned Vic. Mark sighed and looked a bit intimidated. "I have to be cautious about sneaking around these underworld places. The image of propriety is important to my boss and all the swivel chair guys that run things in my office." "You mean those pompous advertising agency dudes?" asked Vic. "And you are a big-shot copy writer who takes orders from those stuffed shirts?" laughed Vic. "You're just another big city drudge, a modern day slave, kid." "Come on, Vic, it's a good job writing ads for print media, television commercials, public relations, and that sort of stuff. It takes talent as a writer and lots of creative ability." Mark had surprised himself that his hurt feelings had caused him to brag. Vic spoke, "I think you need me to keep you from becoming a hopeless square."

Mark couldn't wait to see what was contained in the shoebox he had obtained earlier that day at Chang's Import Shop. That evening Vic acquainted him with the disguise items he had ordered. The inventory consisted of black, brown and blonde false mustaches, two small bottles of hair dye, three sets of false eyebrows, some skin tanning cream, three pair of spectacles with simple glass see-through lenses in different frame styles, two very hairy toupees and a few false stick-on warts.

As Mark settled himself in the airliner window seat he glanced back three rows to see Uncle Vic comfortably seated on an aisle seat looking at him with a contrived blank unrecognizing gaze. Mark felt very uneasy about how Kelly was taking his departure without her. The reasons for the trip as described to her by both Mark and Uncle Vic had seemed entirely plausible for the moment, but the more she thought about it more questions seemed to emerge in her mind. Mark fervently hoped that Vic's recent gift to her would dampen any fears she might have. Mark had his own fears about the whole crazy relationship with Uncle Vic, but his fears were trumped by an almost overwhelming sense of excitement, which then seemed to overcome whatever common sense he was supposed to have. Mark's thoughts paused for a moment on Vic's very generous gift to Kelly, a new big screen television, and the giant stuffed animals, which had so delighted his little three-year-old Janna. Three rows back on the Alaskan Airlines nonstop flight from Seattle to Reno sat a swarthy middle aged man with a dark brown mustache, a pair of black horn rimmed glasses, wearing a passive expression. His passport name was Carlos Garcia.

Carlos Garcia and Mark Novak sped away from the Reno airport car rental lot in the heavy duty Dodge Dakota van, headed for Carson City. Mark held the maps furnished by the airport car rental agency in an attempt to navigate to the destination indicated by Uncle Vic. Vic, alias Carlos Garcia, already knew the way but he allowed Mark to keep track of their directional progress. The highway that stretched along the desert between Reno and Carson City allowed for a rapid pace, but the turnoff leading to their isolated destination called for a slowdown and careful scrutiny of the surrounding area. Vic had no patience for error at this point in their journey. The stop at the hardware store before leaving the Reno area had provided Vic and Mark with equipment they would need to complete their mission. Included were a small lantern, two-foot locker style toolboxes, two shovels, two long handled pickaxes, and two pair of snug fitting work gloves.

"That lantern doesn't give enough light," said Mark. "Keep digging kid, the bags are not buried very deep," panted Vic. A few more minutes of furious digging revealed what appeared to Mark as a large canvas bag. "There are three more," grunted Vic, "pull'em out of there as quick as you can." The three huge canvas bags carried the names of banks unfamiliar to Mark. They had to be full of Uncle Vic's money. Vic's voice crackled in the darkness. "Hand me that smaller bag, Mark, and hurry up!" Unzipping the bag, Vic brought forth a .9mm Glock automatic pistol. After checking the clip, he racked a cartridge into the chamber, set the safety and jammed the weapon under his belt with the butt showing at his waist. "Here's one for you, Markie," said Vic, as he pressed a small .25 caliber Beretta automatic pistol into Mark's right hand. "Why do we need guns, Vic?" "Quit whining and do as I tell you," snapped Vic. "Put a round in the chamber and check the safety like you saw me do and keep it in your pocket. Do it now or do I have to do it for you? Now let's get this shotgun and the ammo stashed into the van and the money out of those bags into the footlockers. After that we gotta fill this hole and make it look like nobody's been here, so get going."

At that moment a flash of light appeared in the desert darkness. Mark peered into the distance. "Who would be driving out here at three in the morning?" he asked. "Who the hell knows," growled Vic. "Turn out that lantern and sit right there and be quiet. I think he's driving down this road. Maybe he'll just drive on by, but if they are bad-asses and it looks like they want to take us down we will shoot first, ya got that, Mark? If they stop, keep cool and let me do the talking. Keep that gun in your hand inside your pocket. Hell, here they come."

A twenty-year-old Chevy rattled to a stop beside Vic's rental van as two young men emerged, both in their early twenties, both wearing dirty jeans and T-shirts covered by shabby jackets. Obviously drunk, both carried double-barreled shotguns in their right forearms with muzzles pointing down. Walking toward Vic and Mark, the tallest guy yelled out, "What do you guys think you're doing so early in the morning on our land? What the hell is in those bags?" Uncle Vic spoke in a submissive tone, "We're from the Washoe County sheriff's office on an investigation involving some stolen property. We hope we're not creating an inconvenience, sir." "That's bullshit," yelled the tall loudmouthed kid. Crouching down for a closer look, he shouted, "Is there money in them bags?" That's when Uncle Vic quickly pulled his pistol and shot the kid four times in the head and chest, the loud gunfire exploding into the quiet desert night.

Stunned, the other young man was struck motionless in the moment of unexpected violence, just long enough for Mark Novak to pull his little automatic and imitating his uncle, blasted their visitor with three rapid shots from four feet away, two in the chest, one in the head, carrying blood, tissue and bone in a stream from his temple to the ground. Both bodies fell quickly and heavily, sprawling across the huge bags of Vic's hijacked money. Vic spoke sharply to Mark, "Go turn those car lights out and see if the keys are still in the car, then come back quickly and dig some more. We've gotta bury this mess!"

At four a.m., Vic's rental van wound its way down a primitive desert road, followed by the old Chevrolet with Mark at the wheel. Vic soon found a little clear spot where he could get his car turned around, and spied just what he was looking for, a deep ravine covered with desert brush. Standing at the driver's window of the Chevy, Vic directed Mark, "Drive over these rocks to that ravine and roll this piece of junk over the edge. Hurry back to our car. Get moving."

As Vic turned the van onto the highway from the dusty desert road, he glanced over at Mark sitting silently next to him with a stunned expression on his handsome face. "Well, kid, you made your bones today." Vic couldn't contain a chuckle. "Please, Vic, don't talk about it, I'm feeling sick."

The used car lot outside Reno had barely opened when Vic wheeled the rented van into the parking area. After a few minutes of negotiations, Mark, wearing phony eyeglasses and a baseball cap paid cash for the eight-year-old Ford pickup truck into which he and Vic transferred their cargo, covering the foot lockers full of cash, the tools and the weapons with an inconspicuous tarp. "The airport is less than an hour from here. Follow me," said Vic, "after I return this van, pick me up at the passenger load zone."

Cruising along the highway near the northern California border in their dirty blue pickup truck, Vic asked Mark, "How do you like the way I look without my Mexican disguise?" "How can you kid around like that," asked Mark, "after what we've done back there?" "It was a clear cut case of self-defense, kid," said Vic. As Vic drove toward Seattle, always careful to observe the speed limits, he had no intention of stopping except for gas, coffee, or rest rooms. Studying Vic's face as he drove, Mark asked, "You said I made my bones last night. What did you mean by that?" Vic showed his alligator grin. "It means you have become a man. It means you are no longer a prissy little shit without a backbone. It means you have had the courage to kill a man who would have killed you. You have now joined a special society of those who have something very special in common with others who aren't afraid to step outside the conventions of society. It gives you important status and respect among a lot of very powerful guys. I have been there, and I can tell you that it's real."

Their next stop was at a Denny's restaurant on the highway about an hour south of Mark's Seattle home. Seated in a corner booth, they sipped their coffee, each was aware that this conversation was to be a vital one for both their futures. Mark spoke first, "Ok, what do we do now, Vic, now that you've made a murderer out of me and probably damned me to hell." "Grow up, kid," growled Vic, "you're a big boy now. Here's what we are gonna do. First you are to buy a couple of nice presents for your wife and little girl. I'll tell you what to buy. We'll stop at a department store right here in Tacoma. I'll stay in the car while you do it. Come back in fifteen minutes.

Then we drive up to your house and unload the car. We hide everything in your garage for now except for your million in cash. Tomorrow we sell the pickup truck to a used car dealer and go to three banks where you put your money in their safe deposit boxes. You must keep the bank information in a very safe place always. After that, we buy two big suitcases for my cruise and fill them with cash. I can probably squeeze about five million in the big bags I have in mind. I can smuggle them on to a cruise ship, but if I can't, I'll get to Australia on a fishing boat. You keep the guns; I won't be able to keep them. That'll leave about three million in our footlockers. Later I will have you divide the money into smaller amounts and deposit the dough through a certain kind of securities certificates through a bank in Belize that I know about. I don't think we have to worry about numbered money because the heist consisted of outgoing cash from the casinos to the banks. I expect to be ready to travel in two or three days. After getting settled somewhere I will instruct you how to wire it to me in smaller amounts. We've trusted each other so far. Can I trust you to keep your word from this point on?" Mark studied the bit of coffee in the bottom of his cup for a long moment. At the same time his right hand rested on the deadly little Beretta pistol concealed in the pocket of his jacket. Mark ran his fingers over the handgrip, felt the smoothness of the barrel, and touched the safety and the trigger. He raised his head and locked eyes with Victor Luchinski. In a very quiet voice Mark said, "I'm your man, Uncle Vic."

RAINIER BEACH

Sometime during the last years of the nineteenth century a wooded area in the county just south of the big city was annexed and became a suburb. The big city was Seattle, population about eighty thousand. The new suburb near the south shore of Lake Washington was nicknamed "Rainier Beach." It was at the southern terminal of the old streetcar line. Sparsely populated, the settlers were mostly farmers. Rainier Beach had originally been covered with bountiful stands of fir, cedar and hemlock trees, but had earlier been aggressively logged, leaving brushy open areas with stands of smaller deciduous trees.

As the years passed, the population increased resulting in hundreds of bungalow style homes, concrete streets, sidewalks, schools, churches, parks and small businesses. Never becoming completely urbanized there remained vacant lots and blackberry patches. The earliest occupants of this countrified area, miles from the city, were no doubt attracted by cheap land for homes and investments. As time passed, the area was populated mostly by families tending their small farms and orchards and later by working class commuters. In the 1930's there was an interesting mix of residents, which included some affluent families. There was a feeling in the Rainier Beach neighborhoods of an easygoing independence. The people all seemed proud of their community but in a sort of laid back way. The kids were typical American small town kids, mischievous and rascally at times, but rarely destructive or seriously mean to their peers. All in all, Rainier Beach, during the depression years in the 1930's was a great environment for families.

The following tales seem to me fairly typical reflections of suburban American life. The fact was that the Rainier Beach population was virtually all white. The strange ironies, the hypocrisies, and the sometimes-quirky behavior as depicted I regard as typical. Each tale about the characters in this story has had special meaning for me. I hope this will also be true for you.

Nicknames

Many of the kids in Rainier Beach had nicknames. Some of the nicknames disappeared as the kids grew older but some of them stuck for life. It still seems amusing to recall the funniest and the most appropriate nicknames the kids hung on one another. Some nicknames seemed to fit, like the one imposed on the strapping twelve year-old kid with a huge shock of dark red hair. Red Dog Barker was the perfect name and it stuck, even when he grew up, earned a PhD and a pretentious title, Randolph Red Dog Barker, PhD, chairman of the prestigious International Organization to Eliminate Worldwide Poverty.

Some of the nicknames were a product of someone's sicko sense of humor like the three-legged, one-eyed, ragged eared dog called "Lucky." Lucky was a clownish loveable oaf of a mutt, an incongruous mix of Airedale, terrier and German shepherd. Strangely marked with black, brown and white hair, Lucky easily made friends with both dogs and people. Lucky did not hesitate to fight fiercely with any dog he regarded as a threat to himself or any kid confronted by a dog in the neighborhood. Lucky was one of a group of dogs that regularly accompanied six-year-old Jimmy Bronkowsky on his walks to and from the local grocery store. In the depression days of the 1930's Jimmy lived with his widowed mother in a dilapidated four room shack, three blocks from the local grocery store. Every other day or so, little Jimmy would set out for the store with enough change in his pocket to buy a few groceries for him and his tired old mom. Using the same route to the store each time, Jimmy passed the same houses, most of which contained a resident dog. The dogs expected Jimmy to come by at about the same time each day. They loved to join him as he sauntered along in his ragged clothes consisting of blue overalls held by one shoulder strap, a little newsboy cap and beat-up sodbuster shoes. Usually whistling as he walked, hopped and skipped along, Jimmy welcomed each dog as they joined the group, tails wagging and smiling as only happy dogs smile. Lucky was always in the middle of the pack as Jimmy continued to the store, the dogs that lived along the way joined the dog parade, fancying themselves as Jimmy's protectors.

When Jimmy entered the store his twelve-dog retinue patiently waited outside the store until Jimmy came out with his sack of eggs, bread, milk, or whatever. The neighbors always enjoyed watching Jimmy's dog procession. As he walked home the dogs headed into their own yards, eventually leaving Jimmy with only Lucky, Jimmy's dog.

People referred to little Jimmy as the "dog boy." Later dubbed "Dog," eventually in his teen years, he became "Mutt" Bronkowski the toughest kid in the Rainier Beach neighborhood. Mutt had to work at after school jobs but he was able to squeeze in some time to join the Rainier Valley Boys Club gym. The gym offered various activities, including team sports. The sport that most attracted Mutt Bronkowski was boxing. Fortunately the club's boxing instructor was experienced in working with teenagers. A former athlete and amateur boxer, Teddy Brown was a perfect role model and coach for the Mutt. The gym was located about four miles north in the neighborhood known as Hillman City. Mutt was able to attend the gym activities and boxing lessons by means of his bicycle, an old rattletrap balloon-tired vehicle.

A stickler for detail, Teddy Brown convinced Mutt, his protégé, of the importance of proper training, developing strength, coordination, quickness and technique. Mutt was an excellent pupil and soon became a skilled boxer. Also packing a powerful punch, Mutt rose to the very top in Golden Gloves competitions in the region. Mutt never grew to more than 145 pounds and five feet nine inches in height. Fighting as a welterweight, he had the perfect attitude and disposition. Mutt enjoyed the rough give and take never losing his poise in the ring. When facing an opponent, Mutt fought with a combination of skill and ferocity. In spite of his docile demeanor outside the ring, on fight night, the Mutt always came to fight.

When serving in the navy during World War II, he was a champion on boxing teams wherever he was stationed. During the Big War, navel stations around the world maintained sports programs for Navy personnel. Some offered not only boxing, but also other self-defense classes. Mutt availed himself of off duty opportunities to learn all he could about jujitsu and judo. Although Mutt was essentially a gentle spirited boy he loved the physical challenge of the combat sports. Besides, it prepared him with the means to defend himself if necessary.

After discharge from the military, Mutt traveled with two old friends from Rainier Beach, Turk Perkins and Eddie Mooma to Alaska. In those years it was easy to find good paying jobs in canneries and on fishing boats. Mutt and his friends were eager to make some fast money. If they could take home enough cash after their summer jobs in Alaska, they could buy cars, start chasing girls and perhaps settle on some kind of career.

By chance one night in a Ketchikan bar, all three were challenged to a fight by a huge drunken local character. The three boys seemed to have no choice but to go outside to the parking lot and face the guy down. It seemed only natural that Turk and Eddie appointed Mutt to take care of the loud mouthed, insulting drunken slob named Benny. A crowd gathered around the two combatants as they squared off on the rain soaked asphalt. Some of the spectators began to bet as to how long little Mutt would last against Benny, who seemed twice as big.

Before blows were struck, Turk and Eddie entered the betting, taking advantage of some heavy odds offered by the locals, who of course had no idea that Mutt was a very tough and experienced boxer. Two feints and four rapid powerful punches put Benny flat on his back with some very sore ribs and one broken very bloody nose. Mutt and his friends shared four hundred dollars for the evenings work.

After that every free night found the three boys from Rainier Beach at a smoky bar in the Ketchikan area, teasing some local strong-boy into fighting their smallish passive looking friend, a little guy who looked like he couldn't hurt a flea.

The three boys eventually quit their cannery jobs in order to travel to Anchorage, Homer, Valdez and Fairbanks. In each place they turned Mutt loose to knock out the local champions. They developed a very effective little act to entice the local bullies into a challenge. Bets were arranged, always with favorable odds before the battle. Mutt was always underestimated, but always victorious even though there were some of the fights in which he took some hard punches before putting his opponent down. As often as not Mutt was required to adapt his fighting technique since many of his big clumsy opponents were vicious street brawlers and were completely unaware of the Marquis of Queensbury rules.

At those times, Mutt reverted to the judo techniques he had learned in the Navy. Boxing skills were one thing, but the use of judo (martial arts) provided Mutt with an impressive arsenal using tripping, body slams, judo chops, knee kicks and blows to the vital organs. The old cliché always applied, the bigger they were, the harder they fell.

At the end of the summer Turk, Eddie and Mutt came home to Rainier Beach, each feeling rich with several thousand bucks apiece.

Later on Mutt was enticed into turning pro. He won a few local fights, and began traveling to other cities for bigger purses. It was heard later that after only a year or so Mutt quit the ring and got married. All that happened back east. Eventually, his old friends lost track of Mutt Bronkowski. He was a sweet guy, a brave guy. His old pals from the neighborhood liked him a lot and all admired him as a real warrior.

A family moved to Rainier Beach from England in the 1920's. In 1926 they proudly named their firstborn son Wellington Jonathon Jones. In Rainier Beach, the boy was dubbed Duke Jones, his nickname forever afterward. When he was ten years old the nice little guy from the neighborhood went on a camping trip with his Cub Scout pack. The boys camped on a strip of land on the shores of the Cedar River about 10 miles south of Rainier Beach. At night most of the boys slept in pup tents, but Elwood Merkle chose to sleep on the ground outside his tent. In the morning his sleeping bag had hundreds of little earwigs, many of them attempting to establish nests in

Elwood's hair. From that moment on he was known as Earwig Merkle. Earwig was understandably unhappy about his new nickname (to say the least) especially later in his teen years. This nickname was a big disadvantage when attempting to impress the girls.

A few of the neighborhood boys' nicknames were assigned at the local swimming beach. It wasn't really a beach, but a secluded space at the foot of a steep brushy hill leading to the shore of Lake Washington. A flat little dirt platform extended out from the shore into deeper water where a dock once existed at a time when commerce was conducted by boat to the far flung little communities around the lake. A few pilings were still in place in the immediate area, making it a perfect spot for small groups of boys to skinny dip, since the brush and trees kept the site hidden from the street above. This place was fondly known as Boy's Beach. Swimming nude the boys were subject to lots of teasing from one another, sometimes about their exposed body parts. Morton Nichols was a puny little ten-year-old who occasionally joined his peers at Boy's Beach on warm summer days. It wasn't always a happy experience for undersized Morton, as his rascally cohorts often teased him about his skinny physique. What they really ragged him about was his tiny little penis, which one of the rude little devils referred to as a shriveled up miniature pickle. At Boy's Beach one warm summer day, Morton Nichols became "Pickle" Nichols.

Boy's Beach was also the place where Monty "Jockstrap" Coker became famous, at least temporarily

104

amongst his teenaged peers. Monty was always the biggest kid in school. At sixteen, he reached six-foot six inches in height and was big all over. Young Monty Coker rarely indulged in fighting or rough horseplay. He was a gentle spirited even tempered boy, but he did enjoy showing off. In his own quiet way he seemed to need attention. One sunny day in July, sixteen-year-old Monty Coker joined his mates at Boy's Beach where some furious swimming and diving was occurring in an atmosphere of teenage yelling, teasing and cussing. The boys took special delight in carousing in their brazen nakedness. "What's Monty up to?" yelled Red Dog Barker. Monty had appeared preparing to take his first dive wearing a jockstrap. Required for gym class worn under gym shorts, all the boys owned one. "You'll see," shouted Monty, as he swam about twenty yards into deeper water toward the tallest piling sticking about eight feet above the surface. At the tall piling Monty climbed to the very top using the protruding spikes, which affected a kind of ladder. Once on top big Monty carefully balanced himself and stood tall, well above the surface of the lake. With a big grin he faced the hill above the swimming area. Monty was so far out from the shore he could actually be observed from the highway above the beach. His huge white body sporting the bulging jockstrap was so bizarre and comical the other boys couldn't stop laughing, surely the people in the many cars passing by that day had to be shocked, amused, titillated, surprised or horrified. Monty enjoyed the attention waving enthusiastically at the passing cars, as if to say, "Look at me!" Monty was henceforth referred to as Jockstrap Coker, a new oft-repeated tradition was also born that day at Boy's Beach.

Young Robert Gruber was about seven when crossing a cow pasture he stumbled and fell. It was not unusual for boys to tumble every now and then, but Robert fell on his chest and stomach directly into a pile of wet cow manure. His friends helped direct him to his house after picking him up, keeping their distance from poor little Robert along the way. His peers found the experience to be simultaneously hilarious and obnoxiously odorous. Smell Gruber was unable to be free of his nickname until he left home for college.

Ralph Horne was a cute little guy at age eleven or twelve. There didn't seem to be a clear reason to attach a nickname to Ralph. There came a time when his parents forced him to take lessons on the trumpet. Thus, the little fellow with a narrow birdlike face close cropped black hair and a shy smile was awarded a lifetime nickname, Toot. Toot Horne, another colorful nickname.

When Sven Johnson moved into Rainier Beach, he was about thirteen. As the kids in the neighborhood became acquainted with Sven everyone knew he needed a nickname. His peers soon learned that he carried a nickname from when he lived previously in an Italian community. There, he was considered an outsider mainly because of his appearance. How could he be anything but an outsider with his blonde hair, ice blue eyes and rosy cheeks? The wops had nicknamed him "Squarehead." Yes, Squarehead Johnson, and it stuck. The name Squarehead was a common pejorative for a Swede or

Norwegian. Even so, it was better than being called a "herring-choker," thus, Sven Johnson was known by everyone as Squarehead. He got used to it and didn't seem to mind.

Some of the girls were given nicknames. Mostly the names were used in a somewhat secret way. Privately, among the gutterminded teenaged boys, behind the girl's backs. For example, a cute teen named Dolores Tilley, who had "developed" a bit early and sprouted enormous boobs, disproportionate for her age. Therefore, her secret nickname was "Tits Tilley," seemed only natural.

Another local teenager was named Betty Bosworth. She was always nice to everybody. Even though possessing a happy outgoing personality, unfortunately, Betty was a bit over weight. So it followed that she was subject to a mean-spirited insulting nickname. Actually she had two, either "Big Butt Betty Bosworth," or "Little Miss Lard Ass." Take your pick.

When seniors in high school some of the kids were taken with the story of a girl they occasionally saw at the school dances. She attended a different high school, but the boys were quite fascinated by the story (or rumor) about a sexual encounter in the back seat of Sheik Miller's car. As Sheik told the story, he and the girl, Tamara Toober, were playing kissy-face in the front seat. One thing led to another and Sheik maneuvered the two of them into the back seat. On the verge of "going all the way," both were inclined. They went for it. What she didn't know was that it was the Sheiks very first time. When the big moment came, he got so excited that he kicked the back window out of his 1936 Plymouth. When relating the story later to his friends, Sheik admitted that he was way too quick. "It only took two pumps," he laughed. Forever after, poor Tamara was known as "Two Pump Tamara Toober."

The practice of shoplifting was fairly common amongst the teenaged scoundrels in the neighborhood. Charles Peterson, through intensive practice, carried the evil hobby of shoplifting to a high art, so much so that his pals would sometimes present a list of items they wished to acquire. Charles was always happy to sell them the stolen goods he had cleverly swiped from various stores in the downtown Seattle area. Items may have included portable radios, clothing, sporting goods, candy bars, cigarettes and pint bottles of cheap wine within reach on the wine rack at the local drug store. The little thief became known as "Light Fingers Charley." Eventually Charley grew up, married and moved to California. Charley and his father ran a successful rental equipment business in a bustling little city, and became prominent in community business and politics. Many years later, as an adult, pickle Nichols visited Charley in California. As it happened, he invited Pickle to lunch with a group of his friends, all of whom were either prominent business leaders or big-shot local politicians. After two or three drinks before lunch, Pickle made a big mistake by kiddingly referring to Charles Peterson, the local chamber of commerce president and favorite to become the next mayor as "Light Fingers Charley," his old nickname. Pickle has since contended that Charley never returns his calls.

The Hermit

Tucked away in a remote corner of Rainier Beach there existed from early pioneer times, a tiny log cabin adjacent to a little orchard. Inside a surrounding fence were full-grown apple and cherry trees, each fall loaded with succulent fruit.

It was a beautiful fall afternoon the day the leaders of the little gang of pre-teen troublemakers decided to raid the cherry trees near the log cabin. The older boys in the group boasted about "raiding" these particular trees each year in late summer. The idea was to climb into the trees (loaded with juicy cherries), eat all you could gobble, fill your pockets as fast as you could, jump to the ground and run like hell. It was an exciting adventure any kid could be very proud of. Just getting away with it without being caught was a big deal in itself. "You have to watch out for the hermit!" warned Ducky Waters, the leader of the group of little rapscallions. "Who's the hermit?" another kid asked. "An old guy who lives there by himself," offered Billy Tilley, a fat kid about eleven years old. "Be careful, you little fart, because he has a shotgun and he killed a kid a couple years ago." "Bullshit, that's a rumor," hollered Ducky. "It is not," said Greaseball Vacca, grimily. "It's a true fact!" "The damned old hermit's not even home," yelled another boy. "Let's get those cherries." The group of raggedy young scamps broke into a run heading for the trees. The smaller kids lagged behind but ran as fast as they could and climbed the easier lower limbs of the nearest trees. Reaching for the clusters of luscious blue-black bing cherries, the boys were furiously chomping cherries and filling their pockets when they abruptly stopped, shocked as they heard the terrifying blast of what they knew was the roar of the feared shotgun. Terrified, they jumped out of the trees as another awful shot rang out along with an old man's voice shouting, "I caught you varmints, now I'm gonna shoot every one of ya!" The kids were dashing out of the orchard in a full uncontrolled panic, crying and sobbing, some pissing their pants, cherries falling out of their shabby little jacket pockets, running for all they were worth for safety, almost sure that the next shot would kill one of them before they could reach a place to hide or escape. "Oh my god, please save me!" screamed Greaseball. As it turned out none of the little cherry robbers were shot and none would dare tell their parents about their adventure at the Hermit's orchard. About six months later, Ducky's mother described a conversation she had earlier that day at the local grocery store. Ducky's family was seated at the dinner table. "She was a young pretty woman named Sally," said mom, "Turns out she was settling the estate of her late father, the old man who lived down the road over in that old log cabin next to the cherry orchard. I'm glad you never played over there Donald," she said to Ducky. "Her father used to enjoy watching the kids come over and raid his cherry trees because he loved to scare them. Can you imagine that?" "They called him the hermit," Ducky murmured. "How did he scare the kids?" asked Uncle

George, seated across the table from Ducky. "Why with a shotgun, of all things," said mom. "Imagine, enjoying the act of frightening little kids." Uncle George's face showed an amused expression, thought Ducky. Later as George was heading out by himself for the evening, Ducky stopped him just as he was opening the front door. As a kid of only eight, Ducky was aware there was a lot about life he had yet to learn. "Why would the old hermit like to scare people with a gun?" the kid asked him. George looked sideways at him, winked, and said, "Well kid, some hermits are like that. Hermits have to act out their parts just like the rest of us." Uncle George paused, and then walked off into the night.

The Wheelbarrow

There was an interesting kid in the neighborhood about ten years old named Ronnie Wilson. He lived in an old house on a big lot. The lot was at least two or three acres in size, probably what was left of a farm from years before. Ronnie's family included his older brother Creemo, about fifteen, his mother Alta, and her brother Uncle Judd. Creemo, whose real name was Arthur, got his nickname from a brand of cigars which, after swiping from the grocery store, he and his teenage buddies loved to smoke in secret. On occasion they got lucky at times when nobody at the drugstore was looking they sometimes were able to acquire a pint or two of cheap wine as well. Loganberry or apple fortified were favorites of the young lawbreakers. Ronnie and Creemo's Uncle Judd seemed very old to all of the neighborhood kids.

He was probably only in his late fifties but was rickety and stooped over, with a corny cowboy accent. One day in the late afternoon, Creemo was playing monopoly with Ronnie when their mother yelled to them, "Go out and pick up Uncle Judd." The boys headed out the door to the tool shed out back. Stopping at the shed, Ronnie rolled out a big wheelbarrow. It was an old relic with an iron wheel and wooden sideboards. It was the kind that was used to carry sacks of feed, fertilizer, or crops from the garden. Pushing the big clumsy wheelbarrow, the two boys wheeled their way along a rough path to the far end of the property. After a walk of maybe five to ten minutes they came to a little wooden hut in the far corner of the pasture, half-hidden by some large maple trees. Behind a huge boulder next to the tiny hut appeared two legs lying in the tall grass. The feet and legs belonged to uncle Judd. Creemo felt around the grass until he retrieved an empty wine bottle, which he threw into a nearby blackberry patch. "Take this leg," ordered Creemo, pointing to one of Uncle Judd's coveralled legs. "Now take the other one Ronnie and I'll take his arms. On three." said Creemo. After flopping old Judd, who was passed out and didn't feel a thing into the old rickety wheelbarrow, Creemo began wheeling Uncle Judd back to the house. "This is the third time this week," giggled Ronnie. "I think he gets most of his wine from Mr. Yazzalino over on Gazelle street. Mr. Yazz makes it himself. They call it "Dago Red." Let me do the wheeling for a bit," asked Ronnie, heading for the house where Mrs. Wilson was waiting to roll Uncle Judd into his bed. Time passed by and Uncle Judd died. The Wilsons moved away. A few years later, a couple of our neighborhood boys played football against Creemo when he played on the Ballard high school football team. He was still very friendly. He had grown into a big strong guy. Maybe he developed some of his strength from pushing Uncle Judd around in that old wheelbarrow.

The Bear Trap

During summer vacations in the 1930's, the local boys living at Rainier Beach were able to spend their time having fun. Aside from a few chores, the boys went swimming, played baseball and fished in the local lakes and streams; some were lucky enough to participate in hiking and camping trips. From age seven to thirteen, a kid named Ned Stewart was especially fortunate. He spent a month or two each summer in a remote mountain cabin. It was located about 300 miles east of Seattle on the Colville Indian reservation in eastern Washington State.

As a World War I Navy veteran, his Uncle Mike was in 1922 or 1923, offered an opportunity to acquire eighty acres of reservation land as a homestead site. The land was free. It simply required an approved application, and after that, a fence surrounding the entire property and a house of some sort. After spending some weeks exploring the area, Uncle Mike and his father, Ned's grandfather, built a log cabin overlooking a magnificent view of pristine meadows and blue mountain peaks in the distance. A more ideal wilderness setting could scarcely be imagined. The freshest water in the world came from an artesian well and the lighting in the cabin came from old-fashioned kerosene lamps. The stars on a summer night were uncountable, they seemed so bright and so overwhelmingly awesome and infinitely mysterious that at times it scared the hell out of little Ned. He didn't much care for the outhouse in back of the cabin because he was quite sure that the many resident chipmunks scurrying about were planning to attack him whenever he sat on the rustic old outhouse throne.

It was very hot every day and surprisingly cold at night, sometimes freezing but Ned thrived on it along with his grandfather Carl and Grandmother Sophie. Some years they kept a horse for Ned to ride. There was a barn about eighty yards back of the cabin and a cool storehouse dug into the side of a bank nearby containing shelves filled with food, enclosed by a heavy wooden door. Ned's activities at the "Frosty Meadows" homestead included horseback riding, fishing in a creek teeming with fish, hiking the mountain trails, or enjoying riding his horse through the grassy meadows, or sitting on a log daydreaming and loving the feel of being a very lucky human being in God's primitive domain. Ned loved it all.

At ten, Ned was allowed to take a companion from Rainier Beach with him, a kid named Roger Wise. At first Roger had some difficulty getting used to Ned's grandmothers cooking and his grandfather's gruff ways. Roger got used to it after a couple of weeks.

It was unusual to have company since the cabin was about twenty miles from the nearest town, a wide spot in the road named Keller. The winding dirt road to Keller was a narrow one lane road featuring steep hills, switchbacks, streams running across the road, deep ruts, patches of quick sand, and the occasional boulder or fallen tree blocking the road. Every so often they had visitors. There were groups of Indians who rode through on horseback from their village thirty miles away near the mighty Columbia River. These native people would ride the trails up to the cabin and continue to travel further up higher trails near the "Gold Mountain" area where the really good huckleberries grew in abundance. After filling huge sacks with the berries, they would load their pack mules and ride miles back to their camp. It was probably a three or four day trip. They usually stopped and camped near Carl's cabin. They always filled their canteens at the spring and cooked very carefully over open fires. Usually only one or two of the group of eight or so could speak English. They all seemed to accept Ned's grandpa as part of the local environment, and he seemed to know just how to relate to them. The way they dressed always interested Ned. It was something like being in a western movie. In the 1930's these native people existed very much as they had about a hundred years earlier, living mostly off the land. Actually, the land was bountiful, since down at the river each year they harvested enormous numbers of salmon, especially twice a year during the spawning times. Wild game was everywhere in the surrounding hills, near the big river.

Other occasional visitors were sheepherders who moved their flocks from day to day or week to week into the best grazing areas. The owners of the sheep business had worked out lease agreements with the Colville tribe allowing them summer grazing rights. Most of the sheep owners were from around Yakima in central Washington State. Each spring they trucked hundreds of sheep to the sparsely populated forests and meadows on the Colville reservation. The sheep were separated into manageable flocks attended by one or two herders. The herder's job was to move their flocks from place to place, keeping them safe, healthy, and allowing them to fatten up on the grassy hillsides and meadows. This required the herders to continually break camp and set up a new tent camp almost each time they moved the herd. Most of the herders were guys in their twenties. Some were relatives of the owners. Most had French names, as the owners were usually French immigrants.

As the only kid for miles around, the sheepherder's always gave Ned some attention as they sometimes made brief stopovers at the cabin. They seemed to enjoy teasing the kid about one thing or another. Sometimes they took Ned for rides on their horses where he sat behind them hanging onto their backs. Ned said they always smelled strongly of sweat. Bathing wasn't the usual thing with these guys. In general, they were happy spirited and fun to be around. They enjoyed visiting Ned's grandpa, as he treated them with wine and home brew beer. Grandpa always gave them some "greens" from his garden, and often they rewarded him with a leg of lamb or some venison. What the young guys really liked was some conversation, since they were alone much of the time.

Alone, that is, from human company. Occasionally they had unwelcome visitors, usually at night. Coyotes, wolves and bears sometimes attempted to prey on the sheep. It happened often enough in this wild country so that the herders always carried guns, usually .38 revolvers in holsters, and .30-30 rifles in saddle scabbards. Ned always enjoyed looking at their guns. At about age ten, grandpa taught his grandson to shoot a .22 rifle. Shortly after that Ned received instruction in the use of the old man's .38 pistol and later, his twelve gauge shotgun. At age twelve, Ned was given his own .22 single shot rifle, which, in late August, Ned was allowed to use to shoot grouse. When fishing around the big creek two hundred yards below the cabin, Ned was taught to carry the pistol in a belted holster, right on his hip, just like a cowboy in the movies. This was in case he happened to stumble across a mama bear with her cubs in the brush somewhere around the creek. What a place for a young boy to spend his summer vacation. A place in the wild country riding horses, catching fish, shooting guns, and hanging out with some big strong guys who were like heroes to a young boy.

One sunny morning Ned's friend Roger and he had just returned from the spring with big buckets of water. Nine-mile Charley, an Indian just passing through, had spent the night in the cabin with the family and had just finished breakfast. Charley was twenty something, and rode a great looking bay gelding. Ned enjoyed Charley's rare visits even though the dark-skinned full-blooded Native American didn't say much. Ned was fascinated with Charley's long black braids, a beaded vest, a cowboy hat with a high rounded crown, and big noisy spurs on his boots. About that time, Grandpa Carl was scanning the meadow two hundred yards down the hill with his binoculars hoping to see some deer. All of us were suddenly shocked to see grandpa lower his binoculars and burst into tears. Ned was shocked as he had never seen an adult cry before and it scared him. "Duvall has been shot," the old man exclaimed. Squinting through his binoculars down the hill into the meadow, he could make out two riders, one leading the second horse on which the second rider appeared to be slumped over the saddle. No one knew quite what to do, but Nine-Mile Charley mounted his horse and galloped down the hill to see if he could be of help. As the horses approached the cabin, Roger shouted, "He's all bloody!" The three men lifted Louie Duvall from his horse and carried him inside the cabin, where Grandmother Sophie had prepared the bed and fetched the first aid box, some water and clean towels. Louie Duvall's left side and left leg were covered with blood, the result of a shotgun blast. It turned out that Louie and his partner, Pierre La Belle had been occupying the tiny cabin at the "buck camp," two miles north. The buck camp was a sort of base camp for the sheepherders, featuring some large corrals and loading gates. It was a place for separating bucks, ewes and lambs, and for keeping numbers of sheep corralled at various times. Frequently, there were raids by predators, mostly bears. At times the herders set traps designed to kill the invaders. That morning, Duvall was attempting to install a bear trap, armed with a twelve-gauge shotgun loaded with double-aught buckshot. The trap was set up like a booby trap, set off by a trip wire. Apparently, Louie got in his own way or committed some kind of serious error because the gun accidentally fired a round into his left side. Louie was in his early fifties and part owner of the sheep business. He and Grandpa Carl had become friends. Everyone present was extremely worried that Louie might bleed to death. It was quickly decided that Charley would ride as fast as he could to Keller, twenty miles away and phone for an ambulance. The nearest hospital was at Wilber, a tiny little town twenty-five miles from Keller. The twenty-five miles included a ferry ride across the treacherous Columbia River. There was no choice. Charley mounted and rode off at a fast gallop. Ned's grandparents went to work attempting to stop Louie's bleeding. In an hour or so they had him disinfected, cleaned up and bandaged, but were still worried that Louie would not survive. Pierre, Roger and Ned sat around outside not knowing what to do. The ambulance finally got to the cabin after hours of anxious waiting. Louie was in and out of consciousness as everyone waited. As all present learned later, Louie Duvall survived. Ned's grandparents were heroes for saving his life.

Ned and Roger had been stunned and shocked to observe the bloody sheepherder and the expectation that he might die before their eyes. What about Nine-Mile Charley? He was a hero also. His wild ride over the dangerous old mountain road must have been a real feat of horsemanship. As they heard later, as Charley galloped up to the Keller store to call for an ambulance, his horse fell dead from exhaustion. Charley's horse was a hero too.

Ditch'em

The kids in Rainier Beach played pretty much the same games as those in other suburbs and small towns anywhere in the USA. During the depression years board games like monopoly were played in every home, in recreational centers and clubrooms. The usual games were similar to board games of today. Swimming pools, beaches and vacant lots were popular venues for other activities. The girls had their games such as hopscotch. The boys might play football in vacant lots or roller hockey on neighborhood streets or vacant tennis courts. At one time or another all the kids in the neighborhoods played kick the can or hide and seek. At the ages of about ten to thirteen, the neighborhood boys at Rainier Beach invented a game they called "Ditch'em." It was like hide and seek played on bicycles. The game started with two teams, call them team A and team B. Each boy had a bicycle. All agreed on the boundaries, roughly three blocks by three blocks. Rainier Beach was hilly but the boys played Ditch'em in a fairly level area of about nine square blocks. It started at "home base," one of the boy's front yards. Teams were made up of anywhere from two-to-six boys on each team. When all were assembled the rules were reviewed, and the boys on team A would then ride their bikes rapidly off in different directions. They were given about three minutes to "hide out" within the established street boundaries. After that, the kids on team B would ride furiously from the home base – often a street corner or some neighborhood lawn – after them, in an attempt to "ride them down." This meant closing distance between the chasees, (team A) and the chasers (team B). Each paved street always had certain "separations," or "sections," marked by tar strips extending horizontally from curb to curb. The horizontal tar line sections were about eight yards apart. Their rules held that if a rider from team B could ride fast enough to catch a rider from team A, he needed to get within two tar lines of the rider from team A. After the boys from team A were "run-down," or "caught," they were out of the game, and had to return to home base. While waiting at home base, the team A boys would sometimes play mumble-peg on the lawn, or Indian wrestle. The kids didn't usually like "sitting around." It was always exciting to chase another kid on bicycles, both pumping as hard as possible, each attempting to gain speed and outride the other. Riders from team A were prohibited from actually concealing themselves by hiding behind buildings or brushy areas. This kept the action going. As soon as all the boys on team A were caught and assembled at home base, it was team B that rode off to be chased by the team A kids. There were some risks when riding at high speed and attempting to negotiate sharp corners, rough or slippery spots on the streets, sidewalks, parking strips, curbs, wet pavement, alleys and vacant lots. Sometimes these contests of Ditch'em lasted two or three hours. There were no winning or losing teams. The whole idea was to have fun riding bikes as fast as they could while enjoying the competition. Fortunately, there was never much traffic. An occasional car might drive through, but the streets in the neighborhood were generally quiet. There were sometimes some very strange looks from people in the occasional car passing by. The look was usually a mixture of puzzlement or shock as they watched the bike riders madly pedaling after one another. The boys rode furiously over curbs, lawns, sidewalks, across driveways, through gates, flower gardens, ditches, gravel, boardwalks, grassy fields and muddy alleys, swerving, skidding, and recklessly chasing each other around the neighborhood. What fun!

Sometime around age fourteen or so the kids seemed to get involved in other activities, and the game of Ditch'em phased out. The strange thing about this wonderful game was that the next generation of pre-teen kids did not continue the fun. Apparently it was not known about in other neighborhoods, other towns or anywhere. As far as anyone ever knew, Ditch'em was a unique game originated by the Depression-era creative little roughnecks at Rainier Beach. In commenting about the game of "Ditch'em" in later years as adults, the guys who had participated were of one opinion. The game never existed that was more downright exhilarating or "more damn fun!"

The Circle

Small towns traditionally have a town drunk. The Rainier Beach village drunk was a guy named Johnny Mayhew. No taller than five-foot five, Johnny was slightly built, on the skinny side. Wringing wet, he weighed no more than 130 pounds and a bit wizened looking, at forty-something. The local drug store was kind of a hangout for some of the local smart aleck teenagers. Johnny was often seen around the drug store where he usually availed himself of pints of cheap wine. The bus stop zone was directly in front of the drug store. Johnny often caught the bus to downtown Seattle from the bus stop. Sometimes when attempting to board the bus, drunken Johnny received assistance from others at the bus stop. There were times when some of the teenagers would help him up to the first step. Johnny Mayhew was always belligerent, nasty, insulting, loud and obnoxious. The kids thought he was really funny as he yelled out insults to anyone nearby, especially those who had stepped forward to help him. There were several occasions however, when they went out of their way not to help him, but to tease him. At these times a group of six or eight boys would form a circle around Johnny and return his insults by yelling at him with the filthiest cuss words they could muster. Then the fun really started as the teenage devils would grab him, shove him back and forth across the circle, all of them whooping, laughing and giggling. It was like pushing a rag doll from one side to the other, then roughly passing him around the inside of the circle from one boy to another until they tired of the game. About the same age as their parents, Johnny was a pathetic old guy, even as he hurled insults and tried to spit in the boy's faces. "God damn you," he would shriek, "I know you guys! I've screwed your mothers! Every one of them. Your mothers are dirty whores!" he would yell, "I've knocked them up, you rotten little bastards!" Johnny would continue yelling epithets as he was being roughly pushed, pulled, and tossed back and forth. As the bus arrived, the boys would then push him aboard where he would wander up and down the aisle, cursing and being an obnoxious pest. After the action the young bullies would chortle and titter over the pride they felt after manhandling and humiliating drunken, helpless Johnny Mayhew.

A few days after performing their circle act with Johnny, one of the young bullies named Homer Blair, happened to be talking to one of the boys who had participated in the infamous circle. "Yesterday my mom asked me to put some old photo albums into the garbage can," said Homer. "I looked through a couple of them, at the old black and white snapshots. Mom told me, "Most of the people in these old snapshots are relatives and friends from about fifteen or twenty years ago, back when I was first divorced from your father, and before I married your step dad." "There was a picture of my mother," said Homer, "and a strange man kissing. Damned if it wasn't Johnny Mayhew. They both looked a lot younger but I could tell it was him kissing my mom."

Fights

Kids growing up in the suburbs of Rainier Beach were fortunate. Generally speaking, it was a pretty wholesome and safe environment, much like any other suburb, village, or small town anywhere in America in the 1920's through the 1950's. There were very few one-parent families. Most kids felt secure in their home environments. Along with contributing feelings of security parents were protective, but at the same time seemed to give their kids lots of latitude. Like kids anywhere, however, sometimes the boys occasionally felt the need to fight somebody. Normally, fighting never seemed to produce serious injury. A bloody nose or black eye was about as bad as it got, but there were a few fights that were somewhat unusual, even bizarre. There was one that Jack Kober remembered from when he was about eight or nine. The fight took place between two adults in a parking lot behind the neighborhood tavern. One of the contestants was an old man, probably forty years old. Jack knew who he was, a man dressed in a three piece gray suit complete with a watch chain across his vest. Mr. Vernon Jonas was ruddy-faced, big nosed, mostly bald and very drunk. He and his opponent had left the tavern after a loud argument and staggered out to the parking lot to resolve their disagreement by means of a fisticuffs contest. Mr. Jonas faced a much younger man, slightly built, with an overhanging brow, swarthy complexion and a flat nose. The crowd that gathered, surrounding the pugilists called the guy Phil. The fight started at a pretty fast pace. It was obvious from the start that Phil, even though pretty swacked, knew something about boxing. He jabbed, feinted, and smacked old Jonas on the temple, then rapidly punched him in the stomach, the eye, and the jaw. Old Vern Jonas did not go down, but took the punches with little defense. Obviously, Mr. Jonas had no boxing skills. The kids who were watching began to snicker. They laughed and yelled in a teasing manner at Mr. Jonas. Phil knocked the old fool down in short order and the fight was over. Jack was late for dinner, so he ran home as fast as he could. At the dinner table that evening Jack asked his mom, "Don't you know a man named Jonas, a guy with a big nose?" "Oh yes, Vern Jonas is a sort of a friend of ours," said mom, "He is a very prominent man in the community. Why Jack, have you seen him someplace?" "Yes mom, about an hour ago the very prominent man in the community was behind the tavern getting the shit kicked out of him." Mom gave Jack a stern look, and scolded, "How many times have I told you not to hang around that tavern?"

An interesting fight took place on Brownie Clemens front lawn when he was about twelve. Brownie was engaged in a serious game of mumble peg one summer afternoon with two friends. Mumble peg was a favorite game in those days. It was played with a pocketknife, and had rigid rules as to how the knife, with two blades exposed, was thrown or flipped into the ground. There was a scoring system, so the competition was always fun for boys in the neighborhood. The two kid's names were Bink Nabb and Gene Polock. Bink was a big rangy guy, a bit older than both Brownie and Gene. The kids all called Gene Polock "Lunkhead." Lunk was a skinny little guy about a year younger than Brownie. Unexpectedly, Brownie's two friends began a heated argument about the scoring in the mumblepeg game. Suddenly the two boys were slapping and punching each other. Brownie tried to intervene, but could only get them to stop temporarily so they could agree on how they were going to pursue a serious fight. Lunk refused to box with the bigger Bink, so they agreed to wrestle. Brownie wasn't too comfortable about it because both were very angry, saying things like "I never did like you." Brownie was afraid that Lunkhead might be hurt. The two contestants appointed Brownie referee. After removing their pocketknives from the grass, the wrestling match began on the front lawn, with Brownie as the only spectator. Big Bink grabbed wiry little Lunk, trying to pin him, but the smaller kid was surprisingly strong and agile. After attempting several wrestling holds, they rolled around on the lawn, fiercely attempting to gain an advantage. In a very swift unsuspected maneuver, Lunkhead got his legs around Bink's waist in a scissors grip. Watching, Brownie was sure Bink would easily break the hold. Unable to break the scissors, Bink started trying to punch the smaller Lunk in the face, but Lunk's face was out of range of any effective blows by Bink. It was very much like a powerful boa constrictor was painfully squeezing Bink's stomach. Bink's face reddened, as his eyes seemed to bulge out of their sockets. In only a few minutes, Bink was forced to give up. Little Lunkhead Polock was victorious. The two boys quickly headed for home. It seemed big Bink

Nabb learned never to underestimate an opponent. Sometime later, Brownie learned that Bink was treated for something like bruised kidneys. After the fight, as time went on, Brownie had the feeling that Bink went out of his way to avoid him. He swore he never told anyone about that fight, but he calculated that Bink was embarrassed about it. He probably thought it was a matter of boyhood honor.

Sometime at the age of about fourteen, a group of neighborhood teenagers happened to be walking on their way home after swimming at our local beach. The group included Red Dog Barker, Teddy Gatz, Bobby Hoke and Bobby's little brother Joey. Big Bobby was sixteen, about two years older than the rest of the guys. He was an unusually big kid for his age, very muscular and strong as a young bull. Bobby had a shock of tousled black hair and squinty dark eyes under protruding brows. With a thick neck and heavy jaw, Bobby was a pretty nice guy, but not a boy to mess with. His little brother Joey was about ten, and considered a bit of a pest, but Joey loved to hang out with his big brother and his friends whenever he could. Heading for home the group of boys meandered along the sidewalk, sometimes digressing by hopping over the curb into the street and often onto adjacent parking strips, they were startled by a man's loud voice shouting, "Get off that parking strip you little creep!" The man had moved very quickly from his front porch and was reaching out attempting to push little Joey off his parking strip. "I just planted grass there you little shit!" The man was about thirty, average size with curly brown hair. At this moment Bobby shouted, "Get your hands off my brother!" At the same time he dashed toward the guy. The older man turned quickly to meet Bobby's rush, doubled his fist and swung a roundhouse right aimed at Bobby's head. The blow never found its mark, as Bobby ducked and buried his big right fist into the man's belly. The wide eyed kids heard the guy grunt as he staggered backward and lowered his fists. This allowed Bobby to smash the man's face with two quick powerful punches. He fell backward landing on his rump in a sitting position, glassy eyed, his mouth open, and blood gushing from his obviously broken nose. In the meantime the man's wife had emerged from their house, to the front porch with two little kids, a boy about five and a tiny girl about three. The mother was screaming as she clutched her kids, "Patrick, what is going on? Patrick, he's hurting you, stop him somebody, stop, and stop, you monster!" Bobby, the monster, quit socking Patrick when he flopped down on his butt, looked at him, and said quietly, "You shouldn't push my little brother." With Patrick's wife screaming and clutching her horrified little children, and Patrick sitting on the sidewalk bleeding, the teenaged rascals ran off toward their homes, separating along the way. Their dogtrot pace soon evolved into an all out sprint for their houses, keeping their eyes peeled for any sign of a police car. None of the kids would ever think about relating such an event to their parents, but the story of the parking strip fight made its way around the teenage community as a neighborhood classic story. When Teddy Gatz met up with Bobby Hoke a few days later, he exclaimed, "I guess you gave old Patrick a lesson the other day." "Yeah," said Bobby, "He was pushin' Joey." "That's some kinda brotherly love," Teddy snickered. Bobby showed a crooked grin. "It was kinda fun too," he said.

A local kid named Ducky Waters lived in a house with a full cement basement. It was at a time when Ducky and his pals were about eleven or twelve, where they set up a boxing ring. It was a rather small ring, bounded by ropes tied to basement support-posts. Into the corners Ducky had placed folding chairs for the boxers to sit between rounds. Another boy supplied the new boxing gloves he had received as a Christmas gift from his dad. Every so often, the kids would get the urge to punch or slap or hit somebody. At those times the boys would recruit a few others and conduct some semi-serious boxing matches in Ducky's basement boxing gym. Sometimes they would invite an "outsider" to join them, probably because they thought they could beat the hell out of the new guy. They had different ways of organizing these boxing competitions. Sometimes it was purely spontaneous, with challenges from one kid to another, and then they could slug away at each other with little regard for the rules of boxing. They usually fought two-minute rounds to avoid exhaustion and the occasional brutal mismatch. Sometimes they drew names from a hat or bucket to determine an opponent. Some kind of referee was needed so that things didn't get entirely out of hand. Nobody wanted to get into the ring with Big Bobby Hoke, not to mention Mutt Bronkowski. The guys did their best to make sure that those two bruisers didn't know about these boxing events, but when they happened to be there, the two acknowledged champions took it easy on the rest of them. Those boxing matches somehow helped the boys believe that it was "practice" to become competent at fighting. At twelve or thirteen, in their neighborhood, one never quite knew when a fight was likely to break out and you might suddenly be transformed into a street corner warrior, like it or not. In their basement-boxing ring they usually fought two or three rounds, two minutes each with a one-minute rest between rounds. Sometimes it was fun for some to act as "handlers," or managers. The handlers enjoyed giving advice to his fighter as he rested in his corner between rounds. "Punch to the body, hit him in the gut, stay away and keep your left in his face, crowd him into a corner, and let him have it, remember, pop-pop-bang!" Sometimes they would giggle as they forced their fighter to drink a gulp of water out of a coke bottle. It didn't take long to determine which of the boys came to fight, and which ones hated to get hit, but went through the motions so they would not lose face. It was very rare when anyone was hurt, but slamming each other around, taking punches to the face and body, and the enlivening action was beneficial (it was thought) to a group of rambunctious young boys. Occasionally there was a bit of pain, a bloody nose, a black eye, some sore ribs, and a diminished ego that came out of the experience. All in all, it was great sport in which the boys gained experience in how to handle both victory and defeat, to know they could survive some physical punishment, and to have a certain degree of pride in knowing that they had the courage to take physical risks and hold onto their pride, win or lose.

The Mount Baker Rumble

In high school, Rex Darrow enjoyed the social stuff, the parties and especially the dances. He could never describe himself as a ladies man, like some of the boys he knew, but there were a few occasions when Rex was lucky enough to talk a girl into going out with him, usually to a movie or a dance. During one three or four week period, when he was a senior, he dated a cute little sophomore girl named Bonnie who also lived in the Rainier Beach neighborhood. At some social occasion she was introduced to a big senior kid from Lincoln High School which, was located clear across town, about eight miles north of Rex and Bonnie's neighborhood. The guy's name was Chuck Amsterdam and he took quite a fancy to Bonnie who told Rex she wanted nothing to do with this Chuck character. Chuck was aggressive and called her frequently asking her out. Bonnie had informed him that she and Rex were regularly dating and she was not interested in going out with him. After more persistent but unsuccessful phone calls, he became frustrated and angry. It was then that he began to threaten Rex through his phone calls to Bonnie. "I've heard that Rex, this boyfriend of yours, is a regular at the Mount Baker friday night dances," said Chuck. "Yeah, he's always there," admitted Bonnie, "and I'm usually there too." "I'm going to settle this," snarled

Chuck Amsterdam. "I'm going to show up at Friday's dance and beat the hell out of that guy. Not only that, but I'll bring along a bunch of guys to beat hell out of his friends at the same time." "Please don't do that," pleaded Bonnie. Later, when she told Rex about Chuck's threat, she couldn't quite hide her feelings that she was enjoying all the fuss. No doubt Chuck figured that if he showed his manliness by beating up on Rex, it would make him acceptable to Bonnie.

At that juncture, Rex's teenage honor was at stake, so somehow he figured he would have to confront the threat. It was unnerving to know that the gang Chuck was bringing were notorious north-end tough guys, but Rex had no choice but to prepare. He set about to buttonhole every friend and acquaintance at Franklin high school and in the local neighborhood and asked for their support. "If a lot of us show up," Rex kept repeating, "we will outnumber them and there probably won't be any trouble." Rex secretly wished he could have believed it himself. Rex was encouraged when just about every boy he talked to assured him that he would be there to bravely confront the Lincoln gang at the Mount Baker neighborhood community hall. The hall featured a large dance floor and a big fancy jukebox. About fifty or sixty teenagers usually attended the dances. The atmosphere was always happy, safe and fun for the bobby sox set. Most of the kids loved to dance to the music of Harry James, Glen Miller, Benny Goodman and Tommy Dorsey, music perfectly performed and recorded for the social dance fashion of the times.

When the fateful Friday night rolled around, Rex was counting on arrangements with a friend to drive him to the dance, which started at 7:30 p.m.. A half hour before he was due to pick Rex up, he phoned and said he had trouble with his car, so the ride was out. Rex walked to Bonnie's house and the two of them proceeded to the Mount Baker dance hall by bus. Rex had a funny feeling as he and Bonnie entered the door into the hall. Instead of the usual crowd, only three people were lolling around inside the huge interior. The jukebox was quiet. There was an eerie silence in the place. Word about the anticipated rumble had certainly gotten around. Where were all Rex's friends? Where were all the toughest guys in school who had promised to be there? Where were the girls? Where was the lady chaperone that managed the hall? Where were Chuck Amsterdam and his gang of roughnecks from Lincoln? Where the hell *was* everybody? Rex and Bonnie hung around until 8:30 p.m., then left for the local malt shop for a snack and caught the bus home. Later, as Rex pondered the craziness of the previous Friday night, he tried to determine what he had learned from the experience. I guess what I learned, thought Rex, is that you are a fool to depend on your friends when there is a risk involved. All those so-called tough guys at school are gutless phonies. How can any of those bozos look me in the eye when I see them again? It's amazing how fast word gets around.

Naval Warfare

Living through their teens in the early years of World War II, the Rainier Beach kids loved their environment on the shore of the magnificent Lake Washington, twenty-five miles long and approximately two miles wide. Most became good swimmers, loved fishing and splashing around in boats. Any type of boat was fun, rafts, skiffs, rowboats, canoes, paddle craft, sailboats, powerboats and inner tubes. It was at the tail end of the Great Depression. Most people in working class neighborhoods had few luxuries. Very few even knew a boat owner. There was a boat moorage close by where the local boys sometimes would rent a rowboat or canoe, but those times were rare. They did discover however, a good-sized boat moorage about four miles north, along the east shore where boats could be rented for "no money down." Payment was expected only after the boat was returned to the moorage dock. There was a lot more trust in those days. The day the teenage rascals discovered that boats at the Lakewood boathouse could be rented for no money up front was an inspiration to their larcenous hearts.

It happened that on a few occasions they took advantage of a glorious opportunity to enjoy the use of some boats for free. The scam went as follows: a group of five or more of them would take a bus to the moorage and appoint the oldest looking kid to sign up for a big rowboat or a canoe. Sometimes they managed to get their hands on as many as three canoes, or two rowboats and one canoe, or whatever they could get. The kid renting the boats always signed a fictitious name. They would then row or paddle the boats onto the lake, out of sight of the moorage office, usually two or three miles south, closer to their Rainier Beach neighborhood. That's when the fun began. Challenges were issued and the navel battles got under way. A broadside ramming was great fun. Capsizing their opponent's rowboat or canoe was exhilarating. Paddles and oars were used for furious splashing, poking and prying. This sort of raucous activity was just about the most fun a guy could have. With frequent pauses in the warfare, there was always some fun crawling or scrambling over the bottoms of the capsized crafts, or swimming underneath to find an air pocket. There was always lots of shouting, cursing, laughing and taunting amongst the teenage naval warriors. After the fun, often lasting for an hour or two, the little sinners maneuvered the maltreated boats into shallow water, sometimes secluding them into reeds or cattails near the shore. Pleased with themselves after enjoying their water battles, they would scramble to shore, soaking wet and proceed to walk to the security of their familiar neighborhood. What a great summer afternoon!

The Bath House

During World War II, most young men between the ages of eighteen and thirty-three or four either enlisted in the armed forces or were drafted into the military. The absence of young men created a shortage just about everywhere. There was a public swimming beach about a mile north of Rainier Beach on the Shore of Lake

Washington. In normal years, three lifeguards would be on duty each day during the summer vacation months. Unfortunately, during the last two years of the war a shortage of manpower resulted in a limited availability of qualified lifeguards to protect the swimmers at all Seattle beaches, including Pritchard beach. All was not lost however, the parks department found ways to furnish limited lifeguard service. Instead of the usual three, only one lifeguard was assigned to Pritchard beach. One lifeguard could not handle the normal duties. The result was that the bathhouse was closed, and bathers were forced to change into and out of their swimsuits in the restrooms attached to the main bathhouse. Locker room facility access was suspended for the duration. One summer day in 1944, four Rainier Beach teenaged stalwarts happened to mosey over to the swimming beach, doubtless to ogle some half-naked girls. As it happened, one of their buddies from high school, Dane Colville, was a qualified lifeguard and was on duty at the beach. Dane was lifeguarding while waiting to be called into the Navy. "What are you upstanding gentlemen doing here?" was Dane's greeting to them. "We just dropped by to see how many people have drowned since you've been here," grinned Charley Peterson. A friendly chat ensued, with good-natured insults exchanged, and a few dirty stories related by the upstanding gentleman for the amusement of Dane, at that moment our favorite lifeguard. Jake Gilman questioned Dane about the presence of any really sexy teen or preteen girls. "I'll tell you what," said Dane softly, "if you filthy minded twerps can keep your mouths shut I'll show you something." "Yeah, like what?" asked Goodtime Willie Kane. "Follow me," said Dane, and headed toward the bathhouse. "Where's he taking us?" asked Charley. The boys followed Dane through the locked bathhouse door past the locker rooms, the office, and into a large room where the lifeguard's rowboats were kept. The east inside wall stood between the boat room and the girl's restroom. The boat room was unfinished inside. With the studs and wiring showing, the only wall between the girl's restroom and the five boys was a thin sheet of wallboard. The best thing about it was that the wall had some tiny holes, perfect for peeking into the girl's cubicles on the other side. Each cubicle contained a toilet and little bench. Dane gathered the boys very close and whispered, "Don't you guys dare make a sound, or we will all be in deep shit. Keep very, very quiet, and I'll let you look for ten minutes. Then we leave. No arguments, got it?" All agreed, and the boys scrambled to the wall to learn in detail how girls changed into and out of their bathing suits, how they fussed with their hair. The boys carefully observed and remembered in specific detail what girl's private parts really looked like. After all, the girls were only about three or four feet away from the boys with the glassy-eyed stares. The big problem for all of the guys was keeping quiet. There was an irresistible urge to giggle, snicker, guffaw, or laugh uproariously as they enjoyed this magnificent, fantastically quirky, earth-shaking event in their hormone driven teenage existence. Could anyone imagine such a stimulating pleasurable experience? After

138

the prescribed ten minutes, Dane ushered the teenage devils still struggling to contain their constant urge to giggle, out of the boathouse to the front sidewalk. "Now for God's sake," he demanded, "Keep your big mouths shut about this. I did you a favor and risked my job. See you guys later." Shortly thereafter, most of the boys were called into the military, so the incident never got to be a favorite story at the Rainier Beach barbershop.

The Stolen Car

Kids growing up in the neighborhood generally respected their parents. They did however, occasionally get into mischief and indulged in stupid stunts. One winter night for example, three twelve-year-old boys decided to break into the local elementary school. They did not necessarily intend to destroy anything, but did it just to see if they could. It would be a dangerous and stimulating adventure. Ernie Loman, Buns Reynolds and Henry (Bottlebutt) Varner found a window to crawl through. They stole a soccer ball and some color crayons. Not a very big haul, but Bottlebutt Varner did the adventurous thing. He took a dump on the stage in the school auditorium. The boys all had a good laugh over that nasty little act. They could imagine the look on the school custodian's face when he discovered it the next morning. Surprise! For the rest of the day the old sourpuss would shuffle around the school muttering to himself as he always did, mystified at the rotten things those insufferable little brats seemed to love to do just to make his life more difficult.

139

Henry Varner had been an unfortunate victim of infantile paralysis (polio) at age six, leaving him with a grotesque limp. It was as if he needed to throw his little butt around in circular gyrations just to be able to walk. At Rainier Beach any boy who had a physical deformity could expect a nickname, usually of a derogatory nature. Little Henry was dubbed "Bottlebutt."

About three years later, at sixteen, Bottlebutt found himself in the company of the other two school burglars. The three of them were sitting at the soda fountain in Sorenson's drug store when Buns Reynolds asked Bottlebutt, "What are you doing later tonight?" "No plans," answered Bottlebutt. "You want to go with us? We're gonna take a ride in Ernie's dad's car." "Are you old enough to drive, Ernie?" Bottlebutt asked. "Hell yes, I'm fifteen and a half," Ernie snorted. Buns giggled. "Be at Ernie's house at 7:30," said Buns. "We're going to drive to West Seattle and pick up some girls." "I'll be there," said Bottlebutt. At the appointed time, they met on the sidewalk in front of Ernie's house. "Here's the deal," said Buns softly, "We open the garage doors and roll the car out of the garage, but we gotta be real quiet." Ernie's parents were obviously home, since the house lights were on. "We're taking Ernie's dad's car without permission?" asked the little cripple. Does this mean we were guilty of stealing a car? Could I be risking arrest? Forget it, he told himself if it comes to that, I'd just plead innocence and blame it on Buns and Ernie. The three of them got the car rolling down hill, jumped in and got it started. On the way, Ernie informed the Butt that they had met three girls at a skating rink the week before. Buns said he had called the one girl named Charlene and made a date for tonight. Ernie had the address and we were headed to a house in West Seattle, about six miles away. Buns described the three girls as kinda ordinary looking, not really cute, but loud and giggly. Arriving at Charlene's house, the three girls appeared and piled into the car, one girl in the front seat with Ernie, the other two into the back seat with Buns and Bottlebutt. Naturally, the boys tried to work their way around to putting their arms around the girls and trying for some kissy face, but that never seemed to work out. In fact, Buns was sure those silly girls didn't care much for the three irresistible Lotharios. The clumsy attempts by Ernie, Buns and Bottlebutt to grope the three little virgins turned out to be a losing endeavor. In a very short time the girls were ordered out of the car under a street light somewhere on a quiet corner in West Seattle.

On the way home, as the boys were driving on a busy street, they were pulled over by a Seattle police officer. "Roll down your window," ordered the cop. Ernie complied. "Do you know you just drove illegally through three stop lights, ran over a curb, and clipped a stop sign in the past three minutes?" asked the cop. Ernie affected his most innocent look. "Let me see your driver's license." "I don't have one, officer," said angel-faced Ernie. "You don't have a license? How old are you?" demanded the cop. "Almost sixteen," replied Ernie. The cop shone his flashlight into the car and gave Buns and Bottlebutt a careful scrutiny. "I can't believe this," he repeated to himself. "You boys are really something. What in the hell am I going to do with you?" After some thought the cop spoke, "Look, if I let you go, I want you to promise me that you will drive very very carefully and slowly 'till you get home. Does your father know you are out with his car?" "No sir," said Ernie, in a meek voice. "Drive home very slowly. No more than twenty miles per hour all the way. Put this car back in your garage and behave yourselves. Otherwise I will have to lock you up in the city jail. Now get the hell out of here." It was probably the only time Bottlebutt ever knowingly rode in a stolen car.

At the Movies

At age nine, Rollo Manning was allowed to attend movies. For a few years in the mid-thirties there was a small movie theatre not far from Rainier Beach. The cost of admission for kids was ten cents, as time went on the price went up. Downtown movies cost more. About that time, word went around the grapevine that a very important double feature was about to begin showing at a movie house in downtown Seattle. It was the kind of earth shaking movie event that any kid was expected to see, or had to see in order to be relevant to his peers. After some serious begging Rollo was granted permission to take the bus downtown to the Music Box theatre Saturday morning on the condition that he go with a group of local boys. The movie they desperately needed to see was a double feature consisting of two horror films. Although considered campy and corny by today's standards, the two films have become horror classics, "Frankenstein," starring Boris Karloff along with "Dracula," was starring Bela Lugosi.

On Saturday morning the kids (all boys) were lined up in twos for almost a block before the theatre doors opened. All went well on the bus and at the movie, but both movies had the effect of scaring the heck out of Rollo. While he never admitted being scared, it took a few weeks for him to stop experiencing something like the night terrors. Later, in his pre-teen years Rollo was able to see a movie almost every week, most often at the Sunday matinee. Sometime during his teenage years, Rollo ran with a group of neighborhood friends who enjoyed attending free downtown movies. They were "free" because the young scoundrels found a way to sneak into the theatres through the back exit doors. On these occasions one of the boys was previously assigned to bring a small wrecking bar. Using a special prying technique, those clever lads could easily pop the fire exit doors open. Rollo's group of break-in artists would then quietly sneak through the dark passageway just inside the door, into the dark theatre. Keeping a low profile, they would scurry in an exaggerated crouch moving rapidly to find seats.

On one particular occasion after breaking into a downtown theatre (just before the first film was due to begin at 11:00 a.m.) Rollo's gang silently slipped into seats near the middle of the theatre. The four lawbreakers were surprised to see a friend, Bernie Nason, quietly sitting there eating popcorn, waiting for the movie to start. "Hey there Bernie," they whispered, "imagine meeting you here." They all chuckled at the coincidence. "Where the hell did you guys come from?" Bernie good-naturedly hissed. Shortly thereafter, a man appeared dressed in a suit and tie that turned out to be the manager of the theatre. "You boys come this way," he ordered. Having no choice, the four break-and-enter specialists with Bernie included followed him into the lobby. "Now fellows, you are going outside, and don't try to come back in," he growled. "You can't kick me out," whined Bernie, "I paid my way in. Here is my ticket stub. I don't even know these guys!" "I know your tricks you little scoundrels," said the manager. "One of you buys a ticket, then sneaks to the back and lets the rest of you in through the back door. Out you go!" Outside on the sidewalk under the marquee, Bernie was very upset. "The least you guys can do is pay me. Pay me for the ticket I bought. You guys got me kicked out and I had nothing to do with this." As the boys left poor Bernie standing there, they sauntered down the sidewalk yelling, "Sorry Bernie, that's life.

The War Hero

Franklin High School served a big population of students, about two thousand. In 1941, World War II began. The war had an enormous impact on every American. Some of the younger teachers and coaches left for the military, some of the boys enlisted when they reached the age of seventeen. Some were subsequently killed or disabled. The high school served about two hundred fifty ethnic Japanese students. The Japanese attack on Pearl Harbor occurred on December 7th, 1941. One day in early 1942 the Japanese students disappeared from the classrooms, having been rounded up and sent to Internment Camps for the duration of the war.

Old photos and firsthand accounts testified to the fact that the so called "relocation camps" were not exactly luxury resorts. Ironically, as many as half of the prisoners were American citizens born in the USA.

All of the neighborhood teenaged boys anticipated service immediately after graduation from high school either by being drafted or enlisting. They were obligated one way or the other. Those drafted were subject to be assigned to any one of the military services. Frank Sorvino was one who joined the Marine Corps at age seventeen. Frank was very social, mild-mannered and an all-around good guy. It was never clear how he acquired the name "Flash," but it stuck. Flash Sorvino was dark complexioned, with dark brown eyes, wavy black hair and olive skin. Of average height, he was very well built, unusually strong and well-coordinated. Flash always seemed older than the rest of his buddies. His early physical maturity suggested his body was more like a twenty-something man. By enlisting very early in the war, Flash gave up his chance to play varsity football. He had played on the high school freshman team. Frank completed his Marine Corps boot camp training and was sent overseas during the time that battles were raging in the South Pacific. The Army, Navy and Marine Corps suffered enormous casualties in those times. Our thoughts were often of the guys we suspected were in harm's way. Flash was serving over there somewhere. At about this time, most of Frank's old gang were seniors in high school. Home on leave, Flash Sorvino showed up for a week or so after service in the South Pacific. He arrived at Franklin High School decked out in his colorful Marine dress uniform complete with decorations. Flash presented himself as a war hero home on leave from the battle zones in the South Pacific islands. Corporal Sorvino was presented to the faculty and students in a school assembly in his honor staged in two assembly sessions before more than fifteen hundred people. Corporal Sorvino delivered a compelling speech, relating tales of navel bombardments, island invasions, fierce battles, firefights and hand-to-hand combat. He described his experiences as a courageous fighting Marine, and how he had personally slain Japanese soldiers using his rifle and his deadly bayonet. He described how a marine in combat developed the ability to smell Japs at a distance, preparing him for a deadly encounter. His audiences were enthralled and enormously impressed with Corporal Frank Sorvino's heroism. They loved his presentation with the red white and blue of his full dress uniform glowing in the spotlight as he spoke. His swarthy good looks enhanced his compelling presentation. The student body audience departed that day feeling a patriotic glow. They had seen a genuine war hero in the flesh, and it had been an inspiring experience. All of Flash's old pals were excited by his presence. They could not have been more proud, a war hero and one of their own.

Later that week most of the Franklin teenagers

146

attended a special school dance held in honor of the school war hero. A local radio station reported the event, sending out one of their announcers to MC the occasion. Flash was interviewed over the air, and did very well. The largest dance crowd of the year attended the celebration in honor of Corporal Flash Sorvino. Along with all that, there were a few feature newspaper articles about the heroic marine, the World War II warrior. After graduation, most of the teenaged boys did their duty in the various military services. Sometime after the war was over they came back home to work, to school, to marry and assimilate into the post war culture. Flash and some friends saw each other on a few occasions after that, but gradually drifted apart.

Frank Sorvino's name came up on an occasion a few years later at a get together between a few old Rainier Beach friends, all war veterans, in a booth at the local tavern. Red Dog Barker related the story to the guys at the gathering. "I was attending my college master's degree class at the U dub," said Red Dog. "The class numbered only about eight grad students, plus an instructor who led some discussions with everyone participating. During the lunch break, I was part of a group of four other students, all World War II veterans. One guy had lost his left arm at the battle of Saipan in the South Pacific. As it turned out, all four of my classmates were ex-combat marines. At some point in our casual conversation over luncheon sandwiches and cokes, I mentioned my friend Frank Sorvino, the war hero. Red Dog paused and looked at the others in the booth. "At the mention of his name, the other three guys seemed to stiffen and stared intently at me. "What did I say," I asked a bit bewildered by their looks. "Didn't you know," asked the guy named Marv, that Sorvino was a phony?" "What? What do you mean?" I asked. The one-armed guy answered, "Sorvino never saw action. He was stationed in Hawaii doing office work the whole time away from the States." The third ex-marine named Stan chipped in, "He was a lying phony son of a bitch. Made us all ashamed." "And damned mad," said Marv. Red Dogs account of his meeting with those ex-marines resulted in a stunned silence by Flash Sorvinos ex-friends. "So here is the question," asked Red Dog, "Where was the honor?"

Lenny Arrives

Goodtime Willie Kane was one of the more interesting characters in the neighborhood among those growing up in the 1930's and 40's. Willie had a certain magical aura that a lot of his peers responded to. A natural leader, he played his part so well that his followers would tag along like a band of sheep and seemed to hang on his every word. His good looks attracted girls as well as boys. Only average size, his curly blond hair blue eyes and a perpetual expression of perfect confidence assured his popularity. Willie Kane usually captained the pick-up football or softball games at the local playfield. He often led his constituents on weekend forays to the movies, to the beach, or to the roller skating rink. To some, it was unclear how he became the acknowledged leader at the football games with his peers, as he was a lousy passer and a slow runner.

Some of the local kids were fond of recalling an incident at a time when Willie and a few of his followers were stalking around the neighborhood carrying BB guns and plinking at the occasional target. Targets might include cats, dogs, birds, telephone poles, or basement windows. The BB gun gang numbered about five teenage self-described sharpshooters. One of the five was a younger kid, probably about eleven years old named Carl, who was a devoted disciple of Goodtime Willie, the leader of the pack. Willie's lucky shot downed an innocent little sparrow. Standing over the quivering bird laying at his feet their leader spoke: "Hey, this little bastard ain't dead yet. Look at him shake. Somebody put him out of his misery." "Shoot him again Willie," shouted one of the boys. "Nah, I can't do it. Carley, come over here and put this bird out of its misery, he's suffering." "How?" asked Carley. "I don't know, let's see... I've got it, bite his head off." An expression of dread came over Carley's face. "Do I hafta?" "Go on," said Willie, "Do it!" Following the leader's directive, little Carley bit and spit the tiny head along with some blood and feathers onto the ground. The boys all guffawed and teased, but Carly continued to spit for the rest of the afternoon. Leadership is at times a mysterious thing.

Willie's right-hand friend was Jake Gilman. In high school Willie and Jake became accomplished in their relationships with girls. Jake was always very selective and dated only the loveliest teenaged girls. Willie wasn't that particular, he went after the plain ones and the ugly ones as well as the occasional cutie. They usually met girls at the school dances and they were very proficient at picking up girls just about anywhere, parties, skating rinks, and picnics and even, on a rare occasion, at church.

Since World War II was still raging, the local teenaged boys all expected to be called into military service right after high school graduation. Jake enlisted in the Marine Corps. Willie was one of the few boys in the local community to avoid service. His job at a local shipyard provided him with a deferment, which lasted until well after the war. In the meantime, he developed some kind of ailment affecting his eardrum, which exempted him from the Korean War draft.

The two became almost inseparable. They continued to cut a swath amongst the many girls that they met as they partied along in the post war socialization frenzy. Young people in their twenties seemed to be frantically seeking mates, lovers and spouses. Jake settled on one of his girlfriends from high school, Rosie Marnett. In a short time, they became inseparable, intimate and genuinely in love. Jake and Rosie teamed with Willie and his current girlfriend just about every weekend and the days between. In spite of their loving relationship obviously heading for marriage, Jake and Rosie had lover's spats from time to time. A serious argument, complete with shouted insults and hurt feelings, resulted in a break up. Their friends expected it would soon run its course. Jake and Rosie would surely make up. A few weeks went by as Jake sulked and Rosie steamed. Jake was so upset he avoided even temporary connections with other girls.

Jake became a kind of recluse during the three weeks he and Rosie remained apart. In the meantime Goodtime Willie called Rosie with "condolences," as he asked her to accompany him to a party for which he said he needed a date. Surprising herself, Rosie accepted, temporarily satisfying an urge to show spite toward Jake. Turning on his irresistible charm, Willie dated her a time or two after the first outing to the party for which he had claimed he needed an escort. Shortly thereafter, Jake called Rosie. They met and got back together, in love as before. Their friends watched the romantic scenario with interest. They gossiped about Rosie's dates with Goodtime Willie. The rumor was that Rosie and Willie had shared a sexual encounter, intended or not. The rumor seemed to vanish as Jake Gilman and Rosie Marnett were together again. Now engaged they enjoyed planning their wedding.

The marriage post-war bug was infecting most of the young people at Rainier Beach during those years. Some of Jake and Rosie's friends continued to interact with them at parties and other get-togethers. After a few months of marriage, babies began to show up. The last anyone saw of Jake and Rosie before they left town for good was at a social event in which their friends and they showed off their babies to one another. Some babies were newborns, along with older little tykes. It was a grand party, sort of a reunion in which Jake, Rosie and their two-year-old boy, Lenny said farewell. They were excited about moving to California where Jake was offered a partnership in business run by an elderly uncle. Time passed. Most of the old gang stayed close to home, but

Jake and Rosie became permanent Californians. Their old friends stayed in touch off and on through the years but rarely were able to meet.

It was sixteen years later when their friends Pickle and Susan Nichols heard from Jake and Rosie. They agreed to meet at the Nichol's Rainier Beach home on a Sunday afternoon for drinks, dinner and a long awaited visit. "Lenny will be coming with us," Jake announced over the phone before they started on their trip. Pick and Susan were quite overjoyed to welcome Jake and Rosie after such a long separation. "Lenny is visiting his cousins," Jake explained. They will drive him here later." The two couples thoroughly enjoyed sharing information about their families, gossip about their mutual friends and their ups and downs in the recent past. After dinner and drinks, their conversations continued as they sat in the living room on the Nichole's comfortable sofa and easy chairs. Pick and Susan were looking forward to meeting Jake and Rosie's son Lenny of whom they had heard a lot in the sixteen years since they had seen the little guy. "I think I hear a car," said Jake. Footsteps were heard on the front porch. Jake hurriedly threw open the front door and there stood Lenny. Eighteen years old, blonde hair blue eyed all-American boy, a perfect image of a teenaged Good Time Willie Kane.

Walterboro

The following is a recollection from the author's own experience.

In 1945 the Big War ended. Most boys who were teenagers in the 30's and 40's served in the military during the war years. A friend from Rainier Beach was stationed in South Carolina at the same time as my assignment in Georgia. We were keeping in touch and planned to get together. Curt Wells' Air Corps Unit was located in Walterboro, South Carolina. As planned, I traveled to Walterboro on a weekend pass. Since the war had recently ended with the unconditional surrender of Japan, the air force base at Walterboro was in the process of closing down in much the same way as my base at Chatham field near Savanna, Georgia. Surprisingly, when I arrived, my friend Curt was hurting a bit. He was recovering from a circumcision. He chose to have it done in response to an invitation issued to the GI's on the base. Because of the closure many of the ongoing base activities had slowed. Troops were constantly being shipped out and reassigned. Some of the units on the base suffered from inactivity and boredom, even the medical staff, where business was slow. Some of the doctors issued invitations to any soldiers on base to volunteer for a circumcision. It wasn't meant as a joke. The medics simply wanted to keep busy, but circumcisions? It turned out that many of the enlisted men accepted the offer and presented themselves to the infirmary for the clipping. The recovery time was about two weeks during which a twice daily soak was prescribed. Curt said he expected a razzing from the guys in his barracks, but over half of them had opted for the procedure, just as Curt had. Did that mean that the other half – about forty men – were Jewish? "Nobody had raised the question," stated Curt.

Shortly after I arrived at the base, Curt and I took the bus to town, even though he informed me there wasn't much to do, just visit some bars. More than half the GI's quartered on the base (in segregated areas from the white soldiers) were African American. Everyone used the word "Negro" back then in order to be politically correct. As we approached the bus taking us to town, Curt gave me some advice that all visitors like me needed to know. It was about the separation of the races when on the bus. Every serviceman stationed in the southern states in those times knew the rules. The civilian law held that Blacks were to ride in the back of the buses, whites in the front. Somehow, at camp Walterboro, the policy had been changed. The white soldiers were in the minority, so they were pressured to seat themselves in the <u>back</u> of the army buses. No exceptions, no questions, all the whites conformed. Even the southern redneck cracker white guys kept in line, and kept their mouths shut.

Curt was right, the only thing to do in town was drink. There was no USO, no dances, and no entertainment. It was just a spooky little town. Curt and I enjoyed our visit, retelling stories about the characters and events we had known in Rainier Beach. Late in the evening a gang fight broke out in the dingy little bar we were habituating, so we found ourselves back pedaling and retreating into the latrine (men's room). There was some pushing and shoving going on even in there. I found myself bending over to help a sailor out of the gutter-style urinal. I kept trying to pull his legs and feet so that his head would slide out of the slimy, stinking urine-soaked gutter. It appeared that the poor sap's head had landed in the urinal after drinking himself unconscious, or perhaps one of the brawlers had decked him. Maybe it had been one of those obnoxious marines who were presently attempting to kill some of us with their bare hands. At the time I wasn't actually sober myself, but I remember wondering what the little swabby's mother would think about their nineteen-year-old sailor boy, dead drunk, lying flat on his back, his head in the pisserie, and the guys going in and out of the men's room pissing on his head, across his closed eyes, and into his ears and mouth.

The next day I said farewell to my pal Curt. "We'll meet soon back in the old Rainier Beach neighborhood," he said. We both anticipated a return to civilian life in a few months. "Take care of your cock, you're gonna need it," I chortled as I began hitchhiking back to Chatham Field and the big birds. The B-29's were of the kind that delivered the last strike on Japan that ended the war on August 15, 1945.

GUB STADIUM

The big kid stood awkwardly at home plate holding the bat at a crazy angle on his shoulder. "Come on, Gub," shouted the kid at shortstop, "Hit a home run." The pitcher underhanded a nice pitch over the middle of home plate inviting a base hit. Gub's clumsy swing swished past the big softball for strike four. "Okay, Gub," said the pitcher, "the next pitch will be an easy one so let's see you hit it. You have two more strikes left." The neighborhood kids sometimes argued over the rules but once a consensus was reached, their amendments were enforced religiously. They allowed six strikes to the big kid now at bat, and loudly encouraged him to get a hit, any kind of a hit, after which they would all get a kick out of watching the big boy lumber his way to first base. Gub swung his bat at the next pitch in an absurdly clumsy swing. The boys on the playing field watched a comical parody of a baseball slugger gone bonkers. This time the ball met the bat, that is, part of the bat connected with part of the ball, sending the ball out to the pitcher in three bounces. As the hitter dropped his bat and started his run to first base, the boys on both teams began cheering and yelling as loud as a group of preteen rascals could scream. "Go for it, Gub!" "Run like hell!" "Run for second base!" "Hurry!" "Run faster!" The pitcher fielded the ball cleanly and with a big grin, looped the ball out of reach over the first baseman's head. Deadly serious, Gub rounded first base and bumbled his way toward second, and then third, heading for home as the first baseman retrieved the ball and threw it toward third base, too high for anyone to catch. Accompanied by cheers, Gub stumbled, staggered and struggled to run. "Go for it Gub!" "Run!" "Your ass is on fire," the kids shouted. They enjoyed Gub's triumphal home run as much as Gub's rewarding smile.

In the middle 1930's, at a time before computers, cell phones, skate boards, and little league, most boys sought playfields or vacant lots where they would congregate to enjoy pick-up games. These were spontaneous activities in which teen and preteenaged boys played with great energy and enthusiasm. Older teenagers often played on organized teams sponsored by the park department. There were also softball and soccer teams organized by elementary schools playing regular schedules. In early twentieth century America, young boys often organized their own neighborhood teams and competed with rival neighborhoods. There were also church leagues, Boy Scout teams and fraternal club teams. During the Great Depression kids almost always played without uniforms, coaches or parental involvement. They usually played with worn out, used or battered equipment. Games were played on a variety of venues, city play fields and parks, vacant lots and neighborhood streets. At many schools there were gravel surfaced playgrounds where kids played during recess, lunchtime or after school. There was always a big turnout of boys playing sports on playfields and vacant lots just about every day. And so it was in 1937, in a Seattle working class neighborhood that a group of young boys played softball on a vacant lot. The lot was a grassy patch located behind Swanson's grocery store. Sidewalks bounded the lot on two sides on top of steep dirt banks about four feet high. The lot measured about eighty by ninety feet, a flat sunken rectangle of land with a bumpy dirt infield and weedy outfield. The boys in the neighborhood played softball on this wonderful vacant lot at least three times a week during the summer months. Their consensus leader was a thirteen-year-old kid named Les Compton. Les was usually the one who got the games started by assuming the role of captain of team number one. Team number two was led by another kid who would choose his team members, taking turns with Les. Instead of the usual nine (or ten) players, teams might consist of three to twelve depending on who showed up. Despite the usual arguments the boys did their own informal umpiring. Eleven, twelve, and thirteen-year-old kids with names like Andy Harlan, Jay Goodrich, Swede Olson and Pee Wee Conner made sure that the other boys followed the rules of baseball. In the middle of the Great Depression of the 1930's the raggedy boys found ways through baseball to find a kind of fulfillment through competition and exercise channeling their energies in nondestructive ways.

One of the regulars was a kid who was noticeably different from the others. He was obviously older but no one could tell by how much. He was much bigger than the others, standing slightly over six feet and weighing as much as two hundred twenty or thirty pounds. Even so, because of his humble manner the kids all seemed to like him. Despite the differences in size, there was an obvious difference in mental capacity. If the average IQ is about one hundred, the big boy's IQ was somewhere around the middle sixties, thus classifying him as a low level moron. Grant Burton was a gentle uncoordinated giant, but his humility and eagerness to be accepted endeared him to the kids at the vacant lot, at least to those boys who had the emotional capacity to feel empathy for someone as unfortunate as Grant Burton. His full name was Grant Underhill Burton. Upon learning this, the kids nicknamed him "Gub" after the first letters in his name. The nickname in one sense was a bit insulting but was really meant as a kind of affection. In any case, the big handicapped lumbering giant showed up at the vacant lot at every game, eager to be accepted, to be allowed to join the other boys and to play ball.

Since the vacant lot was on a lower level from the surrounding sidewalks and street, it resembled a miniature ballpark, an athletic field, maybe a virtual tiny stadium, minus a grandstand and bleachers. Those were left to the imagination.

On a day when the local boys had just finished a game which ended with a score of twenty-three to thirteen, Les called everyone together and suggested they name their tiny "stadium." Instead of just referring to it as "the lot," why not give it a real name? "Like Yankee Stadium," yelled Andy Harlan. "I think we should name it after Gub," said Les. "Let's call it Gub Stadium." Everyone looked at Gub who felt a bit embarrassed, but sensed that it was an honor. At least that's the way Gub took it as he opened his big mouth in a huge grin. Gub's happy smile revealed two rows of huge dirty teeth that were accompanied by a bit of drool running out of the left side of his mouth. His heavy black eyebrows and round bulging eyes took on a shiny look. His teammates giggled and cheered as they watched Gub's proud reaction. From the top of his battered baseball cap covering his thick growth of wild black hair, his bull neck and huge partly shaven jaw, his generous wide nostrils, to his barrel chest, big clumsy legs, to his clodhopper shoes, Gub was as happy at this moment as he had ever been.

From that time the sunken lot behind Swanson's grocery store was known to everyone as "Gub Stadium." Big Gub was a constant presence at the ball field. Games were played when there sometimes weren't enough players for two teams. Such games as "scrub," "home-run," "workup," and others where the kids could run, throw, hit, catch, pitch, and learn to interact with other. Hardball was not the game. The game was equivalent to present day slow pitch softball. Gloves were seldom used. Swearing and arguments were frequent but serious fights were rare.

Big Gub was regularly hired for short jobs like sweeping the sidewalks in front of Swanson's, the local barber shop, and the drugstore two blocks down the street. He was proud to be paid fifty cents or so each time. Gub could usually be found hanging around Gub Stadium even when there was no action. Sometimes he sat on top of the bank next to the sidewalk looking out at his beloved Gub Stadium. At other times he was observed lying on his back near the center of the field next to second base just dozing away.

Gub wasn't much for verbalizing. It was a struggle just to talk his way through a short sentence. He communicated mostly using two or three words enhanced with awkward gestures. He often grunted, whistled, or uttered words in a kind of unintelligible gargle.

One of the regulars at Gub Stadium was a towheaded kid named Swede Olson. He was the only kid who seemed to know anything about Gub's home life. Swede reported that Gub lived with his mother and father in a small bungalow about four blocks away on the same street as the Olson family. Gub's mother was a quiet middle-aged woman who rarely left their house. Gub's father was a tall heavyset balding fiftyish man who drove to work each morning in a beat-up 1929 Plymouth. He carried a lunch bucket each day and never spoke to his neighbors. In those days it was common for retarded – or otherwise handicapped people – to live with their families. The exception was when disabled people became dangerous to others. In that event they became wards of the state and placed in an "appropriate" institution. In the thirties, such institutions were usually underfunded and understaffed. Those who were familiar with such institutions were prone to refer to them as a disgrace to a civilized society. The Burton's chose to care for their pathetically retarded boy in their own home and suffer the humiliation they sometimes felt when their neighbor referred to their son as a "dummy," a "freak" or a "monster." Aside from those times when the other boys gently teased their retarded friend, in their hearts they respected him as he tried desperately to fit in. All knew that he never really could. The older boys in the group sometimes wondered if the big gentle, happy spirited Gub had a dark side. "Don't you ever get mad?" asked Andy. Gub looked at Andy, grinned, gurgled, threw his head back and gave a loud whistle. Then he said "Yeah, I like a play ball, I like a play ball, ha!" The boys at Gub Stadium seemed to trust him, but his friend Les sometimes wondered if there was a limit to his good nature. If ole Gub ever became violent that would really be something. "If we didn't know him so well he might look dangerous like a King Kong," said Les one day. "I wonder how strong he really is."

The auto repair shop at Rainier Avenue and Alaska Street suddenly erupted with bombastic yells and cheering voices as the old Model "A" Ford sputtered to life in a noxious cloud of exhaust smoke. In these times it was actually possible to repair your own car with your own tools. The four teenaged boys couldn't wait to try their car on the road, a week's work with greasy engine parts and sparky electric wires had finally resulted in success. The oldest boy was sixteen-year-old Blacky Blake. Blessed with a husky build, he stood almost six feet tall. A natural leader, he was good looking with a swarthy complexion, deep-set dark brown eyes and unruly black hair. His followers, all boys about fifteen to sixteen, were charged with teenage energy and prone to mischief which often blossomed into borderline criminal acts. At the local police precinct they were regarded as a gang. "That Blake gang is nothing but trouble," was a quote everyone locally was familiar with. It was uttered more than once by the precinct sergeant, a man named Bill Vukich. The boys in Blacky Blake's motley group were always eager for excitement, and allowed Blacky to call the shots, but each boy was personally afraid of their leader. Blacky sometimes displayed some unnerving mood swings, sometimes a persuasive charmer, at other times a ruthless bully. On the day the car was drivable three of his henchmen took seats in the Ford Model "A" coupe, one next to Blacky in the front seat, and two in the open rumble seat (located behind the main cab). "Where we headed?" asked Tony Ellis, the fifteen-year-old riding shotgun. "Now we have this car, we need to make somethin' happen," said Blacky, shifting gears for the fourth time since they started out. We want to find some kids in one of these other neighborhoods and teach them a lesson." Tony shouted out the cab window to the two young thugs in the open-air rumble seat, "You guys got your batteries?" "Yeah, yeah, we got 'em, you bet," shouted Vern Foley over the engine noise. "Let's bust some heads," he yelled to Pete Kaminski, sitting next to him, grinning as they both opened and closed their fists around two size 'D' flashlight batteries. Vern was a rather timid freckle faced fifteen-year-old. Small in stature, he loved hanging out with Blacky's Alaska Street gang. He enjoyed fantasizing about being important, a tough guy, afraid of nothing, perhaps even earning a reputation as a fearsome bully. Didn't all teenagers need recognition, admiration maybe? Someone the other kids were afraid of. Pete Kaminski, Vern's cohort, wasn't subject to short guy paranoia, since he was seventeen and almost six feet tall, skinny but strong. Rat-faced with buck teeth and squinty black eyes, Pete had been in a few fights in the past with boys from other neighborhoods like down at Garlic Gulch, at Beacon Hill, and Georgetown. He had enjoyed success in fights using flashlight batteries to harden his bony fists. Blacky's followers loved street fights, but only if they had the advantage of numbers, size, location, and weaponry. Beating up other kids gave them feelings of superiority, satisfied the teenage need for excitement, action and sense of power they did not find in school or at home. There was also the perverted sense of importance in getting away with breaking the law, community traditions, and physical things like street signs, park benches and damage to bikes, cars, and whatever else they could get away with. Outwitting their parents, their teachers, the cops, and society in general was of ultimate importance, a kind of upside-down, quirky sense of fulfillment. Finding an outlet in sports or other conventional activities was of no interest to the boys in the Alaska Street gang.

Blacky drove the rattley Model A Ford for a half hour around other Rainier Valley neighborhoods looking for prey with Tony making suggestions. They drove down roads off the main drag looking for the perfect situation where there would be vulnerable unsupervised younger kids. Gub Stadium was the scene of a boisterous group of six eleven- to twelve-year-olds engaged in a softball game they called "scrub." In their midst was big Gub, perhaps ten years older, but mentally five years younger. Gub had become a regular. As inept a player as he was, the boys enjoyed his presence. They laughed and gently teased him often, but Gub laughed right along with them, and was always excited to be accepted. Blacky's Ford eased to a stop at the curb adjacent to Gub Stadium. "Well, look at this, Tony, a ballgame." "This is gonna be fun," cackled Tony as all four teenagers got out of the car and walked to the edge of the bank overlooking the field. "Which one of you creeps gave me the finger? We're gonna come down there and beat the shit out of all of you unless one of you admits it," yelled Vern Foley. "You're all asking for it," shouted Blacky. The boys on the field looked up to see the four cocky older teenagers glowering down at them thirty feet away. "Nobody gave you the finger," said Pee Wee Conner. "I think it was you," yelled Pete Kaminsky, pointing his finger at Pee Wee. As the four bullies invaded the field, the boys on the field just stared, not quite believing that the four big guys from the car were really coming after them. "Who's the freak," asked Blacky, pointing at Gub, "I want him." The chase was on as the younger kids began to run for home with Blacky's thugs in pursuit. Gub just looked stunned, trying to figure out what was happening.

Blacky quickly moved toward Gub and smashed his fist into Gub's midsection with his battery enhanced fist. "Yow!" He yelled as his fist merely bounced off Gub's iron stomach muscles. Blacky swung a roundhouse left to Gub's jaw opening a small cut but with no real effect. After receiving two vicious punches Gub seemed to wake up. Grabbing Blacky by one arm and one leg, he quickly lifted him higher than his shoulders and with a mighty heave, threw him bodily twenty feet through the air, depositing him in a crumpled heap near second base. As he was being thrown, Blacky was able to scream, "Get this guy. Help!" Just as he slammed into the ground the breath was knocked out of his body, and his left leg lay at a distorted angle across second base. As Blacky was flying through the air screaming for help, Pete charged forward to attack Gub, arms and fists poised to smash Gub's face. Gub turned just in time to grab Pete's wrists, using his forward momentum to start him swinging, feet off the ground, in a wide circle, helpless under Gub's powerful grip. Pete's body was swinging ever faster outstretched almost parallel to the ground when his legs crashed into Tony Ellis' chest sending him sprawling backwards into the ground gasping for air. Gub released his hold on Pete. His big lanky body sailed a few yards before hitting the ground, the momentum causing him to roll over rapidly several times before stopping in short left field. With three of the Alaska Street gang invaders lying crumpled on the ball field, Vern Foley stopped punching Pee Wee Conner and stared at Gub, who now moved toward the freckle-faced little bully. With a terrifying glint in his eyes, Gub assumed the look of a huge gorilla with an urge to do some serious damage. Confused about exactly what he was doing, Gub had been moved to violent action. Was it a desire to defend his friends? How did that connect with his sudden impulse to hurt somebody? Yes, to hurt somebody very badly.

After running a short distance to avoid their attackers, the younger ball players stopped to watch the action. As they watched, stunned by the sudden defeat of Blacky's roughnecks, they saw Vern Foley scramble up the bank toward Blacky's car, thinking that if he could reach the car he would somehow be safe. Gub surprised everybody by chasing Vern to where the car was parked. Vern suddenly realized he was not going to be safe from the hands of this crazy powerful nitwit, the goddamned oaf, weirdo, freaky monster. Vern ran for his life down the street, into alleys, between houses, across lawns until he was at least a mile away from Gub Stadium, heading for home.

Gub stopped when he got to the car. These bad boys needed a lesson. He crabbed the bumper and began to shake the Ford up and down, faster and faster applying his enormous strength to the effort, now enhanced by adrenalin fueled fierce energy. As the kids watched in amazement, they saw Gub shake the car in such a way that the right rear wheel actually left the street surface. Faster lifting and heaving got the front wheel to rise from the concrete and then the entire right side of the Ford was lifted just enough to find the tipping point. Big Gub had managed with furious effort and incredible strength to tip the car on its side. With the crashing sound of metal and broken glass against concrete, Blacky's Model A Ford lay on its side out of action. Hearing the noise just to the rear of their grocery store, Gus and Inga Swanson ran outside where they saw the car on its side in the street next to their store. Broken glass, a detached fender and a seat cushion from the rumble seat lay strewn about. Some of the neighbors were emerging, standing on their porches with curious expressions, staring at the car and the boys running for home carrying their baseball gloves. Most alarming was the sight of three teenagers lying scattered around the ball field. Two of them seemed to be painfully pulling themselves upright. Blacky Blake lay motionless across second base. "Call the police," someone shouted, "those kids need an ambulance!" Gub's teammates were scrambling their way home. Confused, he returned to the ball field to pick up his baseball glove (a tiny old-fashioned mitt not much bigger than his hand) and shambled his way home mumbling to himself.

The aftermath involving police cars, an ambulance and excitement in the otherwise quiet neighborhood, called for a police investigation. Interrogations, testimony and accusations followed, with the goodhearted simple minded Gub at the center of heated controversy. On one side were the parents of the boys in the Alaska Street families. They and their attorney demanded a cash settlement for medical expenses and damage to the Model A Ford. Furthermore, they insisted that Gub Burton be confined somewhere in prison or a mental institution. "That big monster dummy freako idiot should be locked up," yelled Morrie Blake, Blacky's irate father. "That big ignorant moron is dangerous. He's likely to kill somebody," Vern Foley's dad kept repeating. "If they don't do something about that oversized bully, I just might do something myself." Similar threats were heard from Ivan Kaminsky, Pete's outraged dad.

The police captain overseeing the controversy was Roy Kendrick, a man with the reputation as an intelligent and decent cop. From his office at the local precinct, he was making a sincere attempt to determine the facts before turning it over to the City Prosecutor. Kendrick was half inclined to urge that assault charges be filed against Blacky Blake and his band of teenage delinquents, but he also felt that Gub's presence in the neighborhood might be a source of future trouble. Big Gub had been passive and gentle since he started hanging around Gub stadium and other neighborhood places. His passivity was now open to question as the result of the recent violence at Gub Stadium. "What should you expect of him, that he let that gang of bullies bent on attacking our kids' on the ball field for no reason other than the fun of beating the hell out of them? Using batteries in their fists, for God's sake, they might have crippled or killed one of our boys if it hadn't been for Gub. He was just defending them the best way he knew how."

After the lawsuits were thrown out of court and the appropriate lectures delivered to Gub's parents along with the parents and members of Blacky Blake's gang, the neighborhood settled into normalcy. Gub Stadium once again was a scene of boyish enthusiasm as they resumed their games. Summer vacation was almost over but the hollering, arguing, and laughter continued until the day when the school term began. An occasional after-school game was played with Gub in attendance, basking in his new role as protector, body guard, and hero. As autumn arrived the kid's interest turned to football, mostly played in smaller numbers of players. Touch football was played but mostly it was sand lot tackle. The kids had their own rules about who was allowed to play. It depended on age, weight and maturity. Without such agreed upon rules, somebody was sure to get hurt. Gub vaguely understood why he was not allowed to participate, but he still showed up at all times when the kids were on the field. He just watched. After all it was Gub Stadium and he belonged there.

Sometimes at night Gub was observed walking the sidewalks near his beloved vacant lot, a lonely figure in the darkness. The boys in the neighborhood enjoyed having the big guy close by. They thought of him as their defender, in spite of his vacant look, his ever-present dopey smile and the glob of drool at the corner of his mouth, a big loveable oaf. Woe to any outsider foolish enough to tease their hero.

Swanson's grocery store closed at 6:00 p.m. At 5:30 p.m. on a day in late October, Gub was finishing his sweeping job at a far corner in the empty store. Empty that is except for two customers and Mrs. Swanson. Gub took his eyes off his dust pan to look toward the checkout counter. The two customers wore hooded parkas covering their faces. Gub spotted the flash of a knife blade held by the bigger of the two who were obviously threatening Mrs. Swanson. He began moving quietly toward them. Unobserved as he stalked forward, Gub suddenly let out a whoop and ran at them brandishing his push broom like a baseball bat, "Get ya," he growled as he hurtled toward them. Completely surprised, the two would-be robbers scrambled for the front door. "It's him, let's get out of here," yelled the tallest guy. The two hoodlums took off running down the sidewalk, across the street, disappearing into the darkness. Gub and Mrs. Swanson watched as they disappeared. As news of the failed grocery store robbery made its way around the neighborhood, Gub was again acclaimed a hero.

Sergeant Vukich carefully reviewed the police report of the failed robbery attempt at the Swanson store. He recalled the invasion of Gub Stadium by Blacky Blakes Alaska Street teenage gang. Could this be an attempt by those scumbags at retaliation? The more he thought about it, the more he was convinced that there was some connection. Any number of Blacky's gang would certainly be up to it. We'll probably never know, he thought.

Drizzly days in the late fall often found Gub walking slowly on a lonely walk in the area around the local drugstore, the barber shop, and the deserted vacant lot. Sometimes Gub could be seen sitting on the bank or next to home plate at the ball field the kids had named after him. Who could tell what thoughts went through his impaired brain? How could anyone understand what emotions were coursing through his mind? Was he sad for himself, proud of his status as a heroic protector? Was he happy in some simple-minded way? Was he somehow secure in his private world?

Using a black crayon, Pete Kaminski had just finished printing his name on Blacky's leg cast. "Not finished," Pete said as he drew a crude skull and crossbones under his name. "I should'a thought of that," cried Tony, "Gimme that crayon and I'll draw a rattlesnake." A get together on a dark night in December seemed a good time for a cast signing. The empty garage at the Alaska Street gas station was a good enough meeting place as long as the heater kept working. Six of Blacky's gang was on hand to sympathize and sign Blacky's leg cast. "A broken femur takes at least three months to heal," declared Blacky, "but now we gotta plan to pay him back." Pete's dislocated shoulder and Tony Ellis' cracked ribs had healed since the unfortunate experience at Gub Stadium. Vern Foley spoke up, "What we should do is go back there with guns and shoot that big lunatic." "And blast those damn kids, at the same time," suggested Stumpy Curran, another member of the gang. "We gotta plan it," said Pete. "Plan it so we're sure not to get caught." "We could take our other car," offered Blacky. "Do it at night," said Bobby Cole. "I hear he skulks around that ball field almost every day, but Sunday night he's always there sitting on home plate."

The 1928 Willys sedan rattled slowly through the neighborhood. It was Sunday evening. Except for the usual dimly lit street lights, it was dark and unusually gloomy on the streets around Gub Stadium. Inside the car, the four teenagers wore dark stocking caps and rain coats which concealed several pistols. Vern Foley was proud of his .22 caliber Browning automatic which he had stolen in the course of a burglary last summer. Stumpy Cole and Carlo Berman each carried .22 Colt revolvers. Binky Strunk was armed with an old army .45 automatic borrowed from Blacky Blake whose father had used it when he had served as a World War I doughboy. In the holster on his hip, the gun gave Binky – in his teenage delusion – a feeling of power and invincibility unmatched in any other aspect of his life. Since Blacky was still recovering from his broken leg, Pete Kaminski drove the car, his weapon a mostly worn out twelve gauge shotgun was hidden under a blanket on the floor fully loaded. Pete's jacket pockets bulged with shotgun shells. Shining his powerful flashlight out the front window, Vern Foley suddenly shouted, "There he is!" The flashlight beam revealed Gub standing in the pitcher's box slightly stunned by the light. The car squealed to a stop as the five assassins leapt onto the sidewalk and down the bank to the ball field. Guns in hand, they walked toward Gub who stood confused and staring into the bright flashlight beam. "Now ain't you sorry you broke Blacky's leg, you bastard," somebody yelled. "And my ribs," hollered Tony. "Give it to him," screamed Pete as he fired his shotgun from thirty feet away. As he fired he nervously swung his gun slightly away from his target. The charge struck Gub in the left ankle. As he turned and tried to run, he staggered just as the other three began shooting. Pete's second shot struck Gub in the chest. As he fell, the shooters nervously fired a few more rounds in Gub's direction as they turned to run for the car. With all five quickly aboard the car roared away. Gub lay on his back, arms extended flat against the grass, his chest splattered with blood.

The ensuing years dimmed the memories of the shooting at Gub Stadium but the kids who had played there never forgot their friend and protector from 1937 at the time of the Great Depression.

Nearing retirement, an aging Les Compton could recall the tragic incident of that winter night so long ago. At their annual get together at the Rainier Yacht Club, Les was enjoying an after dinner brandy along with Andy Harlin and Pee Wee Conner. "I see where some of those Alaska Street hoodlums have just recently passed away," said Andy. "I remember that the one they called Blacky was killed in prison many years ago." "Well they all served some years in the joint," commented Les. "Not nearly long enough," declared Pee Wee. "Good thing Gub survived." "Yeah, but only because that idiot Pete Kaminsky loaded birdshot instead of buckshot shells into that damned shotgun," said Les. "After he recovered," Andy recalled, "that was a great place they sent Gub to live, on a ranch in Texas for retarded boys. I heard it was a really nice environment. I think he must have lived a good life. I wonder if Gub turned into a cowboy." The three friends from the old neighborhood chuckled at the thought. Les sipped his brandy. "Hey, didn't we have some great games in Gub Stadium?"

THE MOUNTAINEER

Anita O'Hara was beside herself with worry. Pacing nervously, she couldn't stop walking back and forth in the parking lot, sometimes wringing her hands while anxiously peering toward the open area at the trail head, where the trail began.

Fearing Anita was about to panic, her brother-in-law, Paul, attempted to calm her, assuring Anita that her husband Buff would soon arrive to tramp happily into the trail-head parking lot smiling as always. A small group of hikers, finished for the day, stood anxiously near their cars with a show of concern. Obviously empathetic with the distraught Anita, there was no reason to stay any longer. Tired from hiking the rugged mountain trails, they couldn't wait to get into their cars and head for home. For most of them the Seattle Tacoma area would be their destination, a four to five hour drive. For some, hiking for only a day in the magnificent Olympic National Park was well worth the trip. For others it was only worthwhile if they could camp overnight in one of the many beautiful campgrounds along the trail. This particular trail, known as the Hoh River Trail, extended for at least twenty five miles into very steep primeval mountainous terrain covered with gigantic first growth Hemlock, cedar, and fir trees. The pristine Olympic National Park is enormous, covering about fifteen hundred square miles. The western Washington State National Park is punctuated by snow fields at the higher elevations, cascading streams, waterfalls, rushing rivers, lakes and connecting trails. The higher mountain peaks tower over the wild and unspoiled rainforest at the lower altitudes.

"Listen Anita," said Paul O'Hara, "if Buff doesn't make it down the trail right now, he'll just find a warm place to sleep and trot right down here to the car first thing in the morning. You know my brother, he's the experienced mountaineer. He's the best of the best. Buff knows how to survive in the mountains better than anybody, so calm down everything's o.k., take my word for it." "But it's almost dark," babbled Anita. "He never should have started up that connecting trail just to explore on his own. Why did he do that, yelling out that he would catch up with us? For all we know, he may have fallen and broken a leg or something and nobody will ever find him!"

"Here's what we'll do, Anita," said Paul. "It's just about dark. Buff is not going to hike down here in the dark. Let's drive down to Forks, call the sheriff and find out how to call the local Search and Rescue organization. We'll get something to eat and try to get some sleep in a motel if we can find one. At daylight we will drive back here, at the same time keeping in touch with the authorities using my trusty cell phone."

Edmond (Buff) O'Hara sat in a rare flat spot twenty yards off the trail with his back supported against a huge log. "I'll just rest a few minutes," he told himself. "There is still enough light to travel three or four miles if I keep this pace. I'll sack out at dark and get going at daylight. Beginning a new life will reveal a lot of surprises and exciting challenges. I have to keep making sure all my ducks are in a row." Buff pulled a folded document from his jacket. His homemade map of the mountain trails in western Olympic National Park was the product of some intensive research relying not only on official government maps but the locations of many obscure trail connections within the enormous park boundaries. After carefully studying the map Buff was assured he was on the right trail which would get him to Fairholm, the tiny block long village in the foothills across the park boundary. The timing has to be right, he kept reminding himself. Get there at night. Be invisible. Remember, those search parties and their dogs will be all over the place by tomorrow searching for me. As Buff got to his feet, he became aware of a little stream rippling down a rocky cliff just about thirty yards across the tiny meadow at his feet. The stream flowed into a small pond before resuming its progress downward seeking to spill its contents from the Grand Blue Glacier eight thousand feet above into the blue-gray waters of the straights of Juan de Fuca below. The pond invited a quick inspection. "What's this?" Buff said aloud as he observed some huge bear tracks in the mud at the edge of the pond. Buff was aware of the presence of bears in the Park. The Black Bear species shared the remote forests in an idyllic protected existence with large numbers of elk, mountain goat, Pacific Coast blacktail Deer and dozens of other species. Bears were sometimes spotted by hikers who invariably gave them a wide berth. Everyone knows that a wild bear can never be trusted to keep their distance. At the sight of the bear tracks, Buff went into action, shucking off his jacket and removing his shirt. Using his knife, he began to cut into the shirt, allowing him to rip and tear as if an attacking bear might have torn the shirt off an unfortunate hiker named Buff O'Hara. "Now for some blood," he said to himself. Reaching into his pack, he retrieved the items needed. Looking intently at his bare left arm, he doubled his left fist and squeezed. A nicely swollen vein appeared on the inside upper forearm inviting Buff's razor-sharp blade. As the blood ran down his arm, he directed the glossy red stream into and across the ripped-up shirt lying on the ground. "Not too much," he murmured, "just enough to make it look like 'ol Buff lost a wrestling match with yogi bear." With the disinfectant properly applied and the arm wrapped tight with a gauze bandage, Buff hoped the flow of blood would be stopped soon with no subsequent problems. Placing the battered shirt on the ground as if it were randomly abandoned, he tossed his baseball cap into the brush next to the shirt. Buff took another look at the stream which seemed to get wider and swifter as it aggressively tumbled down, picking up momentum. This is just what I'm looking for. This little stream will flow into the Sol Duc River, and then the river will take me almost to Fairholm, that is if I can stand the icy water and keep afloat across the rocks and the rapids. I have to be alert for the point where the river passes under the bridge. That's where I will swim to shore if I'm not dead from hypothermia or collision with a floating log. If the search people bring in dogs and cover this area tomorrow or the next day, they'll track me to here, but when I float down as planned the dogs won't be able to track me. Then those search guys will have to declare me missing or dead. My compass tells me precisely where I need to go to get to my motorcycle.

Rapidly exchanging his hiking boots for the tennis shoes in his pack, Buff secured the contents in his waterproof lightweight packsack and began his descent, wading, clambering and stumbling his way down the rocky, slippery, unpredictable mountain stream. "I should name this waterway," thought Buff, "I'll call it Maria's Creek after my little sweetie." Maria, Buff's adorable three year old daughter enjoyed the unrelenting devotion of her daddy.

Anita O'Hara seemed totally stressed as she and brother-in-law Paul sat tensely in the Clallam County Sheriff's office. "Try to stay calm. Do the best you can, Mrs. O'Hara," said Sheriff Mosely. "Search and Rescue has over fifty men already urgently looking for your husband. They are spread out over an area covering a radius of five miles in all directions from where you last saw him head out on that other trail. We have an excellent record of locating missing hikers, over ninety per cent within two or three days. It sometimes depends on the weather. Unfortunately, the heavy overcast today will prevent the use of the helicopter. But maybe it will clear up tomorrow. Mr. O'Hara is apparently an experienced mountaineer and that's very important. He will know how to keep warm at night." Anita spoke up, "But what if he's hurt with a broken neck or something and can't move?" Anita dabbed her eyes. "If something like that has happened," answered Mosely, "one of that army of guys on the mountain will find him even sooner, so please try to calm down. When we find him today or tomorrow, we will take him immediately to our nearest hospital in Forks. Why don't you consider driving back home to Seattle and just keep in touch with me on the phone. I'll let you know the minute we find him and we can take it from there." "I think that's a good idea, Anita," said Paul.

True to Buff's prediction, Maria's Creek grew wider and deeper as it descended the mountain, carrying Buff along with the current. At this point, Buff sometimes could not touch the bottom of what now had become a very fast-flowing river. Buff struggled to keep his head above water and his body positioned to keep smoothly afloat as he attempted to avoid the boulders, rocks, logs, and other obstructions, any one of which would have ended his bizarre adventure. Buff guessed that the river had carried him several miles down the mountain, and under the Sol Duc River Bridge. Now he wondered if he would be able to escape the pull of the current and climb out of the rapidly flowing river which now seemed intent on killing him one way or another. The first attempt at reaching shore proved unsuccessful as the current was simply too powerful to swim to shore, only thirty to forty feet away. Grabbing for overhanging brush or downed trees proved too great a struggle in overcoming the pull of the persistent tug of the ever faster moving river. Spotting a small backwater created by a huge rock poking above the surface, Buff was able to lean into it, gaining just enough leverage to plow his way to the river bank.

Allowing himself a few precious minutes to recoup, Buff unwrapped the ropes which had secured his small back pack tightly to his body throughout the ordeal. Inside the waterproof flap, Buff found his small towel, a dry pair of hiking socks and his irreplaceable hiking boots. Traipsing downhill through a thickly wooded area for a few miles, traveling ever northwest, Buff stumbled onto a well-used trail, good for another mile or two until darkness required that he curl up beside a tree and sack out until daylight. Buff hiked down the trail at a fast pace, but not too fast so as not to fall victim to rocks, boulders, fallen logs, ruts and slippery spots along the steep trail. Buff's thoughts turned to finding water and enjoying the small ration of trail mix, consisting of nuts, raisins and those delicious bits of dried fruit, all mixed together and waiting for him to gobble it down, hopefully before he starved to death and before he hunkered down for the night trying to keep from freezing.

Now near civilization, the trick was to be invisible. Under cover of a moonless night, Buff snuck along the roadway leading to the deserted farmhouse. The isolated five acre farm had been uninhabited for six years except for a twice a year visit by Vern Stenstrom and his family. Vern had been a friend of Buff and Paul O'Hara since their high school days. Vern's Uncle Ragnar had died six years before and had willed the property to his nephew Vern. Buff had spent a night here with Vern about two years ago when on route to a fishing trip to Westport, a favorite salmon fishing destination on the Pacific Ocean. Buff headed straight for the shed at the rear of the farmhouse. Stripping off the plastic cover, his inspection revealed the Kawasaki 250 in shape to travel, full of fuel, just as he left it two weeks ago on a clandestine trip from his home in Seattle. Lying in a sleeping bag on a bed inside the house, Buff was finally able to relax and anticipate a good night's sleep.

Waking at 5:00 a.m., Buff pondered the remote possibility that anyone observing a motorcyclist hunched low on his bike scurrying south on U.S. 101 could somehow be the same man whose picture was in the morning paper. Lost on a mountain trail in Olympic National Park? A preposterous coincidence, thought Buff. Thoughts of the contents of his precious backpack swirled through his mind as he rode down the highway, the false passports, the phony registration for the Kawasaki, the fake horned rimmed glasses, along with the wig and the counterfeit driver's licenses' and identification cards. Not to mention the ten thousand dollars in cash, wrapped tightly in a plastic container. Buff had escaped from his former world. As of now, he was free.

Buff awoke from a fitful nights' sleep. His Big Six motel room had also hosted the motorcycle which stood, rather proudly Buff thought, firmly on its stand next to his bed. "It's still early," he said to himself. Now I have to think and follow my plan. I suppose by now those SEC investigators are closer to figuring out how much money I was able to liberate from my former employer. Those big insurance companies are ingenious when it comes to scamming their customers. It's about time somebody scammed them. Well, I got away with it so far. The funny part of it is that as a trusted high level CPA, it was remarkably easy. Now the 1.5 million is all mine, safely held in four different numbered private accounts mostly in Caribbean banks. I can't help laughing just going over it all in my mind. I can't allow myself to become smug or too self confident. That's when you make mistakes. Remember, that's what happened to John Dillinger and Al Capone.

It was time to get going. It was 6:30 a.m. There were important calls to make. Buff fondled the cheap cell phone purchased the night before, along with a prepaid long distance calling card. Placing a folded handkerchief over the mouthpiece and effecting a high pitched falsetto voice, Buff spoke as soon as he heard Paul's voice say "Hello." "Is this Seattle City Light?" squeaked Buff. "No," said Paul O'Hara, "You have the wrong number." "Sorry sir," said Buff, and abruptly hung up.

Anita's lovely voice effected a slight shiver down Buff's spine "How I'd love to have you in my arms right now," he thought. Using a low-pitched voice spoken through a handkerchief covering the mouthpiece, Buff growled "This is the pharmacy at Safeway. Is this Mrs. O'Hara?" "Yes it is," she said eagerly. "Your prescription is ready, mam," said the voice. "I'm so very glad you called," Anita replied sweetly in her slightly accented pronunciation and hiding the lump in her throat. "My pleasure Mrs. O'Hara," said Buff in his unrecognizable voice.

Thoroughly disliking the long bus ride from Portland to Santa Fe, New Mexico, Buff kept attempting to occupy his brain by reading magazines and planning his next attempts to lose himself. "My Term Life Insurance is worth about a hundred thousand. After I'm declared dead, after being lost in the Olympics, it will come to Anita. Then there's the Accidental Death Policy worth a cool million. The 1.5 million I've so cleverly embezzled will be the frosting on the cake, or maybe the cake itself. That should be enough to last the rest of our lives if we can manage some safe investments. Since I'll always be incognito, maybe fugitive is a better word, we need to find a nice place to live the good life in a foreign country, maybe Argentina."

"I'm sure I can find a cheap hotel or motel that accepts cash near the bus station. After that, some different clothes so I will be able to look like the other guys around town. Then for some black dye for the hair and the sprouting mustache. The fake horn rimmed eyeglasses along with the new duds and long black hair should be a good disguise. I hate to get rid of this expensive Mountaineer's jacket. Maybe I'll just hide it for awhile. Now's the time for me to start using some of this cash I brought along. The ten big ones on that roll should sustain me for a good while.

Anita O'Hara held the telephone close against her cheek. "Yes mama, I'm just trying to get through this the best I can. My heart is broken, mama, but what else can I do? So many friends have come over and called. It's been a real comfort to have their support. The search teams have found a bloody shirt and Buff's ball cap, but nothing else. They have stopped searching and tell me there is no hope of finding him, only a slim chance that after this winter and the snow clears away some evidence may turn up. The reality is that my Buff is gone." Anita's sobs brought tears to Theresa Salazar's eyes; murmuring prayers in Spanish, Anita's Mother began to wail. "Please don't cry, Momma, I know you are sorry for me, but I am trying my best to adapt, and I am all right and keeping busy caring for Maria. She is helping me, even though she doesn't really know what's going on." My brother-in-law Paul has been my greatest supporter. I talk to him every day."

Buff found that he remembered quite a lot about Santa Fe and how he liked the atmosphere both in the city and the outskirts. It was only five years ago that Anita had brought him to her home area to meet her parents. Theresa, her widowed mother lived about sixty miles north of the city in a rural community of ranchos owned by descendants of sixteenth and seventeenth century Spanish conquistadores and settlers claiming the land in the new world. The descendants of these original settlers refer to themselves as "Spaniards." Most have extensive land holdings and maintain a certain exclusivity, enjoying a kind of elite status in the Santa Fe area.

Buff's plan called for him to pretend to be in town on some kind of business, all the while perfecting his disguise and enhancing his conversational Spanish until Anita and Maria could join him.

Both were enjoying the warm September evening as they sat comfortably on backyard lawn chairs watching three year old Maria frolicking on the lawn with Taco, her little Chihuahua puppy. Anita focused on Paul's face with a look of curiosity. "Have you signed the final papers, Paul?" "In another two weeks I'll be officially divorced," Paul said softly. "After ten years, who would have thought that Jennifer would dump me for that fruitcake of a guitar player? I'm not grieving anymore. Looking back on it, I suppose it's a good thing we never had children. I feel good about being able to put it behind me." Anita's expression showed empathy for her brother-in-law. "How could Jennifer divorce a fine man like Paul?" she thought to herself. "Have you had any more calls from Buff?" she inquired. "No, but if I do, you know that l will immediately call you, Anita." Anita frowned and in a shaky voice announced, "This morning I was notified to expect at least three very important hombres to visit me at my house. They will probably be from Buff's old insurance company and maybe from the SEC, the IRS, and the FBI. I wouldn't be surprised to see Sheriff Joe from Arizona or somebody from the planet Alfa Centuri." "So they're closing in," mused Paul. "They will be after his computer and office records." Anita perked up. "Yes, it's a good thing there's nothing there. No computer, no records of any kind, and I don't have any idea where they are." Anita and Paul looked at each other and giggled. "Me either," said Paul. Now that the authorities are finally zeroing in on the embezzlement charges, how much did my little brother manage to stash away in all those exotic foreign banks?" Paul's look had turned serious. "Oh, God, I don't know, pined Anita. "I just wish he had never done it." Her eyes became teary. "Anyway," she breathed, "after about three months or so, after a period of phony mourning, I'm flying to Santa Fe to visit my mother." "And be together with Buff," added Paul. "By now the whole world thinks Buff is lying dead somewhere around Mount Olympus. It's unlikely you will receive any life insurance money for years without a body." "We will still have more than enough," said Anita, sipping her lemonade, "to have a comfortable life in an inexpensive Latin American country. We'll stay with our plan to find a place that's warm and safe and a good place for Maria to grow up."

"Hey there, buddy," yelled a tall athletic-looking man in his middle thirties, "You want to rotate in on my team?" "Yeah," said Buff O'Hara, "I'm coming." As Buff strode confidently onto the basketball court, the players gave him that "We're sizing you up" stare. The same tall guy offered his hand. "My name is Diego. What's yours?" "Larry," answered Buff, "Larry Santana." More than half of his new teammates appeared to be of

Hispanic ancestry, so it called for another curious look at Buff's white skin and dyed black hair, but a casual shrug was their collective response. The twice weekly pickup basketball program at the local high school gym offered a vigorous workout for the local participants. Most were in their twenties or thirties and all seemed to be experienced players who had previously played in high school or college. In pickup basketball, there are no regular teams. The players show up and are assigned or chosen or invited to play or rotate with a spontaneously formed group of five players. Some who participate regularly while others show up from time to time. Play was scheduled from 7:00 till 9:00 p.m. twice a week all-year round except for high school game nights during the season. Larry (Buff) enjoyed the action in which he felt he held his own very well with the other players. In the locker room after the games, Diego Montoya casually invited Buff to join him and a group of the other players at a local bar for a beer. Seated at a large round table in the barroom, the guys engaged in lively conversation enhanced with a bit of mutual teasing. They all seemed respectful of Larry, the new guy, especially since his performance on the court stamped him as a formidable player, an impressive combination of skill and rugged play under the boards. Seated next to Diego at the table, the conversation resulted in an invitation for Buff to meet Diego at another local gym for a racketball match the following evening. Diego Montoya, a six foot tall 180 pound thirty-seven-year-old single man, displayed well-proportioned handsome features, black close-cropped thinning hair, olive skin and a brilliant smile. It seemed to Buff that Diego was a regular guy. His intelligence and apparent good nature marked him as a good companion. Perhaps they might even become friends, although it would surely be a short lived relationship. For the next two weeks the two men enjoyed a number of sports activities together, including not only basketball and racketball, but tennis, swimming, jogging, and bowling. "I think we were meant to be friends," Diego confided to Lorenzo Santana, Buff O'Hara's name on his phony passport. When pressured about his personal history by Diego, Buff made up a story about why he showed up in Santa Fe. "I'm here," lied Buff, "to explore the possibility of setting up an accounting office as a branch of my home office in Portland, Oregon." It took a few meetings before Diego revealed himself as a Jesuit priest, serving at the St. Mary's Cathedral, a few blocks east of downtown. Father Diego consistently managed to adjust his schedule so he and Buff could enjoy their get-together's, not only for the sports workouts, but also for their lunch and dinner meetings in which they enjoyed their discussions which included almost anything, or everything. Buff was forced to confess to being a fallen catholic, while Diego showed a surprisingly liberal view of life, death, politics and morality issues. Buff O'Hara's admiration for Father Diego grew by leaps and bounds. Buff had never known anyone who seemed completely honest, forthright, intelligent and humble all at the same time. His brief relationship with Diego had the uncomfortable effect of awakening his conscience. "Here I sit," Buff thought "with this guy who is everything a good man should be, while I am nothing more than a damned liar and a criminal. I'm not sure I can handle the shame of it.

After some urging, Buff found his way to St. Mary's to take part in the Sunday Mass and watch Diego in action. It left him even more impressed with Diego's sincere spirituality.

The next evening the saint and the sinner met for dinner at a tiny Mexican restaurant at the edge of town. Their private booth was perfect for enjoying enchiladas and a stimulating discussion about cabbages and kings. At a pause in the conversation, Diego found Buff's eyes and locked in. "Larry, I want you to do something for me," he said softly. I want you to come to church tomorrow morning and sit with me in confession." Buff's eyes widened. "Do you think I have a dark secret that I need to own up to, Diego?" When alone together it was Diego, when in public it was Father Diego. The priest smiled, "I say this to you Larry, as your friend and as your priest, "I am very much concerned for your soul. I know you are aware of the fact that any information divulged in a confession is privileged and protected. I am sworn to secrecy by my sacred vow. Ever since I met you I have sensed that your big generous heart is afflicted by a contradiction of conscience. There is something there that needs to come out. I can tell that you are a good and decent man, Larry. It's in my calling to reach out to you and help to redeem your everlasting soul. I feel a personal responsibility to intervene. Please come tomorrow and sit with me in the confessional. A powerful surge of unexplainable emotion swept over Buff. His ears began to ring. A lump formed in his throat. Tears ran down his cheeks. "What's happening to me?" he choked.

The next morning Buff confessed all to his friend, the priest. "One last thing," asked Father Diego, "Why the name Buff?" Buff answered in a low voice. "It's from my football days as a running back. They said I ran at the defense, like an angry buffalo."

Father Diego's voice crackled through the screen in the booth. "Let's get down to business. If you are to redeem yourself in the eyes of God, make restitution, be sincerely contrite and transform yourself into the man I know you can be, you must do it now, before it's too late." Buff's body stiffened, "What do you mean?" "It means," said Father Diego, "that it is later than you think, my friend."

That night Buff found it difficult to sleep. His short periods of restless sleep were punctuated by horrific nightmares. As he tossed and turned, his emotions seemed out of control, surging from worry about his and Anita's future, to profound shame, to trembling with fear. I've never been a religious guy," he said out loud. "Can it be that I am afraid for my soul?"

"I just had a code call from you know who," exclaimed Paul over the phone. "Me too," said Anita, excitedly. "What is your reaction?" he asked. "It was reassuring," said Anita, "but even in code, I thought he sounded a little stressed." "Yeah, I caught that too, but I'm sure he's OK and dying to see you in the next month or so." By the way, can we meet tonight at Pueblo Bonito restaurant?"

Buff deliberately stayed out of touch with Diego for a few days after the confession. At 7:00 a.m. on the fourth day, Diego received Buff's urgent call. "Diego, its Buff or Lorenzo, or Larry, take your pick." "Careful, Larry," chuckled the Priest, "we don't mess with our secrets." "Right now, Diego, I feel really sick. I need a doctor, could you help me find one?" "I'll be at your hotel in a few minutes, Larry, and I will rush you over to Urgent Care at the hospital, just a few blocks away. You wait right there, I'm coming over."

The next morning Buff sat propped up in the hospital bed. Doctor Henry Guzman stood facing him, "Do you have family close by?" he asked. Buff's grim look matched the Doctors. "No, they're all out of state, why do you ask?" "Because," said the Doctor, "the diagnosis may be upsetting, and you will probably need some family support when I tell you about it." Dr. Guzman's expression changed from grim to grave.

The two men stood at the loading gate in the Santa Fe airport. "How could I ever expect anyone to pay for my air ticket on his credit card?" It seemed that Buff was continually overwhelmed by Father Diego's unselfish efforts to help him. "You paid me cash for it," smiled the priest, "so what's the big deal?" Buff thought for a moment. "The big deal is that in order to allow me to not have to use my illegal credit card, you could be in trouble." "What are friends for?" asked Diego. "Trouble," he said, "has a name. It's called pancreatic cancer and the one month of life they predicted for you." Buff blinked back tears. "Buff," said his friend, "I want you to end up in the good place so I can meet you there when my time comes." "Take this," said Buff, as he handed an envelope to his friend. Diego gave the envelope a curious look. "What's this?" "It's a modest contribution for St. Mary's charity program," said Buff. "I did not expect anything like this, Larry," exclaimed the priest. "How much is in here," he asked, feeling the thickness of the envelope. "Not nearly as much as I would like," said Buff, "only ten Benjamins, I wish it were much more." Both men locked eyes and embraced. This time it was Father Diego's turn to shed tears.

Wearing a baseball cap pulled low, his new mustache and his fake horn rimmed glasses, Buff shuffled a bit awkwardly from the arrival ramp into the Seatac Airport reception area. As expected, brother Paul's Buick pulled to the curb at the airport loading area within a minute of Buff's appearance, exactly as planned. Depositing his travel bag onto the back seat, Buff slammed the rear door and threw himself into the front seat next to the driver. "Welcome home, brother, how are you feeling," Paul greeted.

"I've booked you into this obscure little motel in north Seattle," he announced. "Locals wouldn't be likely to stay there, only tourists." "Will Anita be there?" Buff asked anxiously. "She's waiting for you," grinned Paul.

Upon meeting, neither Anita nor Buff had anticipated such a profound emotional experience. Words of love, desperate embraces, kisses and clumsy attempts at sex, all combined and overlapping with constant weeping. In the face of separation and eminent death, two broken hearted human beings struggled to say goodbye, not knowing how.

Anita's departure in the morning left Buff alone for a brief time to contemplate his plans. At times the pain from the cancer was excruciating, but it came and went depending on how frequently Buff took his medication. Funny, he thought, how you know how the end is near. At ten sharp Paul arrived and was a bit shocked at how much Buff's appearance had deteriorated in just a day. "How are you feeling, Buffalo Boy?" "Crappy, sick, weak and pissed off, thank you," Buff retorted in a hoarse voice. "Let's get that computer cranked up so we can do some business." Buff's lap top computer along with the files that Paul had kept hidden from the authorities enabled them to finish their work in only two hours.

"I know you have done the right thing, Buff," Paul said. "Thanks Paul, I feel good about wiring the money I stole back to my old insurance company. Won't they be surprised! Now to plan our last trip together big brother."

Two days later, the two emerged from Paul's car at the Hoh River Ranger Station parking lot. As they changed into their hiking gear, Buff looked up at the cloudy October sky and murmured, "Please, God, no snow for now." As they started up the trail, Paul's nagging hope was that his forty pound pack would contain all that would be needed on this crucial hike. Buff's disguises assured them that he would not be recognized even though he wore the same mountaineer's jacket he wore at the time of his "disappearance." Ordered by his brother to travel as light as possible, Buff carried no pack. Everything needed for this journey was tucked into Paul's big pack. Pausing at the trail head, Paul asked, "How do you feel right now and how is your energy level?" Buff accepted an energy bar as he answered, in a weak voice, "I don't exactly know, but I'm determined. Lead on." Access to the Hoh River Trail to Mount Olympus was to be restricted in only a few days because of the certainty of snow. Buff and Paul would be the only hikers on these mountain trails until the spring thaws.

Two miles up the trail the O'Hara brothers rested and drank water from Paul's canteen. Paul looked intently at his brother's pale and pain-stricken face. "Are you OK so far?" "Yeah," gasped Buff, "but there's a long way to go." "Don't think about the distance. Just let me help you up the steepest parts and stay with me the best you can. I'll get you there by tomorrow afternoon." At mile ten they flopped on the floor of a park campground hut. "I'm exhausted," Buff gurgled. Paul tried to hide his concern. "I know," Paul said, "We'll camp here. You take your pills and I'll fix some chow. Then we'll sleep. Here's your sleeping bag. Be sure to wake up in the morning."

At dawn, Buff was sure he could not continue. "I'm dying, Paul. I can feel myself slipping away." Paul stared at his emaciated brother. "You're not dead yet, buddy." Paul tried to sound encouraging. "You and I are good for one more hike. You're a real mountaineer, remember?"

Hiking forward on the steep trail, sometimes around fallen branches and over deep ruts, they struggled to reach a semi-flat area where they rested. "It's not too far now," said Paul. Buff could barely choke down his medications and his breathing was irregular. "Anita is going to need some psychological support after you get back," rasped Buff. "Of course, Buff," Paul said softly. "I know you will be there to help her," Buff babbled. Buff began gently weeping. "I'm counting on you big brother." "You have my word," Paul assured him. "Maybe you should take my place with Anita," sobbed Buff. "I promise you that I will make sure that things will be o.k. with Anita," said Paul, over the lump in his throat.

The last leg of their journey imposed excruciating agony on poor Buff's cancer-racked body. Upon reaching the High Divide near the summit of Mount Bogachiel, they paused to sweep their eyes across the incomparable view of the peaks, valleys and wild forest of the Olympic Mountain Range. In view was the perpetual ice of the Blue Glacier, and the dramatic snow-capped Mount Olympus just a few miles to the southeast. Their goal the next day was to be a short distance to the northeast near "Maria's creek, not far from the Sol Duc River, at the spot where Buff had "disappeared," a month before. Late the next afternoon, a totally exhausted, pain-racked Buff O'Hara prepared to lie down in a tiny swale adjacent to some huge fallen hemlock trees.

"I'm ready, Paul," he wheezed, "I'm not afraid. This is all for the best. My life is over and I know it. Next spring some hiker will find the body and Anita can get the life insurance to see her through." Paul held the powerful little pills near Buff's mouth. Both men hugged for the last time. Buff whispered into Paul's ear, "Please go back to church, Paul. I want to be with you on the other side."

Paul fetched a hypodermic syringe needle from his pack and delivered his last gift to his lifelong friend. Slipping into a painless and perpetual sleep, Buff O'Hara uttered his last words, "I love you, big brother."

THE DESPERADOES

At a certain point in my working life, I enjoyed a most interesting and challenging job as a college teacher. One of the nice things about a teaching career was getting paid through the various school holidays. In a previous life in the real world it was rare to have as much time off, notwithstanding economic comparisons and other philosophical tradeoffs. One such five-day vacation that we enjoyed each year took place around Easter and was called "Spring Break." It puts me in mind of a rather bizarre experience of thirty years ago. At that time, open gambling existed pretty much only in the state of Nevada, not counting foreign countries. Most other states offered bingo and punchboards, but no table games or the kind of other casino rip-offs that have become common in Indian casinos. Consequently, in those times, there was a continuous flow of suckers to and from cities in states where casino gambling was legal. Trips from Seattle to Reno, Nevada were popular. At the time, a faculty colleague, John Lee and I discussed the idea of traveling to Reno during our spring break. Before we knew it, two other faculty friends joined us in the idea. We elected to drive, stay three days and return. Squaring it with our wives, not an easy matter, we set off to out gamble the pros in little old Reno, Nevada. A couple of us thought ourselves up to the task. After all, we had played blackjack a few times and studied the books on the winning strategy. I laughingly recalled hearing what the casino people in Nevada called the thousands of optimistic visitors who traveled there to try their luck. They called guys like us "Desperadoes." So it happened that the jolly group of college professors found themselves free for a week to let their hair down, gamble, overeat at those fabulous inexpensive buffets, enjoy the free drinks, and just have a fun outing with the guys.

The trip down to Reno was uneventful and the casino games were as expected. John and I found a good buffet in one of Reno's biggest casinos. We played unsuccessfully at blackjack before and after gorging ourselves at the fabulous buffet dining room. We also enjoyed a couple of lounge act performances. While eating dinner we discussed a popular topic of the day. It was about the casino gambling phenomenon: Was legalized gambling essentially "good" or "bad" for the general society? Allowing gambling could bring enormous revenue but the downside argument was that accumulation of great wealth by the casino big shots resulted in their control over civic authorities. It was feared by many that bribes, payoffs, extortion and underworld involvement influenced governors, mayors, politicians and police. Could this happen in our own state if we allowed casino gambling back home? Enough serious talk, let's finish eating and play blackjack. Remember to always double down against the dealer's five or six with a hard eleven or a soft three through eleven. Let the good times roll.

After our first evening in Reno, John and I returned to the hotel room we shared. Our colleagues were hunkered down in their rooms in the same hotel. I awoke from a sound sleep sometime around 3:00 a.m., to a disturbing sound from our bathroom. My colleague John was engaged in some continuous vomiting. It got worse, to a point that it was too often and too loud. After twenty minutes or so, John, between groans, said, "You better take me to the hospital." I quickly got him into the car and drove him to the emergency room. They took him right in and got the retching under control. What could it be? I was worried. I drove back to the hotel, but a few hours later, I sat next to his bed at the hospital. Poor John was very weak but told me the doctor had seen him and had stabilized his condition. The doctor figured it was food poisoning, since there were up to a dozen people in the hospital being treated for the same symptoms. They all had apparently eaten at the same casino buffet the evening before. "It could have been the shrimp," he suggested. John's nurse was also concerned about the patients who had almost certainly suffered food poisoning at the same place. The food poisoning was serious enough to keep John in the hospital for a while. He was told he might be confined for another three days or so. The next day our comrades decided to drive home. I had no car, so I checked out of the hotel and rented a motel room across the street from the hospital. I felt that I should stay close to John so he wouldn't feel deserted. Being sick away from home in a hospital was bad enough. The next morning at his bedside, John was better, but still sick. "Are they going to investigate that casino restaurant with the poisoned shrimp?" I asked. "Funny thing," said John. "This morning I asked the doctor about it. Are the health authorities going to look into it? Will I be able to recoup all this expense from the casino that poisoned me with contaminated shrimp? Guess what his answer was?" said the pale-faced John Lee with a feeble grin. "Tell me," I said. "The doctor just gave me a funny look and said "What food poisoning? I don't know what you're talking about." I got the same innocent look and comment from the nurse they sent in here this morning."

I stayed in Reno two more days. John insisted that I fly home. The day after that, he was discharged from the hospital and flew home. A few days later, at school, my friend John laid some cash on my desk. "This is for your expenses. Thanks for staying over. I have insurance for this sort of thing. The Reno insurance office wanted nothing to do with me, but my home office here in Seattle reimbursed me right away." "Well, I guess we learned something about Reno," John remarked. "What did we learn, as if I didn't know," I said. "They work together pretty well in the State of Nevada, the casinos, hospitals, doctors and nurses." "Do you think that includes the Mayor, the City Council, the Prosecuting Attorney, and the Chief of Police?" I asked. "I think it includes everybody," exclaimed John, now beginning to look as if he was going to live.

Our conversation earlier about gambling and corruption was most timely as it turned out. Now that casino gambling runs rampant in every state, why would we think that gambling revenue is any less a factor in local politics, law enforcement and across-the-board corruption?

My friend and colleague John Lee retired years ago, as I did, and unfortunately he passed away soon after. These days I rarely see or hear of any of my former faculty friends. I take some pleasure however in reminiscing about my past adventures like the occasion when the desperadoes tried to break the bank at Reno.

TRIANON

"May I have this dance?" Tony asked making sure his best smile was in place for the attractive young lady in the tight green dress. Tony Luna swept her into dance position, quickly leading her across the huge dance floor to *I Had the Craziest Dream*, one of the big hits of 1943 and one of Tony's favorite romantic foxtrots.

Three hundred dancers maneuvered around the dance floor, some stepping crisply into intricate dance patterns. Others swayed slowly together, locked in a dancer's embrace, oblivious to other dancers, the music of the seventeen-piece dance band and the cigarette smoke lazily drifting toward the darkened ceiling.

Danny Nathan's partner, a bright-eyed vivacious eighteen-year-old blonde, squealed with pleasure as Danny rapidly pivoted them both down the floor. Their graceful movements, on time with the music, gave her a sense of exhilaration.

"Sometimes I feel like an instrument in the band," said Danny.

"Me too, you're the best, Danny," she exclaimed, her hair glistening as it caught the light from the reflecting ball overhead. When the music ended most of the couples separated and started thinking about the next dance. The single ladies were hopeful they would be invited to dance again with a different partner. With such a big crowd, thought the ladies, maybe Mister Right will show up this very night. On the other hand, there are a great many servicemen milling around trying their hardest to pick up a girl.

Servicemen in wartime Seattle, soldiers, sailors, marines, air corps types, and coastguardsmen soon learned where the city's biggest ballroom was located, just north of downtown Seattle.

The Trianon (tree′-ah-non), built in the late twenties, was patterned after the huge ballrooms in the Eastern and Midwestern United States. Like many of the others, the Trianon was a mixture of architectural styles. The exterior was Mediterranean-Moorish, featuring graceful arches, stucco facing, embellished pilasters, pillars and a tile roof. Inside it was an eclectic mixture of art nouveau and the popular art deco on moldings, windows and doors. The ceiling was a huge glittering dome. Strategically placed light fixtures affected a shadowy glow that could be adjusted to colors that suited the mood of the music. Orange tones of light were sometimes used when jitterbug music was playing. Cool blue tones appeared during romantic music, slow fox trots and waltzes. The bandstand was located in the huge room positioned for maximum acoustical and dramatic effect.

Overall, the effect when entering the huge ballroom was quite stunning. The idea was to create at once an exotic and romantic ambiance apart from the pressures of the outside world. It created a fun place to socialize and enjoy the popular activity of dancing. The Trianon interior presented a relaxed but dignified atmosphere. Besides, as one GI put it to his buddy: "The Trianon is where the broads are."

"What are we gonna do about those rowdy sailors?"

It was intermission and Wade Bryant, the band leader and manager of the Trianon was asking his small group of confidantes for suggestions.

"I suggest a diplomatic approach," replied Gordon Ashby. "There must be a mutually acceptable solution other than throwing the boys out."

An amused smile appeared behind Wade's mustache, as he silently reminded himself that Gordy always talked like an over-educated rich kid from back East, but he's such a great guy. Not only that, but he's a terrific musician too. What would I do without him?

Jaynie Richards, Wade's lovely wife offered a suggestion. "Let's leave it up to Bruno. He's our bouncer. That's his job. Tell him to handle it but leave out the rough stuff." Jaynie, age 32, was the singer who performed every night with the band. She enjoyed an enthusiastic following among the Trianon customers who not only enjoyed her upbeat style but also were enthralled with her sexy appearance. She had long reddish-brown hair, always perfectly coiffured, flawless skin, a perfectly proportioned body, huge expressive brown eyes and lips which smiled and pouted at just the right times.

Wade Bryant, age forty-two, was too old for military

service. Tall and handsome, most people thought he looked like Artie Shaw the famous bandleader except for his black Clark Gable mustache. A highly talented trombonist, Wade was a born bandleader as well. His knowledge of music was legendary and he projected a highly affable professional presence, an ideal combination for a bandleader in the 1940's. Wade Bryant had assumed the manager's job by virtue of his past acquaintance with Hjalmar Nygard, the owner of the Trianon building.

"Another question," said Wade, "any suggestions about our *big* problem?"

Gordy turned to Wade, "Will Nygard be selling the building soon?"

"Probably, within a year we will be out of a job," Wade replied.

Gordy said nothing, but his thoughts turned to the bitter argument he had recently overheard between Jaynie and Wade. Could their personal lives be falling apart just as the fate of the Trianon is in the greatest doubt?

Some time ago Gordy had admitted to himself that he was hopelessly in love with Jaynie. He hated to see her unhappy. He also wondered – as Wade's most loyal friend – what his role should be in this situation.

While he loved playing in the band, it was only a moonlight job. At age 31, his fulltime job was as a supervisor of a production line at the Boeing Airplane Company, which provided a deferment from military service along with a substantial income. His income from the band jobs was of little importance to Gordy Ashby.

He also inherited more than adequate financial resources set up for him by his Grandfather. The Ashby's were descendants of a prominent New England industrialist family, Boston Brahmans, no less.

Intermission was over, the meeting ended and the band assembled preparing to play *The Waltz You Saved for Me*. The dancers took to the floor and under romantic hazy blue lighting, the couples gracefully waltzed to the lovely three quarter time music. They became lost in the music and the emotion of the moment.

Hjalmar Nygard stood in the farthest corner from the band watching and listening, immersed in his thoughts. Nygard had come to America from Norway as a young child and was raised in Ballard, a predominantly Scandinavian district in the Northwest corner of Seattle. Many of the Ballard residents were Norwegian fishermen, as was Hjalmar's father, who introduced his little boy to life as a crew member on a fishing boat at age ten. A highly successful career as a fisherman enabled young Hjalmar to buy in as a partner in a large fish cannery in Ketchikan, Alaska, in 1923. Subsequently, Nygard acquired full ownership and became wealthy enough to pursue some real estate investment opportunities in Seattle. His investment in the Trianon building was relatively unprofitable, at least compared to his other entrepreneurial pursuits. As he had come to realize you cannot be invested in a dance hall and expect to make any real money. You have to do it for love. Since money outranks love Nygard thought the choice was clear.

Danny Nathan's dance partner of the moment, a

pretty twenty-one-year-old olive skinned raven-haired girl, pretended not to hear the group of rowdy sailor's insulting remarks as she and Danny danced by. "Freak!" "Shrimp!" "Stupid little schmuck!"

As the band left the stand for the second intermission, Danny sat in a corner of the dance hall at a small table surrounded by five attractive girls, all friends who often accepted rides to and from dances with Danny in his big four-door Hudson sedan.

"What makes these guys so mean?" asked Joyce, a brittle edge to her voice. The other girls were all expressing genuine concern and sympathy for Danny and anger at his smart-alec, swabby tormentors.

"Wait a minute, girls," said Danny, "We have to understand that these service boys are mostly in transition. They're being sent from place to place and they're in a state of some kind of anxiety, especially the guys headed overseas. They know they have a pretty good chance of getting killed. That's why they come to places like the Trianon, to get it off their minds and have a little fun."

"So what?" said Betty, "That's no reason for being cruel to people, especially to you."

"On the other hand, maybe it is." Danny replied.

During intermission the hall became quieter as people engaged in conversational patter, jokes and seductive blabbering. Many customers left to get some fresh air and smoke outside on the sidewalk, but most headed for their cars in the parking lot next door where the liquor bottles were stashed and that's where the serious drinking took place, except for the servicemen who usually had no cars available.

During the war years the state liquor laws forbade the sale of alcohol in places other than specified restaurants. In Seattle there was a general scarcity of liquor available during the war years (along with gasoline, tires, sugar, meat, and coffee) but there was – as every G.I. or sailor knew – a thriving black market in overpriced booze.

In the alley behind the Trianon a group of sailors loudly proclaimed their drunkenness by cursing, shouting and staggering into each other. On their way from their battleship docked at the Bremerton Navy Yard this group of sailors had encountered a bootlegger who sold them two cases of Rainier beer stubbies and three fifths of rum. They hid their stash behind garbage cans in the alley before entering the ballroom. The intermission period provided the opportunity for the sailor boys to quench their thirst.

Back inside, the group of girls was still talking to Danny Nathan, attempting to shore up his morale. Donna addressed him in a low pitched sincere tone of voice, "Danny we all love you because you are vulnerable. You have a lot going against you, we know that."

Danny made eye contact with each of the girls as he declared, "I have some serious things I have to deal with, but if you think I can't handle it, you would be wrong."

Donna was surprised that he responded the way he did.

"I don't mean weak-minded or weak-willed, Danny,

but I know that you – at times – have to put up with people staring at you because you are so short, not to mention your physical deformity."

With a shrug Danny replied, "Being born with a twisted spine and having to deal with people calling me names all my life hasn't been easy, but over time I have come to terms with it. Would you believe it, I've gotten so I don't think about it much."

The girls listened intently in one of the rare moments when he talked about himself, but weren't sure they believed him. Danny has so many nice qualities, maybe he has overcome his handicap more than we could know, they thought.

Then Dolores spoke, "Maybe that's because you have so many really good things going for you. The girls flock around you to dance, you are unselfish, very witty and very smart."

Danny grew introspective as he answered, "You may be right. I guess I am pretty lovable," Danny grinned, "A loveable hunchback."

As the band began to play the *One O'Clock Jump*, the dancers streamed onto the floor. The jitter-buggers took over the center, as the "slicker dancers" swished their partners neatly around the outside perimeter of the dance floor.

Wade's music program called for alternating fast and slow numbers. Jaynie sang every other song, drawing the usual attention and applause.

Tony Luna took every opportunity to show off his flashy style, especially when he sensed people watching.

As a Trianon "regular" Tony met lots of women, always selective, inviting only the best of the single lady dancers. As the evening drew to a close, however, Tony gave up being particular and concentrated on women he thought he could pick up. Tony got lucky fairly frequently which served to increase his confidence and the arrogance that went with it.

As the single ladies accepted – or rejected – the men's offers to dance, the conversation openers were characteristically childish statements or questions. "May I have this dance?" "Do you come here often?" "What is your sun sign?" "Sure is raining hard outside, isn't it?" "You sure look pretty tonight." "May I take you home?"

When ladies refused an offer to dance, men reacted in a variety of ways including disappointment, seething anger, resentment, feeling insulted and sometimes almost unable to deal with their feelings of rejection.

When women spent the entire evening attempting to look available and never were asked to dance, they experienced some of the same feelings. On this particular evening, as it got close to the 1:00 a.m. closing time, the crowd had thinned out but the same drunken sailors were still there.

Bruno Orloff, the bouncer, had busied himself in the back room, so no one in authority was present to keep watch during the last hour. The young sailors became even more mean-spirited as they realized that their chances of picking up girls had just about run out. At this time the gang of navy roustabouts invaded Danny's circle demanding that the girls break away from their group and go off with them. Danny was well aware of where they would take the girls if they could. No doubt one of the smoky all-night dives that served illegal liquor, mostly located in the seediest part of downtown Seattle. The next move would be to some cheap skid road hotel room.

The verbal conflict got louder and louder as the sailor's rudeness overcame whatever good sense they may have had before this evening, before the liquor-induced over exuberance rendered them completely stupid.

First it was a push, then a slap alongside Danny's head. In a sudden rush, four of the drunken roughnecks punched and kicked Danny who was knocked to the floor directly in front of the bandstand.

The nearest Trianon employee was the clarinet player, Gordy Ashby, sitting on the bandstand with his music stand and his clarinet. Suddenly aware of the scuffle, he saw Danny, whose head hit the floor knocking him unconscious. Without hesitation, Gordy jumped from the bandstand to the dance floor and with one sweeping movement grabbed the nearest sailor by the front of his uniform collar, kicked his feet out from under him and slammed him viciously to the floor in a perfectly executed jujitsu throw. Gordy moved quickly like a big cat as he kicked, judo chopped and body slammed two of the other three sailors to the floor where they lay stunned, too surprised to react to the attack. The fourth sailor slunk away toward the outside lobby.

Danny's girls got him on his feet, cleaned him up as

best they could and started for home.

The musicians in the band sat in their places wide eyed and stunned at what they had seen.

Andy the bass player exclaimed, "I can't believe what I just saw. Can you believe old Gordy?"

Jerry the drummer grinned at Andy and replied, "Gordy's pretty handy all right. He learned all that judo stuff in that private prep school back east. There's a lot about him you guys don't know."

The band members, including Jaynie and Wade, sat in a large booth enjoying breakfast at a nearby late night restaurant after the closing. As one might expect, the conversation was mostly about the fight and Gordy Ashby's courageous act in defending "that hunchback guy we see every Saturday night with his covey of chicks."

There was no mention of the dreaded impending closure of the Trianon. Both Wade and Jaynie could not help feeling worried and anxious, even though they made a big effort to hide their concern. Gordy noticed the obvious tension between them.

As the breakfast came to an end, Jaynie and Wade paused at the exit door where Gordy observed them arguing, at first quietly, but the argument developed a bitter and intense tone. It ended as Jaynie, close to tears, stomped back into the restaurant booth next to Gordy and began to sob.

"Did Wade go home?" Gordy asked.

Jaynie nodded, "Will you take me home Gordy?"

"Of course," he replied, with an expression of genuine concern. "Of course I will take you home, Jaynie, or anywhere else you want to go."

The conversation in Gordy's car on the way home was uncomfortably awkward for both of them, but particularly for Jaynie, who had suspected for quite some time that Gordy was secretly in love with her. She tried to keep the dialogue contained to trivial comments, small talk about music, the boys in the band and some of the characters they both knew in the music business. Gordy felt a growing desperation, a need to talk to her about his feelings. As Gordy's car pulled up to Wade and Jaynie's apartment building Gordon could not contain his feelings any longer. Impulsively he asked her if she was unhappy with her marriage.

Taking Jaynie's hand, Gordy said, "Jaynie, I'll take you anywhere you want to go, live any kind of life that you want. I will love you, adore you, and take care of you forever. God that sounds so corny, Jaynie, but I mean every word of it."

Taking his hand in both of hers, her words came in gentle tones, "Gordy, you are about the sweetest, kindest man I ever met, and I am so flattered I am at a loss for words, but sweetie, I won't, I can't leave Wade after everything we have meant to each other." Bursting into tears, Janie abruptly ran from the car through the rainy drizzle to the front door, unlocked it, and disappeared inside.

Gordy sat thinking. After a few minutes, he started his car and drove slowly down the street.

Saddened and very much surprised by his friend's sudden departure, Wade could only say, "Our loss is the

Marine Corp's gain."

The next day he called the musician's union hall for a replacement. Andy the base player declared, "We ain't gonna be as good without old Gordy."

Four months had passed. The night that Wade and Jaynie dreaded had finally come. They had been informed that Hjalmar Nygard had indeed made arrangements with a potential buyer to purchase the Trianon building. This night in November 1943 was to be the beginning of the end.

"Unless," stated Nygard looking intently at Wade Bryant, "someone can afford to make a higher bid than I have at this time from my buyer. He intends to make the building into a furniture warehouse and the papers are being prepared now." Wade remembered every word from his meeting with Nygard just three days ago.

Standing on the stage in her long glittering gown Jaynie rendered each song with a special energy. No doubt, she thought, because the impending closure of the Trianon caused her to reflect on how much she loved her music, her work and her life in the past few months. She and Wade had mostly overcome their misunderstandings. Their performances had never been better. The attendance at the ballroom was excellent and the relationship with Wade seemed at last to feel warmly intimate. There was trust between them as never before. As Wade looked across the dance floor he could see Danny happily dancing with each of his girls in turn. Tony was present, showing off as usual. Flirtations continued between the dancers. The other "regulars" were there, elegantly dressed, combed and perfumed, still looking for Mister or Miss Right. As usual there were infatuations, rejections and unrequited affections.

This ballroom, thought Wade, in a way is like a microcosm of life in America. People learn a lot about themselves in places like this. It's a thrill to bring music for all these people to enjoy, as they work things out in their lives. Wade's thoughts phased out as the band finished playing *When the Lights Go On Again All Over the World*.

It was intermission time. As Wade and the other musicians approached the private anteroom at the back of the ballroom to relax, an unfamiliar figure appeared. A heavyset middle aged balding bespectacled gentleman greeted Wade.

"Mr. Bryant, Mrs. Bryant? I am Roger Bolton, Attorney at Law just in town from Boston. Can we talk in private?"

One half hour later, looking somewhat shocked, Jaynie stepped up on the bandstand leading a flush faced Wade by the hand. As Wade stood at the microphone, he asked for the attention of everyone present. Three hundred dancers stood facing the stage as the lights were turned on. An expectant hush settled over the room.

"Ladies and gentlemen," announced Wade, "Perhaps you remember one of our band members, a wonderfully accomplished clarinet player. His name was Gordon Ashby. About four months ago Gordy joined the Marine Corps. After training, he was sent overseas to the South Pacific. Sadly, I must report to you that Gordy lost his life in battle three weeks ago. Tonight we have been informed that Gordy has left a large amount of money in his will to Jaynie and me. Most of this bequest will be used to buy the most precious thing in our lives. Perhaps you have heard the rumors that the Trianon has been sold and would soon be out of business. This was our understanding until tonight. In my phone call of just a few minutes ago the present owner, Mr. Nygard, has assured me that our bid to buy the Trianon building is acceptable as of tonight. This means we will keep the Trianon operating just as it is!"

The explosive roar from the crowd was almost overwhelming. Wade basked in the excitement of the moment as Jaynie tried to keep from crying.

As the band began the next number, a lovely waltz entitled *Remember*, Wade shouted into the mike, "Dance this one for Gordy Ashby!" Eight bars into the song, a smiling Danny Nathan whirled his partner, Dolores, across the floor. Tony Luna approached an attractive forty-year-old divorcee. "Care to dance" he asked?

FAMILY MAN

Ralph Brundage took a deep breath as he took his seat in the board room. Laying his sheaf of papers on the conference table he smiled as if to acknowledge the other board members seated around the table. "Greetings everyone," he smiled. "I believe I have the results of my committee's opinion on the membership issue. Recognizing the importance of establishing a continuing and committed interest and involvement in our church affairs, it seems advisable that we immediately assign each new member a place on a specific committee. The new member must be informed of the purpose and the nature of the duties. They will be given the names and phone numbers of the other committee members. Now we need to appoint someone to put this policy into effect." As Ralph sat down, someone shouted, "We'll call it the Brundage policy." As Ralph stood to leave, the board members chattered and babbled about the new policy revisions along with various church affairs and local gossip.

As Ralph hurried to his car, his thoughts were focused only on his next meeting at the warehouse. A mile away only a block or so from the waterfront loading docks, stood the old warehouse. A large two-storey building, it appeared to be abandoned and falling into disrepair. In spite of a few broken upstairs windows and a very large dark interior, there was a dingy little office on the alley side which was still in use. The owners of the old building obviously were willing to collect the rent for the decrepit little office, perhaps to partially offset the property taxes, with no questions asked. As Ralph parked his car close to the warehouse office, he looked in all directions before hustling to the door. Ralph's voice crackled in the dimly lit room. "Hey Faro, how's it going?" The huge man seated in a battered old recliner responded, "Everything is just the way you wanted it, boss. She's downstairs in our little dungeon watching TV." The young man named Faro boasted a three hundred pound body enhanced by a clean shaven head, punctuated by a sallow complexion, snaky black eyes, a flat nose, irregular teeth, and a hugely disproportionate jaw and neck. Faro sat half reclined, finishing off a can of beer. Ralph cast his eyes around the messy little office, observing the wastebaskets overflowing with half-eaten pizza crusts and beer cans along with other scraps of worthless dreck. A beat-up desk, a very old goose neck lamp, one tiny window, two small tables, the TV set, two waste baskets, a worn out broom and dustpan in a corner completed the scene. Ralph Brundage fixed his gaze on the glowering Faro. "Now you're gonna tell me you haven't touched my little girl friend. Is that right, amigo?" "I swear, boss, I ain't touched a hair on her head.

All I did was feed her just like you told me to. She's all yours." Ralph drew himself closer, his face only inches away from Faro's left ear. "Listen to me you moron, and do exactly as I say. I'm going to pay our little Mia a visit. I'll be about an hour. You wait here. Afterwards, you keep everything just as it is until you hear from me. In the meantime, get off your fat ass and clean up my office."

"Don't hurt her too bad, boss, she's only about fourteen or fifteen."

"Shut your mouth. What I do to her is none of your stupid business," snapped Ralph. As he descended the stairs, Ralph experienced a sense of quiet exhilaration, anticipating his mastery over the terrified little Mexican runaway, picked up as a hitch hiker just three days before by big Faro. "Now she's all mine for the next hour," he thought, "subject to my every whim and command, that sexy little brown body, all mine to enjoy."

It was after dark when Ralph arrived at his home in an affluent Seattle suburb. "Is that you, honey?" Darcy Brundage walked quickly to greet her husband at the front door. "Too bad you had to be late. Your supper is in the oven. Did you have anything to eat?" "Thanks sweetheart, I'm starving. How are our two little people?" "Timmy gave up and went to bed. Debby is in her room studying, I think. Did your meeting work out well this evening?" "Yeah, it worked out OK. I think it will result in an option on a big piece of property between Everett and Marysville." Darcy studied her husband's face as he ate. It's such a handsome forty two-year-old face, she thought. Light brown hair, dark eyebrows, good solid cheekbones and a gorgeous big jaw, as close to a movie star as you could get, six feet tall and a perfectly proportioned body. God, I love Ralph so much. Maybe he'll be too tired tonight to maul me and jerk me around. I wish we could just cuddle. I still do not understand why Ralph, or any man for that matter, needs sex more than a couple of times a month or so. It's so dirty. It makes me ashamed every time we do it.

Ralph's first meeting the following morning was at the Holly Hills Presbyterian church. "Good morning, Ralph," greeted Reverend Welty. "How are you doing at this early hour?" "Top of the morning, Tom, I would like to get on with our meeting as soon as we can, I have a busy day." "Of course Ralph, we can get right to it. Coffee's right here on the desk. Here's the problem: I haven't been able to convince everyone on the board about the importance of our new policy on vouchers." "You mean the vouchers that our charity volunteers give to needy families for furniture, appliances and the like?" Ralph asked, already familiar with the policy. "Who are the holdouts?" "Only one," said Reverend Welty, quietly. "Margo Monson. You have such an influence with our board members. Could you talk to her and get her to change her mind and go along with my wishes?" Tom asked. At that moment a noise was heard in the hallway outside. "That's probably Margo now," said the Reverend, "Please talk to her, Ralph." "Good morning, Margo." called Ralph, "how nice to see you." "Good morning gentlemen," said Margo, sweetly. The preacher smiled and said, "So glad you could make it. Unfortunately I am needed elsewhere right about now, so I have to run, but I would like the two of you to discuss the voucher issue and come to a conclusion and make a recommendation we can all live with. Ralph, I would appreciate it if you would call me tomorrow, OK? Gotta go, thanks to you both." As the preacher rose to leave, Ralph's eye's locked with Margo's. "How have you been, dear?" he asked. "Ralph," she sighed, "I haven't heard from you in weeks. Why have you been avoiding me?" "I haven't been avoiding you, Margo," he said, "It's just that I have been so darn busy with business, the church, my family, and a million distractions." Margo's expression reflected doubt. "I feel that you are exaggerating, and it hurts me so much," she said softly, as she attempted to look deeper into Ralph's eyes. "I've been so anxious to talk to you, Ralph," said Margo, "You and I have that special bond and you can't ignore it. It's been just a year since my abortion, our abortion. You owe me something, Ralph." He spoke consolingly, "I know, Margo. I have a deeply heartfelt regret about the whole experience, but life must go on. We both have to put it in the past. It's over. This is now. Let's do our best to forget and move forward. Now what do you want from me?" Margo's lips quivered as she spoke, "I need to be closer to you, to be with you, I need your arms around me again. Don't you love me?" Ralph spoke softly, "I promise to call you in a week or so and we will plan to get together soon, but we must be discreet. If your husband ever found out about us, all hell would break loose. Now let's talk about you and how you are doing." A long pause ensued before Margo overrode the lump in her throat, "I've been pretty busy with my garden club, the PTA, and my bridge buddies along with keeping track of my other friends. Three of those girls are about to leave for a two week trip to Hawaii next Sunday. You know Norma and Susan and their husbands. Well I'm the cat sitter for Susan. As if she couldn't afford to pay somebody to look after Fluffy. Everybody knows she and Harold are loaded. She must have at least a million dollars worth of diamonds along with priceless gold and silver doodads." Ralph looked intently at Margo and said, "I suppose she keeps them in a vault somewhere." "No," said Margo, "she keeps all her valuables in a little wall safe in their bedroom. I guess I'm a little jealous of my friend Susan Moneybags."

Driving toward his downtown office, Ralph knew he had to find a way to scare Margo into keeping her mouth shut. Either that or get rid of her for good. Ralph Brundage thrived on challenges and was certain he would prevail as always.

His two business partners gathered around the large conference table. As they seated themselves in their usual designated places, Ralph sweptd into the conference room. "OK guys, let's get to it," he called out in greeting. "I've got a busy day." Ralph's two partners sat and listened intently to his comments and instructions for the day. Andrew Marsh felt fortunate, although with a few silent doubts, to be a partner with Ralph Brundage and Larry Cordova. Andrew's tall dignified demeanor lent an air of stability and professionalism to the sometimes harried atmosphere in the busy real estate office. Middle aged, tall and balding, wearing rimless glasses, Andrew reminded Ralph of the famous Grant Wood painting *American Gothic* depicting a grim Iowa farmer staring out at the viewer. Larry Cordova's bright smile and happy spirit were enhanced by his swarthy complexion, even features, shiny black hair, scholarly horn rimmed glasses, and a short well-proportioned figure. Ralph's rules required a dress code which set a highly professional standard of appearance by all in the office. "OK guys," Ralph began, "This is about that forty-acre tract up in La Jolla, and the offer must be in by tomorrow. Larry, you are responsible for the escrow, everything in our favor. Andrew, you are to handle the title insurance and our bid. See how much under the table the agent wants. I need to see the figures first thing in the morning. If it goes right we can steal the property for half its value, any questions? I have a busy schedule, so I'll see you boys in the morning."

About a half mile north of the Woodland Park Zoo was where Ralph parked his car on a neighborhood street, a block away from Tony's bar, which also served as the local pool hall. Two thuggish looking young men stood near the entrance casually talking while smoking suspicious looking cigarettes. Ralph entered the dark interior as the bartender acknowledged him by growling, "In the back."

Ralph maneuvered his way past the smoky little barroom, the pool room, and the dark hallway, to find a beat-up office door. The area around the door was occupied by two heavyset, swarthy, dangerous looking men. Sitting in chairs sipping coffee, they looked Ralph over quickly, nodded, rose and opened the office door. "Hello, Ralphie," shouted Alfonso Sciavoni sitting behind a giant desk. "What's up, kid?" Glancing quickly around the cluttered office, Ralph responded good naturedly, "How's it going Skeets?" Only five feet nine, Skeets carried his two hundred thirty pounds as if he was the leading authority wherever he went. At a younger age, at times, he felt embarrassed by his short stature, his swarthy skin and his big nose, but over time he had developed the ability to intimidate and frighten those around him. "When you called earlier you said you might have something for me," said Skeets. Ralph pulled up a chair and sat facing Skeets. "I do, it's an easy jewelry heist," Ralph said, describing the jewelry he was convinced was locked in Harold and Susan Monson's bedroom safe. "It should be a piece of cake," exclaimed Ralph, "they will be gone for two weeks." Skeets carefully read the information sheet that Ralph laid on his desk. "I'm interested," declared Skeets. "If it goes right, I guess you'll want the usual third." Ralph grinned, "When was I ever greedy?" Both chuckled as Ralph rose to leave. Skeets raised his arm and pointed to his desk. "Got time for a drink?" "I'll take a rain check, Skeets, I have a busy day," said Ralph over his shoulder as he reached for the door.

Faro Sanchez sat on a chair leaning back against the outside wall of Ralph's warehouse office. Faro blinked and stood up as Ralph approached. "Hi boss," greeted Faro. "Hello, Faro, everything shipshape? Let's talk inside."

Ralph spoke slowly to Faro who was seated in front of Ralph's desk facing him eye-to-eye. "I couldn't make it before today. How is she?" Faro nodded assuredly, "She's OK, boss. She doesn't like being cooped up, but she eats her meals and looks healthy enough." "Listen carefully," said Ralph. "A big ugly Chinese guy will be coming here tomorrow about noon. I want you to bring Mia up here to the office. Tie her hands and ankles and tie her to that chair in the corner. Clean her up the best you can. Tonight you are to call your buddy Paco and tell him to come over here at eleven and bring his sawed off shotgun loaded with those double-aught buck shells he likes so much. I want the three of you here to meet the Chinaman. He'll probably have another Chinese goon with him. You take his money and count out twelve thousand and then give the little bitch to him. Watch him carefully the whole time. Don't let him get an angle on you. Have Paco stand in the corner holding that shotgun. Keep your gun in your belt where he can see it. After they've gone call me and confirm." "What will happen to her, boss," asked Faro. "Did you ever hear of an Asian brothel?" grinned Ralph. "Anyway, it's no concern of yours. Tomorrow night at eight, you are to bring the money to the pool hall and I'll give you a bonus. After tomorrow, I want you to follow a guy for a few days. Pick a likely spot for a nighttime lesson. Here's his name, address and picture." Faro perked up at the thought of some action. "What are we doing to the guy, boss?" "We," said Ralph, "are going to break one of his legs and put out his left eye." "What did this guy do to us?" asked Faro.

"He cheated me on a business deal for one thing, and he hasn't paid me the money he owes me," growled Ralph. "Do it next week sometime and call me as soon as it's done. Call me at night, it's OK." Faro thought a moment and asked, "What do I use for his eye?" Ralph stared at Faro for a moment and said, "Use your imagination. Now I have to visit my little sweetheart down below."

Little Mia crouched in a corner away from the shabby bed and the wastebasket overflowing with empty TV dinner trash when she heard the locks on her door rattle a warning. "Buenos Dias my little muchacha," said Ralph, "Como está?" Quivering with fear, Mia cried, "Please do not hurt me again, señor, do not do those bad things, do not beat me," she begged in a plaintive trembling voice. "Why do you slap me and bite me? Please let me go," she pleaded. "Because you are my little sex angel, and you must do exactly as I tell you. Don't be concerned about a little blood. I will probably cut you again, but it won't be too bad. I really love you, you know. Just don't fight me or resist me or I might choke you to death." Ralph couldn't contain a fierce grin as he felt the goose bumps run down his spine as spit gathered at the corners of his mouth.

Lying next to Darcy, at 5:00 a.m., Ralph lay wide awake, watching her sleep blissfully in his arms. A good time to think. In his drowsy state his thoughts ran together as in a stream of disconnected impressions. Yes, I'm the guy who needs a certain kind of sexual fulfillment. So what? A voracious sexual appetite that's only natural, that's who I am, a powerful stud, a man's man, a driving need for power, for prestige, a hot desire to impress people, those hypocrites at church, I am better than any of them. I want to shove their phony religion up their big fat Christian asses. Why do I get such a rush when people fear me? I thrive on the crooked real estate deals, to outsmart those idiots I deal with every day. I got a huge kick out of the fire that burned my office building last year. That stupid building was nothing but a drain, a loser investment. The insurance money paid for my family's vacation, a new Mercedes, and an addition to our summer cabin. I have to be careful in dealing with Skeets and those mugs at the pool hall, but I take them over the jumps every chance I get. Why do I keep thinking about capping one of them? I can still count on Faro to do my dirty jobs, but sooner or later he will betray me like all the others. I kinda like Faro and the other slimy bozos that I deal with, but I wouldn't hesitate to kill any of them. I need to keep working for the church, it's important for my image, I want people to admire me, to worship me. They love me. I could probably start my own religion – Hail Ralph, our savior, hah! What thinking person could believe in that nonsense anyway? I like my wife and kids well enough, but I have some work to do to enhance my image as the perfect father and husband, a pillar of the community. I have to make sure of the reservations for the kid's activities next summer. It's too expensive, but I have to do it, the campfire girl's retreat, the baseball camp for the boy. Why are they such brats? Then the stay at the beach, a week at the mountain cabin, it goes on and on.

I'm getting fed up with it.

The next morning Darcy, Jennifer, aged twelve, and Timmy, age nine, sat at the breakfast table with Ralph, intent on their bacon and eggs. "I have something to tell you all," announced Ralph, "how would you all like to go to Disneyland next weekend?" The table erupted with cheers. "Yay daddy," yelled Timmy. "You make us all so happy, dear," said Darcy. "It's like Reverend Welty said to me just last week, your Ralph is the model of a really wonderful family man."

THE FACULTY RETREAT

I must admit that I cringe when I think about telling my secret. It is about an event which took place thirty-five years ago. It was a despicable crime. Ever since, I have been unable to overcome my constant feeling of unredeemable shame. I often secretly cry when alone at night. There have been times when I have unexpectedly vomited when recalling my inexcusable act of so many years ago. I attribute these physical and emotional manifestations to a version of post traumatic stress.

It is my hope that relating this story may serve as a catharsis, which might alleviate my feelings of guilt, assuage my conscience or result in some kind of soul-cleansing repentance.

In 1973 I was serving as a chemistry professor at Seattle University. I loved teaching and the satisfaction that invariably comes with a successful teaching career. Along with it comes the ego enhancement of being part of the intellectual community.

With the end of the spring term eminent, I looked forward to a happy and productive summer with my wife Deena and my stepdaughter Marcy. When Deena and I were married, Marcy was only three. Over time she accepted me as her daddy and was pleased when we changed her surname. It was easy enough to legally change Marcy's last name from Jennings to Trayger. Marcy Trayger had grown into a stunningly beautiful sixteen-year-old charmer. She was completely adored by her parents, Deena and I, both in our late forties and enjoying our prime of life.

The last day of school was June sixth, and it was – as always – a busy week since we faculty had lots of paperwork to prepare. The final exam grades were only part of the last restless hours before the deadline. It was especially necessary to complete all the work since my plans called for participation in an annual get-together with some faculty friends. We called it our "Faculty Retreat," and looked forward to spending four days on Decatur Island, about one hundred miles north of Seattle. The beautiful island – four miles long and two miles wide – is part of the San Juan archipelago consisting of about twenty islands just south of the Canadian border. Decatur Island is surrounded on all sides by salt water passages. The entire island-studded area is an extension of Puget Sound which shoreline bounds Seattle, Tacoma and Olympia further south. To the west lies the Strait of Juan de Fuca and the Pacific Ocean.

My close friend and colleague, Professor Mel Forman, was owner of ten acres on the southern neck of Decatur Island. On Mel's property was located a creaky old wooden two-storey building. The building measured about sixty feet by twenty feet. It dated back to 1916. It was built to house workers who constructed small cargo ships at the shipyard site only forty yards to the north.

No shred of evidence exists of the shipyard, but Mel's building is still there. The building (we called it the "cabin") originally served the workers as a dormitory and mess hall. It had running water, a decent kitchen with a wood burning cook stove, a private bedroom at one end, three access doors and a barrel stove in the main room. It still contained benches, chairs, a 1930's radio, a tiny library of paperback books and two long wooden mess hall dining tables. The place had a comfortable feeling about it, possibly because it was so downright rustic. The upper story consisted of a large open space unencumbered by furniture. Mel's guests used the upstairs as sleeping quarters often employing air mattresses and sleeping bags. Outside was a small apple orchard, a large area overgrown with blackberry bushes, an outhouse, as well as a good sized lawn and wild rose bushes galore.

Since it was only accessible by boat or airplane, Mel Forman had arranged for us to meet at the marina in Anacortes, a small town on the mainland about one hour away from Decatur.

Mel Forman had acquired the Decatur property some twenty years before and had always been generous about sharing his cabin and the surrounding property. Each year Mel had hosted a get-away party for his faculty friends. This we called the "Faculty Retreat." Little could anyone have foretold what a peculiar and dreadful conclusion was in store.

The activities were not really planned but they were

always pretty much the same each year. First there were the obligatory "chores," which included anything that needed repair. This might include the roof, chimney, windows, hinges, outhouse and the always overgrown lawn and berry bushes.

This year Mel's guests, beside myself, included five other men, all well ensconced educators at Seattle University. The Faculty Retreat in no way was concerned with discussions of educational issues but simply offered an opportunity to spend four days on a faraway pristine island, let our hair down and have some fun.

After the "chores," the guys looked forward to clam digging, chess competitions, shooting contests (using .22 rifles), beachcombing, and gorging themselves with booze and scrumptious meals. The late night poker games confirmed the event as a bunch of good ole boys enjoying a bonding experience for a few days away from the real world.

Existing in tidelands in the Puget Sound area is a giant clam called the goeduck, pronounced "gooeyduck." At an earlier time some wag had nicknamed Mel's group the "Goeducks" and it stuck.

The Goeducks always enjoyed the boat trip from Anacortes through the lovely waterways between the islands. Unloading the supplies at Mel's dock, we were always surprised by the amount of gear and supplies we brought with us, especially the large quantity of food and drink.

Just one week prior to the faculty retreat, I arrived home late Friday afternoon to receive shocking news.

My wife Deena, distraught and tearful, informed me of an incident so despicable that it just about knocked me flat. It appeared that our daughter Marcy had been raped. It had happened a week earlier.

Marcy had apparently been so traumatized that she had become unusually quiet and withdrawn, too terrified to tell her parents or anyone else. I was profoundly shocked to learn who had committed this unforgivable deed, none other than my best friend and closest colleague, Eldon Stark.

Living in the same neighborhood about a half mile away, Stark's wife had hired our Marcy to baby sit their two younger children for the evening of the previous Friday night. According to Marcy, Eldon Stark had forced her to have sex as he was returning her home in his car at eleven thirty that night. How could this have happened to our little girl with the innocent blue eyes and lovely blond hair, our giggly, vivacious, outgoing sweetheart?

I had to utilize all my willpower to control the feeling of rage I felt sweeping over me. When I was able to calm down, I demanded to know all the details. Understandably, the most intimate details were not fully described to Deena and me, but there was no doubt in our minds that Eldon Stark had forced himself on our precious Marcy. I tried and failed to convince Deena and Marcy to contact the police.

I felt the authorities should deal with the crime. Even though we had heard of other rape cases in which the victims were demeaned and humiliated in the process of seeking justice. Such cases were often unsuccessful in obtaining convictions. Marcy was already shamed enough in her own mind. She was horrified by the possibility of her dreadful experience becoming public knowledge. It was, to her mind, simply unthinkable to report all this to the authorities.

I was profoundly saddened, but confused about what action I should take. That evening I called my old friend and attorney Myron Zelnick. After relating the circumstances and facts, as I understood them, I asked Myron for advice. "What should I do Myron, I have to do something. Can we get a conviction if we press charges?" Myron's voice was calm and deliberate. "It's very doubtful, Adam, that there would be enough evidence to convict based on what you have told me. I'm terribly sorry, but my best advice is to get her in for counseling."

I felt that in my fury I was about to lose control of my senses. What was I supposed to do next week in the presence of Eldon Stark?

The Goeducks were in an especially happy mood when arriving at Mel Forman's Decatur dock. After a busy, sometimes stressful school year, we felt free to have a few drinks, tell some raucous jokes and enjoy the camaraderie.

I was hoping the dark cloud hovering over my head wasn't obvious to the others. As to how I was relating to Eldon Stark, I just kept trying to avoid him, even in close quarters as we played our games.

The chores came first. Mel enjoyed appointing teams

to accomplish his assigned work. Four of the seven of us were PhDs. Mel liked to assign them to the dirtiest jobs. He always made sure the outhouse repair team was made up of two or more PhDs. Outhouse chores fell to Ramón Garza, professor of art history and to me, Adam Trayger, the chemistry professor. Garza was a great companion along with being a handsome Latino. A black-haired, mustachioed, swarthy guy, he was fun to work with. We spread the contents of a bag of lye to cover the excrement in the hole of the outhouse and replaced the plywood seat. After inspecting the outhouse, Mel grinned, "I don't think your outhouse expertise is up to standard, but it'll do for now." Then with a twinkle in his eye Mel swilled a large gulp of scotch and winked at me.

Mel's animated facial expressions had become a trademark. Looking thru his horn rimmed glasses, he might give you a quizzical look, a dark expression of disapproval, or a smirk that challenged you to guess what he was thinking. Even with a slightly stooped posture and baldness rapidly taking over, Mel Forman's essential good looks garnered respect.

Along with a crackling sense of humor and keen intelligence, Mel seemed to collect a surprisingly motley group of friends and followers. As a professor of American literature, he sometimes quoted Mark Twain. One of his favorites was "Life is just one goddamned thing after another." I always thought there was a lot of Mark Twain in my friend Mel Forman.

After chores, we went beach combing. The east side of Mel's property was part of a long beach. It extended for about a mile and attracted some fascinating driftwood along with odds and ends of great variety which had floated in on the tides.

Sometimes the Goeducks explored as a group and sometimes individually. Often they returned with flotsam interesting enough to tack up on the outside walls of the cabin or the outhouse. You never knew when you would find something from the beach of kooky interest and good for lots of laughs.

Ken Jarrel and Rob Amherst often hung out together on campus and were, along with Mel Forman, close social friends. I stayed pretty close to Rob and Ken as we explored the beach. I wasn't ready to confront my erstwhile friend Eldon Stark. Ken Jarrel was our African American colleague. About fifty, Ken was a big guy, very imposing, always with a big smile. Ken served the college as a lecturer in the accounting program. His hobby was cooking, fishing and women, not necessarily in that order.

Dr. Rob Amherst was a criminology expert and headed the department at school that was concerned with law enforcement, criminal behavior and incarceration issues. I enjoyed Rob Amherst as a friend and admired his insight in his area of expertise. A rather small man, Rob's round face carried a ruddy appearance in accordance with his dark red hair. His squinty, dark brown eyes sometimes took on a kind of glitter.

Eldon Stark was the jock in our group. I never saw anyone so happy in his job as administrator in charge of the physical education facilities at Seattle University. His authority extended not only to the management of the gyms, swimming pools and athletic fields, but also to intramural sports programs and all physical education classes. Eldon Stark stood six feet two, two hundred pounds with a perfectly proportioned athletic body. Stark's dark good looks featured a large masculine jaw, a slightly protruding brow with thick black eyebrows and deep-set dark blue eyes. His styled blond hair and flashing smile earned him admirers galore. Eldon Stark, my best pal, how could you have betrayed our friendship? My own daughter, you filthy bastard!

Even though the thought of what had happened to my daughter Marcy was continually on my mind, I found I was still able to participate in the Goeducks activities, especially the terrific meals mostly served by Ken and Rob.

We all got a big laugh Saturday afternoon after the rifle-shooting contest. Eldon Stark enjoyed being the winner almost every year. Mel always got a kick out of awarding some silly prize to contest winners. His prize for the shooting contest was a ceramic sculptured whiskey bottle. The sculpture was the figure of a romanticized version of Jesse James, crudely wrapped in gaudy wrapping paper.

Mel arranged a "formal" award ceremony in which he made the presentation in his usual semi-inebriated condition. It took place on the big lawn (which also served as the rifle range). As the whole Goeduck gang looked on, all expected some sort of craziness and a quick speech, but never suspected that Mel would drop his pants and, accompanied by raucous laughter, urinate on Eldon

Stark's trophy.

The same evening we took advantage of the low tide to dig clams on the beach at the west side of the property. By this time everyone was in their cups. Some had difficulty standing, not to mention the actual digging for the tasty Puget Sound butter clams. Afterward Ken Jarrell was heard to yell, "Hey, Garza, you are the only one I ever saw who could dig clams lying on their side!"

Mel Forman usually won the chess tournament. This year was no exception, which meant he was bound to award himself a prize. Two bottles of expensive champagne were revealed and made short work of by the group of thirsty college professors.

The poker winner kept his own prize after cashing in his chips on the last night. I modestly accepted the honor and the cash.

The bad thing was what I did the very next day. On our last day we always did our final explorations within a mile of the cabin. There was still a beachcombing jaunt on the outside beach. Another choice was on the south shoreline. The magnificent stretch of woods on the hill just south of the cabin featured deer trails leading to some big cliffs, a rocky spit connecting a tiny peninsula to the main part of Decatur Island. The whole area to the south was uninhabited and set aside as an official San Juan Islands preservation site. The guys usually split up and did their own final tour after packing up and devouring a huge breakfast. All were due back at the cabin before noon for a snack. Our chartered boat was due at that time to pick us up for the cruise to the mainland.

"Let's you and I hike to the south end," I suggested, speaking to my former friend, the slimiest bastard on earth. I was carefully packing items into my small hiking pack as I spoke. "Great idea," said Stark, "We haven't had any time to catch up. We can check out those deer hideouts down at the south end by Lopez Pass. There's still plenty of time until the guy shows up with the boat at noon." Stark was eager to talk as if making up for lost time.

After hiking through the woods, winding our way down the steep cliffs, across the picturesque driftwood covered spit, we reached the thickly wooded peninsula at the far end of the island. We stopped to rest. "It looks like there will be lots of deer for our hunt this fall," said Stark enthusiastically. "Yeah, it looks good." I tried to match his tone.

We sat against a log on the beach as Eldon jabbered away about old times. "Remember that time in church during Christmas week a few years ago when our wives insisted that we join in with all those people singing Christmas carols?" Stark laughed as he recalled how we took liberties with the lyrics. "Yeah, I remember," I retorted, "instead of jingle bells, the two of us sang "shingle nails." Stark giggled as he recalled singing "Deck the Halls with Poison Ivy." Sometimes it's a great feeling to act like kids again. I guess that's why we like these faculty retreats so much.

At a pause in the conversation, I offered Eldon Stark a swallow of Mel's brandy that I had stashed in my pack. "Sounds great," he said, as I passed the flask into his outstretched hand. "Damn, that's good," said Stark. "Take another big swig before giving it back," I warned, "you may not see it again." After a huge swallow he handed it back to me.

"I know what you did to Marcy," I growled, looking Stark in the eyes. "What the hell are you talking about," he asked? "You don't fool me, you filthy rat," I hissed. "Wait a minute," gasped Stark as he grabbed my shoulder. "Something's wrong with me, I feel like I'm passing out!" "Yes, and before you pass out, you're gonna confess," I said through clenched teeth. "You bastard," I added. "Before I pass out? What does that mean? Did you put something in this brandy?" "Yeah, I sure did. I'm the chemistry guy, right? But don't pass out just yet. Not until you tell me the truth which I already know, you son of a bitch."

With a horrified look in his eyes, Stark realized I had drugged him, as he made a grab for me. Too late, his grasp was weak. He trembled as his eyes began to roll back in his head. I pushed his arms aside and punched him hard in the face. I jumped to my feet and gave him two or three vicious kicks to the stomach and groin. "Now what do you say hot shot, tell me why you ravaged my little girl?"

A wind had come up as the tide was changing. The tide flow at Lopez Pass generated a very strong current at such times. The water was only about six feet away as it swirled ever faster against the shoreline, easily carrying anything afloat rapidly toward Rosario Strait, a body of water as treacherous as any in the Pacific Northwest.

In my unthinking fury I continued to beat the

helpless rapist until he completely passed out from the effect of my own Mickey Finn concoction in Mel's brandy.

Filled with hate, my anger led me to drag the unconscious Eldon Stark to a nearby log, which was temporarily stuck between rocks on the shore. With a small push I figured I could easily free that log to the fast-flowing tidewater. I somehow managed to drape Stark's big body over the log. I figured by pushing the log into the tidal current, Stark would be washed off the log fairly soon, but his position on the log seemed secure enough to float him into deeper water. With some effort I managed to disengage the log and push it into the swirling water. From the straits the tide and current would probably carry his body into the Pacific Ocean. It was likely he would never be found. That's what I hoped for. "Justice," I murmured as I watched until he disappeared into the distance.

Arriving at the cabin I acted panicky, faking a kind of hysteria. "Eldon saw something floating by in the water that he wanted to retrieve and he waded out to grab it," I cried. "The tide got hold of him and just carried him away!"

The Goeducks were transfixed as I lied about Eldon Stark's fate. I put on a pretty good act, I must say. All the guys seemed to fall for my story, except Rob Amherst, who looked questioningly into my eyes as I repeated the story over and over. "We have to use the radio on the boat the minute it gets here," said Mel who appeared extremely upset.

The boat arrived on schedule at 1:00 pm. Mel couldn't wait until he got his hands on the radiophone to call the sheriff. All agreed to meet at the dock on the mainland in one hour to await the sheriff's arrival.

Sheriff Merle Harding, middle aged with the obligatory mustache, potbelly and stern expression, promptly began his investigation by interviewing each of us. Releasing the others, he informed Mel Forman and me that we would be returning to Decatur Island, along with two deputies, where he would examine the site and continue his investigation. Sheriff Harding also issued directives to his search and rescue resources, and informed the Coast Guard. An intensive search was made over the next week or so for Eldon Stark's body.

Mel and I would likely have to stay on the Island for another day or two so Sheriff Harding could garner all the facts. It is hard to explain my feelings at the time. There was certainly anxiety along with a devastating fear. It took all my will power to keep from having an emotional crackup.

I desperately needed to call Deena. Finding a public phone near the dock, I spoke into the mouthpiece. "Hi, Honey, we just arrived at the dock here on the mainland and I have plenty to tell you." "Oh, Adam," she cried, "Something terribly important just happened yesterday. It's about Marcy. Can you believe this? Her story about being raped by Eldon Stark was not true. She made the whole thing up, it was all a lie!"

Eldon Stark's body was never found. I was never charged with any crime. Since that day my life has been a lie. A terrible lie...

A GUY WALKS INTO A BAR

A brisk March wind whistled down the street rattling the windows of Pete's bar. Located in the Georgetown neighborhood near Boeing field in Seattle's south end industrial district. Most Seattleites considered Georgetown nothing more than a dismal, gritty little neighborhood, but the local working class residents considered Georgetown a decent enough place to live where they knew all the local shopkeepers by their first names and were thankful for their cheap rent. Most became used to the constant sound of aircraft landing or taking off, less than the length of a football field, directly overhead.

The regulars at Pete's Pub in Georgetown especially enjoyed the Saturday morning get-together which they thought of as both a kind of refuge and a gathering of a convivial group of peers. The group consisted of roughly two dozen men whose ages varied from mid-twenties to around sixtyish. The numbers in attendance at Pete's Bar rotated from time to time. No matter how many showed up at any particular time, the atmosphere was always friendly, punctuated by joking comments and loud laughter.

The total area of Pete's Pub was about twenty four by forty feet and featured a traditional bar setup with the essential back wall mirror, a glossy display of liquor, swivel bar stools and old fashioned foot rails screwed into the floor. On one wall were two small windows with a limited view of the street. The same wall contained the outside door. Three tables with appropriate chairs filled out the room. Attached to the walls were a few signs encouraging the patrons to guzzle Heidleburg, Michelob or Rainier beer.

One particular twenty-first century Saturday morning in late March found Pete's Pub occupied by four customers along with Pete, the owner. "Come on you guys, start drinking faster. You guys are the world's slowest drinkers. You're making me lose money hand over fist!" The guys chortled and yelled back. "That's what you get for serving watered-down beer," hollered a young guy named Mark. "That goes for the wine, too," yelled Johnny. "Liquor too," chimed in a grinning Luke. "Okay, okay," gurgled Pete, "quit ganging up on me."

At that moment the door opened and an unfamiliar man walked into the bar. Pete the bartender looked him up and down as the stranger made his way toward a bar stool. The man appeared to be in his early thirties, well-proportioned, wearing a pony tail with glossy brown hair trailing part way down his back. On closer observation, the man displayed a four day old beard and a good looking countenance enhanced by deep-set dark brown eyes. The regulars, slurping on their beers, stared at the stranger's attire. No surprises there, he was dressed almost exactly as they were, jeans, Dockers, plaid shirts, jackets and baseball caps. "Greetings, welcome to Pete's Pub. My name's Pete. What can I get for ya?" "A glass of Bud Lite," said the stranger. "You can call me Jesse." Pete and Jesse locked eyes as they shook hands. Sitting two stools away, the man named Johnny turned to greet Jesse. "My name's Johnny. We haven't seen you in here before, where you from?" "Nowhere in particular, I've drifted around a lot," said Jesse. "What's your line of work?" asked Johnny. Jesse thought for a moment. "Insurance," he said. Johnny pointed to the closest table, about eight feet away. "Hey guys, meet Jesse. Sitting over there are some of Georgetown's most sophisticated community leaders. On the left is Luke, the smart guy, next to him sits Mark, the dumb one, then Matt, the ugly one!" Each raised his hand in a kind of greeting and murmured "Hey, Jesse," or "How ya doin?" "Have you got a joke for us, Jesse?" hollered Mark. "Come over and join the crowd," said Luke, the smart one. "It's dangerous over there," said Johnny in a loud voice, as the guys at the table giggled and cackled. "I'd like to join you guys," said Jesse, "if Johnny here would come over and protect me." The guys at the table laughed and yelled at Pete to bring more beer. Jesse and Johnny left their bar stools and headed across the room to join the others, who shuffled around to make room so that Jesse would be seated in the middle of the group. Jesse's big friendly smile signaled that he anticipated a good natured third degree as soon as he got seated.

At that moment the door opened noisily admitting a big man who seemed to be almost dragging a small woman clumsily across the floor toward the bar. Over six feet tall, he wore an aggravated expression along with a fedora hat with an oversized brim. A turtleneck sweater, and a long trench coat and two-color wing tip shoes completed his outfit. The woman appeared to be only in her teens, a pretty girl with long reddish hair and excessive makeup. Vaguely resistant to the man, she was obviously confused as she was pushed, pulled and dragged across the floor by the big powerful brutish young man. Johnny and his group of regulars, including Jesse, were temporarily taken aback as they stared. Jesse's friendly expression abruptly disappeared. "Hey Freddy, what's going on?" said Pete from his place behind the bar. "Give us two straight vodkas, Pete, and make hers a double," growled the man called Freddy. "She looks underage, Freddy, I can't serve her," exclaimed Pete. "What's the idea, are you up to your old tricks? Are you about to put this girl on the street?" "Come on, Pete, this is business. Just serve our drinks and we'll be on our way!"

So quickly that his new friends scarcely noticed, Jesse shot from the table to the bar and seized Freddy's left wrist in a vise like grip. With a lightning fast movement, Jesse locked Freddy in a combination choke hold and hammerlock that rendered big Freddy helpless in Jesse's steel grip. Jesse spoke quietly, "You're leaving now Freddy, so come along and don't make a fuss." Pete, Johnny and the others looked on in a stunned silence as

Jesse walked big Freddy quietly toward the door. Jesse turned Freddy's body, still maintaining his hold, to look directly into both his eyes. Unused to maintaining eye-to-eye contact with anyone, Freddy attempted to look away, but Jesse's intense gaze held him motionless. Freddy had never seen a look like Jesse's deep, inescapable darkly ominous glower. Outside was heard a thunderclap followed by a sharp flash of lightning, which seemed to add to the dramatic scene. Freddy heard Jesse whisper into his ear, "Have nothing to do with little Maggie ever again." Freddy blinked as he asked, "How do you know her name? Who the hell are you?" "If you ever see her again, Freddy, I'm the guy who will put you in the hospital in a world of hurt you can't even imagine." Freddy's mouth went dry and he felt genuine fear. "Do you understand me, Freddy?" "Yeah, I get you," mumbled Freddy, as he stumbled out the door.

Turning to the onlookers inside Pete's Pub, Jesse smiled and removed a cell phone from his jacket pocket and made a brief call, lasting only about thirty seconds. He moved quickly toward the bar where the girl was leaning with her lovely head hanging low. "Come over here," said Jessie, quietly. Sitting at a corner table facing each other, Jessie spoke. "What's your name, dear?" "Madeleine, but everyone calls me Maggie." Jesse looked deeply into Maggie's eyes. "Your days as a hooker are over. Your life is precious and you must not waste it. From now on you will meet people who will protect you and genuinely love you. Make it your goal to find fulfillment with dignity and love overflowing in your life from now on. In a few minutes some people will be here to pick you up and take you to a place where you can live and be safe. You must go along with the program and never think about returning to the streets. Freddy is out of your life." Tears formed in Maggie's blue eyes. "I don't know why," she said, "but I believe you. I will do as you say, I promise. What's happening to me?" She sobbed a bit and wiped her tears. "Hear they are now," said Jesse. "They will take good care of you and your life will change." A middle aged woman and man entered Pete's Pub and with a brief, knowing look at Jesse, left arm in arm with Maggie. As the door closed, the group of regulars shouted their admiration of Jesse, who quietly acknowledged their applause. As he took his seat back at the table among the others, Matt yelled, "This calls for a drink." We want to buy you a beer, Jesse!"

"No need for that, guys," exclaimed Jesse, as he sat in his chair among the group. "Now where were we?" he grinned. His companions couldn't stop asking questions. "What did you say to Freddy?" asked Luke. "What will happen to that girl?" demanded Pete. "What was that all about?" shouted Mark. Jesse maintained a calm demeanor as he answered, "Everything's OK guys, Freddy won't be back and Maggie's off the streets in a safe place. She won't be back either." There was a pause as the guys stared at Jesse. "You must have a special kind of ability or talent with people," offered Luke. "Can I take your pulse?" The guys all laughed. "Luke is working in a hospital to become a physician's assistant," hollered Pete from behind the bar. "What do some of the rest of you do?" asked Jesse. Johnny spoke first, "I'm a ship fitter at the shipyards right over there at Harbor Island on Elliott Bay." "Ever hear of the Boeing Company?" teased Matt. "Mark and I both work there putting airplanes together." "I used to be a commercial fisherman until the fish ran out," yelled Pete. "So you're all honest to God working stiffs," commented Jesse with an unmistakable twinkle in his eyes. "Right now I'm trying to help some people with a petition." "What petition?" asked Matt. "It shouldn't be controversial," Jesse explained. "Some college kids will be in the neighborhood in the next few days getting signatures asking the government to be more involved in global warming." Mark spoke up "I've heard that global warming is only a hoax." "The truth is," said Jesse, with a sincerity that attracted everyone's attention, "that hoax nonsense is special interest propaganda. Aren't you guys informed enough to realize the danger to the planet and everyone who lives on it? I ask you fellows to sign the petition. Please do it for me if not for yourselves." The guys all ogled Jesse with puzzled expressions. As if an exclamation point, the storm outside seemed louder as they all heard a clap of thunder and saw a flash of lightening through the window.

The door flew open unexpectedly to admit a man who staggered into the bar room. "Hey Larry," called Pete, "What's up? You been out jogging in the storm?" Throwing himself onto a bar stool, Larry, in jogging togs, ordered a beer and waved to the regulars as they stared at the soaking wet, overweight, middle-aged guy sitting uncomfortably at the bar. Jesse's eyes narrowed and his body seemed to stiffen as he focused on Larry. Larry's head seemed to roll in circles as he fell heavily to the floor, apparently unconscious or worse. The regulars quickly ran to their prostrate friend. "Looks like a heart attack," someone yelled. "Call 911." Jesse was the first to reach the unconscious Larry. "Please keep back." He ordered. As Jesse knelt beside the unfortunate Larry, the men surrounding sensed that Jesse seemed capable of responding properly to the crises at hand. They watched fascinated as Jesse placed his hands on Larry's chest. Pete looked amazed as he thought he observed a special sensitivity in Jesse's strong hands. Jesse touched Larry's face on both cheeks; the carotid arteries on his neck and his forehead on which Jesse traced some vertical and horizontal lines. Were they symbolic numbers, figures, designs, or what? Jesse put one palm on the top of Larry's head, and the other on his chest. As lightening flashed outside, Jesse spoke quietly, but all could hear. "Get up Larry." Larry's eyes fluttered open. "What happened?" he asked in a raspy whisper. "You're alright now, Larry," Jesse said. "Let's get you up on your feet."

Larry's wife Rachel was just arriving in response to Pete's earlier call. As she rushed into the bar room, Luke and Johnny greeted her. Obviously distraught, she asked, "What happened is Larry OK?" "He's OK," said Johnny. "Jesse seemed to bring him around after he passed out." "I was sure he was a goner." exclaimed Luke, "but he seems alright. It's like a miracle."

Leaning on his wife for support, Larry and Rachel

left for home. "The emergency is over," stated Pete. "If you all sit down, I'll come over with some refills." Relieved, the inhabitants took a collective deep breath and babbled back and forth about Larry's close call. "Jesse," yelled Matt, "How did you do that? What exactly did you do?" "When Larry fell off the stool, he looked stone dead to me," said Luke. "How long have you been performing miracles?" All were silent as Jesse, wearing an amused expression, answered, "This is only one of many," then gave a hearty laugh. All the guys politely joined in. "Hey Jesse," exclaimed Mark, "besides signing that petition, what else would you have us do?" "Believe in it," responded Jesse. "You may not realize it, but this planet is in mortal danger." "Oh, come on, Jesse," said Johnny, "God wouldn't let the planet die just because of a little too much carbon dioxide." Jesse looked into each man's eyes and murmured, "It's out of God's hands, don't any of you understand? It's now in *your* hands and it's almost too late." The words were barely out of Jesse's mouth when the shaking began first the rattle of glasses behind the bar. Then the chandelier's began to sway, then the windows quivered and vibrated. In a matter of seconds, the ceiling and walls trembled violently. Jesse sprinted toward the door and stood with his back to the door as the floor swayed under his feet. "Stay where you are," he shouted. "Nobody goes outside. Do not panic!" Everyone seemed to know it was an earthquake and all were terrified. "Run for it," someone shouted, but Jesse, guarding the door, seemed to puff himself up to appear as an oversized security guard. With arms and legs extended and his back against the door wearing an "immovable object" expression, Jesse assumed control. As Pete's pub shook violently, Jesse shouted orders. "Control yourselves, do not be afraid, get under those tables and be quiet! Do not be afraid. Hear me! You are not going to die! You are safe in here with me! Settle down. It will be over in a minute or two. Have courage! Quiet down. You see it's diminishing. Brace yourselves. It may shake again for a minute. Just keep still, until it's over. Nobody goes outside. Things may still be falling off these buildings!"

From behind the bar, Pete raised his head. "I think it's over. Get up guys, and let's all have another beer!" Rousing themselves the regulars stood and walked around in little circles, some shook hands as if to congratulate each other for surviving the terrifying earthquake. "I saw these walls actually bend and waver," Johnny testified. "Scared the holy hell out of me," admitted Matt. "Me too," they all seemed to say as they looked strangely at Jesse. Jesse's dark brown deep set eyes were calm, his pony tail in place and his smile was no less than beatific. "I told you that you would be safe," he said quietly. "Get over here and sit at this table," ordered Pete. "The beer is on the house." The regulars all cheered as they sat and reached for their cell phones.

For the next fifteen minutes the cell phones were hot with earthquake babble when wives, children, girlfriends, mothers and distant cousins were accounted for and safe, the guys felt free again to seriously pursue the beer drinking and peer bonding that continued to draw them together. Fortunately, there were no important sports events on this day to distract this group of typical working class American men. When the flurry of computerized telephone calls subsided, the drinking continued in earnest, and so did the conversations.

The main topic seemed to be about the charismatic newcomer, the big handsome dude with the week-old beard and distinctive pony tail. "We need to know more about you Jesse," someone said to everyone seated at the table. "What is your last name, your life story, and your philosophy of life?" This brought a laugh from the guys. Actually three tables had been pushed together forming one long table with Jesse perched in the exact middle. Jesse's expression showed a benign gentleness. He seemed a bit amused as he readied his response. All conversation stopped as Jesse spoke, "You guys should all know that last names are not really important unless you are looking for an ethnic connection. Would it make any difference to you if I told you I had a nice Bar Mitzvah at age thirteen, or if I said I had spent some time as a Christian Monk at a monastery located on a steep cliff in northern Greece, or if I am fluent in Spanish, or Norwegian, or Comanche? My life story is full of connected stories, but you don't want to hear all that. My philosophy of life may be of more interest, but some of you may think me a little crazy if I advised you to go home and sell all your possessions and then I would tell you what to do with the money. See what I mean?" "Let's have it, Jesse," yelled Pete, "we're all interested." "Okay," said Jesse, "Short and sweet. As I have been telling you, the threat of extinction is very real because of global warming. Even if we take the proper steps to cope with it right now, it will take another three or four generations for the many forthcoming natural disasters to subside as the result of man-caused alteration of natural forces. In the foreseeable future, we here in Georgetown and everywhere else on earth will have to adapt." "Adapt to what?" someone asked. "Violent hurricanes, storms, tornadoes, tsunami's, droughts, wildfires, typhoons, floods, extreme heat and extreme cold, completely disrupting weather and climate everywhere around the world."

"Atomic war, if not avoided, may wipe out civilization as we know it." All were silent until Mark asked, "What can guys like us do about it?" "Look to your leaders," Jesse exclaimed. "Only elect those with high moral standards enough to fight corporate greed, corruption in government, and phony partisanship. Wake up to the hypocrisy going on around you. I've talked enough."

"I think we should run you for president," yelled Luke. Jesse displayed his enigmatic smile. "We may have to run him for Mayor first," offered Johnny. "Mayor of Seattle?" asked Matt. "Jesse's been a hero today, right here in Georgetown, how about mayor of Georgetown?" Everyone yelled as a chorus. All laughed and cheered as only the regulars in Pete's Pub could cheer.

As the cheers subsided, another customer burst through the door. "Hi ya, Pete," he called. "How's business?" All turned to stare at the man they all knew as Jules, the Bookie. At fifty, Jules was imposing, standing over six feet and carrying over two hundred fifty pounds with only a slight pot belly. Jules revealed a squareish face, adorned with black horned rimmed glasses, a double chin and shifty black eyes. His head was mostly bald with a black fringe left to grow long, part way down his back. Pete glared at Jules. "Business is holding, Jules, what'll you have?" "Give me a pitcher, Pete, and I'll sit at the table over in the far corner." In a loud voice, Jules announced, "Maybe some of the boys over there would join me," gesturing toward the regulars and Jesse seated at the long table near the center of the room. "Okay, Jules, here's your pitcher," growled Pete, "but I don't want any bookmaking in here today!" Jules paid, picked up his pitcher, gave Pete his most captivating snaggle-toothed smile, winked, and walked to his table in the far corner. Matt was the first to wander over to Jules' table. Mark turned to Jesse. "You want to visit Jules? He always has betting pools and charts so you can bet on games, mostly final four and NBA basketball this time of year." " Isn't bookmaking illegal in a place like this?" asked Jesse. "Yeah," said Mark, "but Jules gets away with it." "That's a problem," said Jesse. "I think I'll go over there and see what's what," murmured Mark, as he headed over to Jules' table where charts and lists were appearing. "Are you hungry, Jesse?" Johnny asked. "Pete has some of his famous pizza he could warm up." "Any time," chortled Pete, "how many?" Johnny quietly encouraged Jesse. "You should try the pizza, Jesse, aren't you getting hungry?" "I'm starved."

Jesse's gaze remained on Jules at the far table.

"Sure, Johnny, order enough for all of our guys. It'll be my treat." Jesse spoke quietly, "Ask Pete if he has some wine to go with the pizza." The group at Jules' table now included Luke and Matt, who seemed to be participating in Jules' gambling scams. Cash from the player's wallets was rapidly being transferred to a pile of bills in front of Jules. "Believe it or not," he was saying, "the odds today are in your favor. You boys stand to win some real money!" "Don't our guys know that bookmaking and that other stuff is illegal in bars and other places like this?" asked Jesse. Johnny just nodded. "Why doesn't Pete stop it?" demanded Jesse. Johnny shrugged. Jesse got up from his chair and quickly strode to Jules' table where his friends seemed totally engaged with basketball team rankings, betting pools and the odds of chance. The horse racing charts were yet to appear. Jesse assumed a confrontational stance as he glared at Jules. Jesse raised his voice, demanding the attention of all in the room. "Jules," he shouted, "I won't allow you to cheat these men with your illegal gambling racket! Stop it now or you will have to deal with me!" Jules quickly stood to face Jesse. "Just who the hell do you think you are?" snarled Jules. "Get out of here before I break you in half!" Jesse's eyes flashed as he rasped, "Where I come from we whip people like you. If you don't leave now I will put you under the lash!" Everyone in the room stared in disbelief as Jesse instantly drew his belt free from his trousers and brandished it before Jules' astonished face. "Wait a minute," called Pete from behind the bar. "This has gone far enough!" "You're right, Pete," cried

Jesse, "just stay out of it." In the same breath, he lashed out with his belt, catching Jules across the face causing him to stagger, a fiery red welt appearing on the left cheek and jaw of Jule's astonished countenance. Roaring with anger, Jules charged toward Jesse, but nimbly sidestepping the larger man, Jesse continued to viciously slash Jules with rapid, powerful blows, each sounding like sharp pistol shots which reverberated around the room. Jules expressed his pain by loud curses, then by roaring oaths, culminating with screams of pain and humiliation while crouching on the floor in subjugation. Bending low toward his victim, Jesse growled, "Now get out of here Jules, and don't come back." On hands and knees, Jules scrambled across the floor toward the door, then half rising, screamed, "Where do you get off doing this to me? I'm not illegal. I've taken care of all the cops on the beat!" Poised at the door, he yelled, "Give me my money!" Jesse glared. "Go!" he shouted, as he moved toward the hapless Jules who dove through the door to the sidewalk outside. Pete and the others attempted to catch their breath, as Jesse spoke sharply to Luke and the others still sitting at Jules' corner table. "Pick up your money guys, and let's go back to our table and have some pizza." As the regulars seated themselves, mumbling to each other, Pete cried out, "I just found some good wine I didn't know I had. So wine and glasses coming up!"

As the regulars settled around the table for lunch, the thunder and lightning outside seemed to accentuate their comfortable situation, enjoying a tasty meal in the presence of friends.

Jesse sat at the table with the others enjoying the new found wine and Pete's delicious pizza servings. The lights were low in Pete's pub except for the glow from the overhead light which shone directly on Jesse providing a glow. The conversation was spirited, mostly about the food and drink, but became more subdued when talk of Jesse's earlier exploits became the main topic. The guys seemed poised to ask Jesse about his puzzling behavior. "I think we may all have something to learn from you, Jesse," said Johnny. "Can you tell us who you really are and any comment about today's events?" Jesse gave each man a serious look before he spoke. "I have a few things to talk to you about. The things that happened today that I was involved in must speak for themselves. You may think of them as symbolic acts if you wish. Then again much of our normal behavior you might think of in the same sense. I have something else of importance to discuss. We all must realize some essential facts about the world we live in. In the near future a sea change of awareness is coming. A new enlightenment is sweeping across the planet in which our notion of materialism will be relegated into a more rational perspective. This new worldwide tide of social awareness will penetrate all levels of intellectual competence and will have the effect of changing behavior of both leaders and followers in all cultures around the world. Rationality and critical thinking in all levels of society will be greatly enhanced by means of education and dissemination of information. It will have the effect of stimulating the consciousness of everyone. This universal philosophy could insure the well-being of all, extending into the future, but there is a hitch." A distinct pause ensued as Jesse continued, "Just as the world is subject to counter forces of every description – think of yin-yang – the present world is also in mortal danger of destruction from man's own hands. It is like an irresistible force. It is a combination of zeal on the part of the very rich and powerful to impose their materialistic philosophy on everyone, including the three billion souls who exist on the edge of starvation. These two forces must be placed into a balance in which the new technology will be used for the best interest of those gentlemen wearing three-piece suits in our downtown skyscrapers as well as you guys here in Pete's pub." Listening intently the five men couldn't take their eyes off Jesse. "The last important component," said Jesse "has to do with your personal lives and your ultimate fate." His companions stared almost as if hypnotized, as Jesse continued. "Have you fellows ever heard of meditation?" Two heads nodded. "It's a way – through relaxation and silence – to quiet your mind and allow you to think. You should look into it. It's a lot like prayer. Please take up prayer and meditation. It will bring great enlightenment for you. Take my word for it. Start today. Your spiritual development is of utmost importance to me. Please consider Church, Temple, or whatever religious meetings may be of interest. I have spoken enough. We do not have much time. Do you have questions?" "Speaking of religion," asked Matt, "what do you think about the second coming?" Jesse locked eyes with Matt and replied, "If this prediction would come true, do most people assume that Jesus would make his appearance in Yankee Stadium, or the United Nations Headquarters, or Vatican Square? Maybe a visitation might take place at a lunch counter, or a chamber of commerce meeting or someplace like Pete's Pub." Mark asked, "What do you think about unconditional love?" "By that," answered Jesse, "you mean love for another without expectation of return? The noblest form of love starts with affection for an acquaintance. Then, for someone you love. And then, for those you dislike or hate, and after that it becomes love for oneself. Finally, one extends this love to all beings everywhere, providing you with a loving, blissful heart." Luke politely raised his hand, "Jesse, how did you become so smart? You are amazing the way you whip the hell out of bookies, stop earthquakes, bring dead guys back to life and reform hookers." Everyone giggled. Jesse maintained a peaceful half-smile. Johnny spoke up, "Where did this amazing insight come from? I have to ask you again, Jesse, where the heck do you come from?" "And who are you?" demanded Mark. As he stared intently at Jesse, who was sitting at the table holding his wine glass as if offering a toast, poised in the overhead spotlight. Pete felt a shiver run down his spine. Pete's face suddenly turned white, his jaw dropped and his eyes bulged unnaturally as he bellowed, "Use your imagination, you idiots!" Thunder rumbled loudly outside. At the same moment, the door burst open admitting two very wet Seattle police officers, followed closely by a bedraggled Jules, the erstwhile bookie. "This is the place, officers! This is where I was assaulted and robbed!" screamed Jules. The biggest cop confronted Pete, who was standing behind the bar. "Where's the guy you call Jesse?" he demanded. Pete recoiled, threw his hands over his head, backed up a few steps and whined, "I don't know any Jesse." The big cop stuck his face within inches of Pete's. "You had trouble in here today. That makes you responsible for this man's charges." "I never saw the guy in my life before today." Jules yelled over the cop's shoulder, "They're all guilty of assault and grand larceny!" Turning toward the group at the table, Jules pointed at Jesse and shrieked, "That's him over there, the guy with the pony tail in the middle!" "Cuff him," commanded Big Cop. Smaller Cop dashed toward Jesse who extended his wrists in front of him as the handcuffs were roughly applied. "I got him," exclaimed one of Seattle's finest, at the same time pushing and jerking Jesse toward the door. Jules swaggered to within ten feet of the handcuffed Jesse and snarled, "You're not so tough now, you jerk! Now you're gonna go to jail where you belong!" Nearing the door with both cops grasping his arms, Jesse halted and turned to address the group, still gathered at the table in a stunned silence. "Money for everything is on the table, Pete. Please hold it a minute, officers, I want to say something. I have grown to become very fond of you all, in fact I truly love you. Do not forget me and what I have taught you."

In the next instant Jesse was dragged through

the door and was gone. In the awkward moment that followed, Johnny stood, paused, and asked of the others, "Do you guys think we'll ever see him again?"

The story above is an allegory based on the biblical promise of the second coming.